HIGHLANDER'S DESIRE

Called by a Highlander Book Five

MARIAH STONE

"Nothing is impossible to a willing heart"
    — John Heywood

PROLOGUE

D elny, Ross, January 1310

A HEAVY STONE WEIGHED IN ANGUS MACKENZIE'S STOMACH AS he rode past the granite gate of Delny Castle. The sharp iron stakes of the portcullis hanging above his head didn't look as menacing as the heavy stares of the guards and men-at-arms standing on the curtain walls and in the courtyard.

Swordsmen rested their hands casually on their swords' hilts. Archers held arrows to their bows, and crossbowmen gripped their weapons with charged bolts facing down.

Cold pinched the insides of his nostrils, and the smell of manure and the blood of some recently slaughtered animal in the mud-churned snow assailed him. Reaching the courtyard, Angus suppressed his instinct to grab the reins of the horses his brother and his sister were riding and gallop the hell out of here.

"Catrìona, stay behind me," Angus said quietly. Then he turned his head to Laomann, chief of clan Mackenzie. "God's blood, brother, they didna look like they're waiting for welcome guests."

Flanked by men-at-arms, three richly dressed figures and a priest stood before the rectangular keep that shot into the leaden sky like a dark mountain. The battle-clad warrior in him noticed the well-thought-out defenses that could threaten his clan: the parapet with holes for pouring hot sand, the four defensive turrets at the corners of the tower called bartizans, and the slit windows where archers and crossbowmen could hide.

"Calm down," Laomann muttered through a strained smile directed at their hosts. "The Earl of Ross is our suzerain. He wilna threaten us as long as we pay our annual tribute. And we're bringing it."

But the tension in his voice told Angus he wasn't so sure of his own words.

"Only half," Angus said.

Given the chilly welcome, it was possible they may not ride out of here unharmed.

Or alive.

Riding farther into the courtyard, Angus caught the gaze of William II, Earl of Ross, and knew he wasn't just imagining the tension. The threat was in the stony face of the earl himself, in the arrogant angle of his raised chin. The man in his late thirties looked freshly groomed with his thin mustache and a small blond goat-beard. The long fur cloak sat on him more like armor than protection against cold.

Angus's fist clenched as he stopped the urge to reach for the sword in the sheath on his back.

The only one who studied the Mackenzie band without a trace of tension was a woman standing by the Earl of Ross's left shoulder. This must be Euphemia of Ross, William's sister, Angus thought. She was a little older than him, her blond hair still shiny under the fur-trimmed hood of her rich, woolen cloak. Her blue eyes sparkling and firmly on Angus, her rosy, full lips parted, she fiddled with her cloak's fastening brooch. Somehow, that interest unsettled Angus more than the antagonistic gazes of the surrounding men.

Next to her stood a young woman, probably Catrìona's age, with ashen skin and dark circles under her eyes. This must be Euphemia's daughter, Malise. She glanced around at the Mackenzies, then dropped her gaze to the slush under her feet.

"But they dinna ken we only have a half," Laomann retorted.

Angus pulled the reins and brought his horse to a halt.

"And yet they look at us as though we're the enemy," Angus muttered. "'Twas a wee bit over a year ago that William submitted to the Bruce, but I am nae sure he's come to terms with that decision."

Laomann halted his mare. "I said ye were stupid to offer Bruce shelter four years ago."

Angus descended and helped Catrìona down from her horse. His sister took after their deceased mother and was the only blond member of their family. The fair locks gave her an air of innocence that clearly didn't extend to all blondes. She eyed everything with curiosity. Normally, Angus wouldn't have let her come with them, but she was due to go to the monastery by the end of summer, when she would be twenty-four, and she wanted to see as much of the world as possible before then. She had no desire to marry, and was already older than most lasses were on their wedding day, but Laomann still hoped she would change her mind before the end of summer. He hoped she would be as happy being married as he was.

"Thank ye, brother," she said with a sweet smile.

Angus couldn't stop himself from smiling back. She'd always been his gentle, young sister. How could he not try to shield her from every harm? He didn't like this chilly reception one bit. He should have insisted she stayed home.

The rest of their men descended, alert and watching for a sign of an attack. Laomann was greeting the Earl of Ross, who offered a pinched smile. With a heaviness in his gut, Angus approached their hosts. Slush slurped under his shoes, and he already felt the dank wetness seeping into the seams and soaking his woolen hose. Humid cold seemed to spread ice through his bones, or perhaps it was the intensity in Euphemia's eyes as she studied him with undisguised interest.

He clenched his teeth and brought his attention to William. "May God bless ye, Lord," Angus said with a short nod. "Lady Euphemia," he added, trying not to shudder as he met her gaze.

William nodded. "Ye're very welcome here, Angus Mackenzie."

But everything else said how false those words were.

"May God bless ye, Lord Angus," Euphemia said, her voice low and slow, as though she were tasting a honeyed pastry on her tongue.

Angus was not a stranger to female attention, but there was something about this woman that made him wary.

He gave a curt bow to Euphemia and greeted her daughter. Then they were invited into the great hall. The room was impressive—large, with columns and an arched ceiling. Braziers illuminated the embroidery of the Ross's hereditary coat of arms: three white lions on a crimson background. Garlands of juniper, which, as Angus knew, was the Ross clan tree, hung on the walls. Tables were set with platters of freshly baked bread and bannocks, small jars of butter, salted and dried fish, boiled eggs, and pastries.

The Earl of Ross and Euphemia sat at the table of honor, and the priest took his seat by William's side, opening a thick book on an empty page. He had a quill and a jar with ink at the ready.

"We prepared a feast in yer honor," William said. "But before we begin eating, I do believe we have the matter of tribute to settle, aye?"

Angus's stomach churned. Laomann cleared his throat and exchanged a glance with him. The pouch containing two hundred and fifty pounds weighed on Angus's belt. It was the equivalent of paying the yearly wages of fifteen knights or building three farmhouses. The Mackenzies needed the latter the most, though they might wish for the former if the Earl of Ross responded badly.

What would the Earl of Ross do once he found out how much of their tribute was missing? The glistening swords and the charged crossbows might provide the answer soon.

Willing the tremor in his fingers to stop, Angus unfastened the heavy pouch on his belt and handed it to Laomann. If they were robbed on the long journey here, Laomann as the laird would most likely be attacked, so Angus had carried the silver.

The Earl of Ross took the purse, his hand sinking with the weight of it. He spilled the coins on the table and carefully counted the tribute. His blue eyes, as hard as rocks, met Laomann's.

"Is this a jest?" William said.

Just as though they were both lads again and stood in front of their father, Laomann shrank and Angus stepped forward, shielding him.

Angus replied, "The tribute is high, and we lost many men who fought for our king." Their eyes locked at that. Angus meant Robert the Bruce, while everyone knew the Earl of Ross had been loyal to the King of England.

Angus continued, "We lack people to farm the land, and therefore, bring rent."

The Earl of Ross leaned back in his seat and crossed his arms on his chest, his chin high.

"We will pay ye next year," Angus pressed and, hating himself, added, "Please, my lord."

He was ready to plead or do anything he must to shield his clan, to take any harm that came their way on himself.

"We could take Kintail." Euphemia's voice was so calm, as though she suggested having the leftovers of a roasted chicken.

"What?" Laomann croaked. "My lady, there's nae need to—"

"Kintail belongs to clan Mackenzie," Angus said through gritted teeth. "'Tis our land. Our home. Our father, Kenneth Og Mackenzie, sinned much. But he did one thing right. He protected the clan lands and kept them. They're rightfully ours."

Euphemia arched one elegant eyebrow. "Rightfully yers?" She chuckled. "Just as Bruce's throne is rightfully his because he killed Red John Comyn and proclaimed himself king?"

"He has the right to the throne by blood," Angus said.

"So did the Comyn."

"Euphemia..." the Earl of Ross said, his voice a weak warning.

But she waved her hand. "New king, new rules," she said. "Ye owe us tribute. We could take Kintail back."

Silence hung heavy and thick like a cloud of fog. Angus's blood felt as if it had been replaced by the coldest waters from the depth of a loch.

"We need to discuss this. Isna it much, Euphem—" William began.

"Shut up, William," she snapped. She gazed at Angus like a bird of prey and tilted her head. "We *could* take Kintail," she repeated slowly.

Aye, they could. Despite the fact that the Earl of Ross had submitted to Bruce last year, probably because he knew he'd be obliterated if he hadn't, they did have a significant force compared to the Mackenzies. Fifty years ago, when their grand-father, Angus Crom Mackenzie, fought William I of Ross, he'd had to secure the support of five other clans to stand any kind of chance. Now, with the wars still going on and their allied clans having lost many men, who would stand by the Mackenzies' side? And even if some would, they'd never gather a force that could protect against such a powerful clan as Ross.

Their father had died six years ago, and Laomann had just gotten a bairn. Angus couldn't stand the thought of something happening to his nephew. And Laomann. And Catrìona. And even Raghnall, who would come to their rescue from his wander-ings the moment he learned of their trouble.

Suddenly, Euphemia's face relaxed, and she looked at William. "We're being bad hosts, brother," she said. "Tribute questions can wait. We have much time to discuss it, dinna we?" She smiled a sly smile as she held Angus in her gaze—a smile that made him wish he had a dagger in his hand. "Please, Lord Angus, Lord Laomann, and Lady Catrìona. Take yer seats. Let's eat and drink, and I'm sure we will find a solution. Nae everything should be decided with swords and axes."

William was still frowning at her. "Aye, she's right," he said finally. "Please. Let us eat and drink."

Angus, Laomann, and Catrìona exchanged long glances. William gestured at the chairs around him. The priest moved, allowing Laomann to take a seat by William's side. Angus had no choice but to sit between the Earl of Ross and his sister, while Catrìona took a place on the other side of Euphemia.

The Mackenzie men filled the tables, and so did the Ross men. Voices hummed quietly, the men from the opposite clans still not trusting one another. Servants came to pour ale, but Angus covered his cup with his hand.

"How about some Mackenzie *uisge*," he said.

William's mouth curved upward. "Ah. The famous Mackenzie uisge."

Angus waved to one of his men, and he brought the cask. Angus served the uisge, and as they drank, Angus felt a cool hand on his thigh.

"Ye make the uisge yerself?" Euphemia asked, her voice husky.

He clenched his jaw and turned to her. "Aye, Lady," he said. "'Tis one of the things I enjoy."

Without breaking eye contact, she took another sip and moaned in appreciation. "A fine drink, my lord."

She stroked his thigh, and he tensed. What, by God's bones, was she doing? She behaved like a street harlot, not like a noblewoman with land and riches and power.

"I am glad 'tis to yer satisfaction, my lady," Angus said with an effort to relax his gritted teeth.

He was a warrior. A protector. He wasn't a diplomat. How would he get out of this without offending her?

"A man who can make such delights for the mouth... Ye're nae marrit, my lord, aye?"

By God's blood. "Nae."

"Neither am I. I'm a widow twice."

The Earl of Ross, who'd been listening to Laomann, turned his head to Angus and chuckled. "One of the poor fools is dead by her will."

Angus frowned.

"Have ye nae heard?" William said darkly. "She ordered her second husband beheaded."

"Ye gave the order, brother," she said.

"I was afraid ye'd have me killed if I didna."

She removed her palm from Angus's thigh and took her cup with both hands. A small mercy. "In any case, I had a reason."

"What happened with yer first husband?" he asked.

"He died fighting on the side of William Wallace at the Battle of Falkirk," she said and threw the contents of the cup down her throat. "That was the time our clans fought on the same side, wasna it?"

"Twelve years ago, indeed." Angus nodded.

"I wonder if they can fight together again," she said. "I wonder if that would be the way yer debt can be repaid...or rather, forgotten."

Silence fell on the table. Everyone stared at her. Angus didn't like where this was going. His gut tightened as a dark feeling of premonition settled over him like a cloud.

"My lady?" he said.

"How about, instead of scrambling to get the debt paid, ye become my husband," Euphemia said.

"Angus, nae!" Catrìona cried.

A playful, lazy smile spread on Euphemia's lips. "What say ye?"

The woman clearly wanted him. Mayhap she was lonely.

Mayhap she wanted Kintail, and establishing family ties would be the closest she'd get to the lands. She wouldn't attack kin.

The decision sank into him like a stone and felt like a noose around his neck. He wouldn't only be protecting his brothers and his sister, but also hundreds of clansmen as well as their wives and children. It was his duty to protect his clan. Besides, he'd need to marry someone eventually to strengthen the clan's connections. And if marrying for love was not written in his future, now was as good a time as any to find a wife.

And what better reason was there than to ensure the safety of his family?

He gave an audible, sharp exhale and rolled back his shoulders. Euphemia's lips gathered like a dried fruit.

"Aye." The word came out as though he spat.

"Angus!" his brother cried.

Devils played in Euphemia's eyes as she folded her arms over her chest. She looked him up and down slowly and licked her lower lip with the tip of her tongue. Angus's hand clenched around the edge of the bench. Why was he so repulsed by her?

"The wedding will be in May," she said. "Right after Lent."

"And the contract?" Laomann said. "We must negotiate the dowry and the payment before—"

She waved her hand dismissively, her eyes sticking to Angus like pine resin. "All those details later. May I speak to ye, Lord?"

Angus cocked his head in the way of agreeing and downed the remnants of his uisge.

He let her lead him out of the great hall. She made a sharp turn behind the corner and dragged him into an alcove under the stairs. There, in the darkness, she gathered his tunic by his collar and pulled his face to hers. Her breath was warm against his neck, smelling of uisge. A rich, intense scent of roses filled his nostrils. But he resisted her attempt to pull him closer.

"Lady..."

"Dinna worry about waiting till the wedding night, my lord," she whispered hotly. "I'm nae virgin. I had two husbands. I ken what is to happen between a man and his wife, and I want it to happen between us very much."

She pulled him to her harder, but he turned his face away. "Lady, I canna."

She paused and leaned back. "Ye canna?"

He cleared his throat. "I wilna. Nae till we're marrit."

She shook her head. "I dinna care about that."

"But I do, Lady. Ye will be my wife before God and that will be the night I will take ye as a man takes a woman. Nae before."

She scoffed, then cupped his jaw. Her cold hand burned against his skin. "I understand, Angus. I do. 'Tis yer right. Ye're a man of yer beliefs." Her eyes turned into two small chips of granite. "But understand as well, my sweet betrothed, that if ye change yer mind about the wedding, the consequences will be dear. I dinna take rejection lightly. I will take Kintail by force, and ye wilna be able to stop me."

"My lady, if I give my word, 'tis harder than steel."

"Good. But even steel can be broken."

"I assure ye, it wilna come to that."

She nodded, and he stepped out of her grasp, a boulder weighing on his heart. How would he live his life with such a woman as Euphemia? But as he walked back into the great hall, he knew that this was his life, to choose the path of duty and to carry it. Everything was worth it as long as his clan was safe.

CHAPTER 1

E ilean Donan Castle, May 2021

ROGENE WAKELEY LAID TWO LONG CANDLES NEATLY NEXT TO each other on the polished antique sideboard. Taking a deep breath, she told herself she was 99.9 percent happy for her friend.

Karin was getting married in Eilean Donan, having her dream wedding to the love of her life in the most beautiful castle in Scotland.

Rogene glanced at the fine painting hanging above the table on a rough stone wall. The portraits of generations of clan MacRae looked at the guests from the walls of the Banqueting Hall, surrounded by rococo and neoclassical furniture. Rogene took the bottle of whisky out of the bag and placed it near the silver quaich, a traditional, shallow drinking cup the couple would use as part of the wedding ceremony.

She glanced over her shoulder to make sure the guests were fine. Fifty or so people sat on the Chippendale chairs, murmuring quietly—elegantly dressed women in small hats with flowers, nets, and feathers, most men in kilts. The happy 99.9 percent of her had been glad to shake the hand of every single one of them as they had arrived and smile so much her face ached.

The happy 99.9 percent of her rejoiced in being the maid of honor, making sure all went according to Karin's German standards: perfectly and by the minute. Which was good because Rogene was the responsible one. The one who had basically raised her brother, David, from the time she was twelve years old, despite living with their aunt and uncle.

David was talking to one of Karin's relatives sitting in the front row. The fabric of his suit stretched across his broad shoulders. He was close to being accepted into Northwestern and was likely to get a football scholarship. Good Lord, when did he start looking so much like Dad?

Rogene's eyes prickled.

That was the 0.1 percent talking.

To distract herself, she turned back to the table and placed the silver candleholder by the quaich.

The 0.1 percent reminded her that she couldn't rely on people. That people could disappear at any moment. That they could die. That people wouldn't take care of her when she needed them the most.

That she was so much better off on her own.

She took the vase that held a gorgeous bouquet of thistle, white roses, and freesias and placed it in the center of the table. As she removed a rose from the side of the bouquet and put it into the center, the unhappy 0.1 percent of her wondered if she'd ever have a bouquet like this at her own wedding. Probably not. She couldn't imagine getting married. How did others manage to be happy and in love and trust another human being?

As she turned the vase a little, she went completely still.

The bouquet!

She whirled around to the arched exit, her heart slamming in her chest.

"What is it, Rory?" Anusua, her colleague from Oxford University, asked. She stood at the entrance to the hall, ready to greet newly arriving guests. Short and full-figured, she looked stunning in a similar lilac dress to Rogene's.

"The bouquet..." Rogene grabbed her hair, likely messing up the intricately woven braids and the chic updo that felt like bread crust under her fingers. She felt naked in the long, mermaid-style, lilac dress with low cleavage. Rogene's usual wardrobe included elegant blouses and turtlenecks with suit pants or black jeans, which made her look like a professor before she even was one. "I forgot to pick up the bouquet."

"Oh, bollocks," Anusua muttered, abandoning her post. "Let me fetch it. What's the address?"

Anusua was an Indian Brit, and definitely more accustomed to driving on the "wrong" side of the street. But Rogene was the maid of honor, and if Anusua made a mistake, Karin would be crushed. There was also the bagpipe player who was due to arrive any minute...

"Come on, Rory," Anusua said. "Give me the car key."

Anusua was right, Rogene could delegate, be part of a team.

But the 0.1 percent stopped her.

David walked towards them and opened the beautiful, massive door under the arched entryway for an old lady to pass through. Too bad the door was only a replica made in the grand restoration of the castle in the 1920s, the historian within Rogene thought distantly.

"Everything okay?" David asked.

He was so handsome in his suit, his dirty-blond hair cut in a simple, classic style that made him look older than he was.

Or, maybe, it was because he'd had to grow up sooner than he should have, especially with her abandoning him in Chicago for her doctoral program at Oxford.

"All good," Rogene said, her voice tense.

"You aren't going to let me help, are you?" Anusua said softly. "You know you *can* rely on people to give you a hand."

Anusua sighed and walked to the old lady who had just come in, no doubt to see if she needed any help. David patted Rogene on the shoulder. "What was that about?"

"I need to go get the bouquet, but the bagpipe player still isn't here."

"Let me get the bouquet. You deal with the bagpiper."

"Is your permit even valid here?"

If he misread the name of a street while driving the car on the other side of the road, she'd need to deal with a lost teenager in a foreign country. His face darkened. He knew she was thinking of his dyslexia, not his driver's license.

"Okay," he said. "Go. I can deal with the bagpiper."

She sighed. That was the lesser evil, even though she did hate to leave the responsibility to anyone but herself.

"I'll be right back. Thanks, Dave."

She opened the arched door into the damp, freezing air of the Scottish Highlands and hurried down the old stone stairwell into the courtyard. Harsh wind blew in her face as she passed through the gatehouse with the raised portcullis and onto the long bridge that connected the island to the mainland. She barely glanced at a couple of tourists who roamed around the shape of the medieval tower back on the island.

Rogene's heels clacked against the bridge as she ran towards the parking area. Damn it, she hadn't taken her bolero, and it was so windy—probably because of three lochs that met here. Her lungs ached for air, and a needle pierced her side, reminding her that she should really get more exercise, not spend all her time in archives and libraries working on her PhD.

But her current discomfort didn't matter. She couldn't let her best friend down on her wedding day. She was already walking on a thin ice by refusing to let other people help with her research. There were two problems with that. One, her thesis supervisor was pissed off. Two, she had a bold topic, and she had no proof for it yet.

Panting, she got into the car. After three and a half years in the UK, she was used to driving on the other side of the road, and quickly navigated to Inverinate, which was ten minutes away. Luckily, there were no problems on her way, and she quickly picked up the bouquet and drove back to the castle.

When she was back in the courtyard of Eilean Donan, she saw Karin on the small landing in front of the arched entrance into the Banqueting Hall. Wind played with the long locks of her blond hair that cascaded down her back. A wreath of white heather circled her head. She was such a beautiful bride. One hand was on her flat, corseted belly, the other on her mom's shoulder. David watched her, looking as if he'd swallowed a frog.

Rogene's legs growing cold, she waved with the bouquet as she climbed the stone stairs, careful not to slip on the smooth surface. "It's here! Don't you worry, everything's all right."

Karin glared at her. "All right?"

Rogene swallowed as she kept climbing. Usually, Karin was sweet, but she was now definitely in bridezilla mode.

When Rogene stood in front of Karin, she handed her the bouquet and plastered a happy smile on her face. "Did the bagpipe player arrive?"

Karin paled as her eyes widened at David. "Did he?"

"Yes, he's already inside," David said.

Karin sighed. Her eyes glistened, and Rogene knew her best friend was on the verge of tears. "Do I look horrible?" Karin asked.

Rogene gasped. "What? No! You look amazing. Where is this coming from?"

"Even with this makeup?"

"What do you mean?" Narrowing her eyes, Rogene studied Karin. This looked like her usual evening makeup. Oh...shoot!

Karin sniffled. "The makeup woman never showed up."

"Doesn't matter," Rogene said. "You look beautiful and Nigel's going to be over the moon. Are you ready?"

Karin exchanged a glance with her mom, then took a deep, steadying breath and nodded. "Yes." She smiled. "I am."

"Okay. Let's go."

She opened the door and nodded to the bagpipe guy, who began playing. Nigel, who stood tall and handsome in his kilt, watched the door like a hawk. When Karin appeared, his face lit up, and Karin beamed as she met his gaze.

The couple lit candles and said their vows, which were beautiful and very Scottish. They drank from the silver quaichs, and finally signed the marriage license—or the marriage schedule, as they called it over here.

There were photos, and more bagpipe music, and cheers and broad smiles. The couple looked happy, and as enamored with each other as they could be.

After the ceremony, everyone descended into the Billeting Room on the ground floor for the champagne reception. As the waiters carried trays with drinks around, Rogene felt like she could finally take a breather. Her stomach squeezing in nervous spasms from the adrenaline that hadn't stopped racing through her veins yet, she took her bolero and her clutch and went out onto one of the curtain walls facing north.

David stood on the circular wall around the Great Well, leaning on the parapet with his elbows.

Rogene knew something was wrong and made her way up to him. His eyes were on the island, which was covered with grass, a few bushes and small trees. A group of four people walked down the pebble-covered path that stretched from left to right.

Rogene couldn't see any sign of the curtain walls that she'd seen on archaeological maps of the islands. There were supposed to be three towers that had been raised here in the first phase of construction, in the thirteenth to fourteenth centuries, and the castle where the wedding took place must have only had the keep building.

David's profile was stern, his gray eyes fixed forward.

"Is everything okay?" she asked.

"I almost ruined Karin's wedding." He swallowed hard as he met her eyes, a muscle in his jaw flexing.

"Don't say that," she said.

"It's my fault. The makeup artist's car broke. Her phone was dead, and she came here. I gave her the address of Karin's hotel..."

"Good."

"Not good. I said 51 Dornie Street..."

The address was 15 Dornie Street. Rogene felt the blood leave her face. He sometimes reversed the numbers or the letters in a word and read things like "left" instead of "felt."

"Karin was upset because of me," he muttered.

Rogene searched for David's hand to squeeze it like she had when he was younger. A dyslexic born to professor parents, and with his older sister receiving a scholarship to do a PhD at Oxford, he'd always felt inferior. That was part of the reason he'd gone into sports and was now a football team captain.

"It wasn't your fault," she said.

He scoffed and shook his head. "Who else's?"

"Mine. I should have never left you. I should have sent Anusua to get the bouquet."

He sighed and lowered his head, looking at his shoes. "Whatever. It wouldn't change a thing about me. My only hope for a good future is a football scholarship, and it's still up in the air. I'm the black sheep in a family of geniuses, and you know it. Mom and Dad were professors. You will be, too, one day."

She wasn't so sure about that. The date of her thesis defense was fast approaching and she still didn't have any tangible proof of her mom's outrageous hypothesis that Robert the Bruce had come to Eilean Donan in 1307 on his way to surrender but something or someone had changed his mind.

"David, come on. You're not a black sheep."

"Stop," he said and pulled away. "I don't want anyone's pity."

He pushed himself off the banister and strode into the castle. "David!" Rogene called.

Guilt weighed in her chest. He was upset, and she couldn't just abandon him, not again.

She went after him, fighting against the icy wind, her heels clacking against the stones. She hurried down to the ground floor, hoping he had gone back into the Billeting Room where the reception was taking place, but he wasn't among the guests. Maybe he'd gone into the kitchens? She turned, trying to think of the best route to get there when she heard steps against stone. The tiny foyer had only three doors, two of which led to the Banqueting Hall.

Could he have gone through the third one? Wrought iron hardware held together the planks of massive wood under the arched pathway. A barrier with a red rope guarded the entrance, but that wouldn't stop an upset teenager. She thought she heard footsteps descending.

There were no museum workers present. She went around the barrier, opened the door, and flicked the switch. Lights came on, illuminating stone steps leading down.

"David!" she called as she made her way down the stairs into the grave-like coldness of the basement.

Downstairs was a surprisingly large space illuminated by electrical lamps. Tables and chairs covered with protective sheets stood along the rough stone walls. The chilly air smelled like wet stone, earth, and mold. Light didn't quite reach the very far end of the hall where she noticed a massive door in the shadows.

"David, where are you?" she called.

Only her echo answered, jumping off the ancient, vaulted ceiling. Looking around, she remembered an old legend claiming the castle's name didn't originate from a sixth-century saint, but from a colony of otters that had inhabited the island. Supposedly, the King of the Otters was buried beneath the foundations of the castle. Cu-Donn meant an otter, or a brown dog, but it was also very likely that a Pictish tribe might have been called this. There had been, after all, an Iron Age fortress here before, which had burned to the ground.

Suddenly, Rogene felt like a little girl again, like the first time Mom had gotten her fascinated with history. They had been on a trip in Stirling, and Mom had told her a ghost story, and then the real story behind it. Life would never be the same for Rogene.

She wished she could spend more time here, but she needed to find David. The reception would be over soon, and the wedding party would head to the hotel for dinner. Huddling in her bolero, she walked towards the dark door.

"David?" she called.

The echo of her heels was loud and felt foreign here, as though she could wake up the ghosts of Bronze and Iron Age people, the Picts, and generations of Mackenzies and MacRaes. She could almost feel their eyes on her.

With a shaking hand, she pushed the cold wood of the door and it opened with a gnash. The scent of wet earth and mold breathed on her from the pitch darkness. Was it even safe to be here?

She stepped in.

For a moment, she had the weirdest sense she had left the world as she knew it and stepped into another one. She also had the sense that someone was there.

"David? Hello?"

The echo greeted her back.

She searched with her left hand against the rough wall and found a switch. A single electric bulb suspended from an arched ceiling illuminated the space, which resembled a dungeon, minus the iron grating and torture instruments. A pile of boulders and rocks rose to her right. Steel columns supported the ceiling.

Rogene shivered and huddled into her bolero.

To her left and straight ahead, the walls of rough stone and mortar were whole. Curious, she walked farther into the room, her heels sinking into the packed-earth floor. She held the edges of the bolero closed over her chest, but the wet cold crept into the marrow of her bones. Her knees shook, but she couldn't say if it was from cold or from excitement.

With her eyes on the pile of stones, she approached it and went completely still. Among rubble, dirt, and sand, a carving on a flat rock caught her attention, and something else...

A handprint?

She gasped and her echo gasped with her. Sinking to her knees, she began clearing the rock. When the carving and the handprint were clearly visible, she tasted dust on her tongue. She realized she was touching her mouth with her dirty hand.

Light-headed, she felt the ground shift. Gently, she brushed the carving with her palm, every indent distinct against her fingers. There were three wavy lines and then a straight line and a handprint, just like the footprint on the inauguration stone of the Kings of Dál Riata in Argyll.

"Wow..." she whispered.

"Do ye ken what that is?" a woman said behind her.

Rogene jerked, lost her balance, and fell right on her behind. A woman in a green hooded cloak stood a few steps away from her.

Rogene sighed out. "Jesus Christ, you gave me a heart attack."

The woman came closer and stretched her hand out. When Rogene accepted her hand, the woman pulled her to stand up.

"Sorry," the woman said with a Scottish burr. "I didna mean to frighten ye. I always forget ye humans get so startled."

Ye humans? She must be the castle worker and had probably gotten a bit too into her role or something.

"I'm probably not supposed to be here," Rogene said.

"'Tis all right," the woman said. "I dinna mind. My name is Sìneag, by the way. And ye are?"

"Rogene Wakeley."

"Well, Rogene, ye found a fascinating stone." Her eyes sparkled in the yellow semidarkness.

Rogene distantly wondered why a castle worker didn't scold

her for being in a prohibited area. Perhaps Sìneag was a bit more chill about the rules...and maybe this basement wasn't as dangerous as it looked.

Sìneag lowered her hood, and Rogene marveled at her pretty pale face and beautiful red hair that cascaded in soft waves down her shoulders.

"'Tis a Pictish carving that opens a tunnel through time," Sìneag said.

A tunnel through time? Rogene frowned.

"I've never heard of a time-travel myth," she said. "Are you sure?"

"Oh, aye." She nodded. "Very sure. The three waves are the river of time, and this line is the tunnel through it. A druid carved it."

Rogene bent down and studied the lines and the curves. "Hm. It does look ancient. Picts, huh? So, between sixth and eighth centuries, probably."

"Aye. That druid believed ye can fall through time and find the person ye're truly destined to be with. The one person ye love. Do ye ken?"

Now Sìneag was clearly inventing things. Picts didn't have written language, so they had no way of leaving such messages. The only tiny accounts of them came from the Romans and Christian monks, who wrote chronicles that were concerned with battles and wars. Not myths of romantic love.

"One romantic druid, huh?" she mumbled, not wanting to confront the woman.

"Aye. He was. This stone has always caused curiosity. When clan Mackenzie owned the castle in the fourteenth century, a certain Angus Mackenzie wondered what this carving could mean."

Rogene glanced sharply at Sìneag. "Angus Mackenzie?"

"Aye."

"The one who married Euphemia of Ross?"

"The very same."

"Their marriage produced Paul Mackenzie, who famously saved the life of King Robert III. Did Angus Mackenzie have something to do with this rock? Did he leave some information about this myth?"

Sìneag laughed. "Nae he didna. But he is the man for ye."

Rogene stared at her in disbelief. Then gave out a loud laugh. "For me?"

"Aye, dearie. Look." She looked down at the rock and Rogene followed her gaze.

The carved lines glowed.

Rogene shook her head, not believing her eyes. The three lines of the river glowed blue, and the straight line through it glowed brown. Blinking, she sank to her knees by the rock and looked at it from different angles. What could glow like that? Puzzled, she ran her finger along the blue line, and a buzz went through her. Her heart accelerated. What the hell was that?

She looked at the handprint and had an inexplicable urge to put her own palm into it. Had the Kings of Dál Riata had a similar impulse to step into the footprint? Something called to her, and she just had to press her hand against this rock.

As though, if she did, everything would be all right in the world.

Blood pulsing in her hand, she pressed her palm into the print.

A shiver went through her. The sensation of being sucked in and swallowed consumed her. She felt as if she were falling into emptiness, hand, then head down, as nausea rose in her throat. She screamed, terror washing through her in a cold, paralyzing rush.

And then she became darkness.

CHAPTER 2

E ilean Donan Castle, May 1310

SHE WAS FREEZING. SHE LAY ON A COLD, WET SURFACE.
Then came the smell. Smoke.

She opened her eyes and went completely still. A man stared at her. A tall, muscular, dark-haired man holding a torch and dressed in a medieval tunic that reached his knees, with a belt around his narrow hips, and breeches and pointy shoes. He had a short beard—a bit longer than a week's worth of stubble—and hair that curled around his ears. He was handsome, with a slight bump on his otherwise straight nose and intelligent, steel-gray eyes that bored into her.

Was he another museum worker, like the woman, Sìneag? Then she remembered the glowing carving and putting her hand on the rock. What in the world possessed her to touch the artifact without gloves, without anything...

Holding her throbbing skull, she scrambled to her feet.

"Sorry, I'm not supposed to be here, I know," she said.

He slowly looked her over with his wide eyes, and even in the long dress and a bolero, she felt naked.

"Don't look at me like that, sir. I'm leaving. Where's Sìneag? I'm not sure what happened. I must have passed out..." But why would she? She'd had a sensation of falling, so perhaps she'd hit her head? Gosh, how much time had passed? "Are the guests still there, or did they already leave?"

"Guests?" he asked. "Ye must be with the Ross clan... I'm Angus Mackenzie. Ye ken, of course, I'm the groom."

He had a beautiful voice, low and husky, like distant thunder after an exhausting heat wave, promising sweet release. Distantly, Rogene realized he'd called himself Angus Mackenzie. Angus Mackenzie, the man Sìneag told her would be her destiny... How weird was that? A shiver ran through her. He must be the descendant of the historical figure Sìneag had mentioned. Perhaps he meant he was *with* the groom...

"No. I'm with the Fischers," she said automatically.

She hugged herself, warming her arms. He stared at her bare arms and her cleavage, and then some realization seemed to cross his face and he visibly relaxed.

"Oh. I've never used the services of *a fisher* before," he said. "Is that a new, secret word for what ye whores do?"

She gasped. "What did you call me?"

"Is 'fisher' another word for a whore?" he said slowly.

Blood scalded her cheeks. A whore? Her hand flew up before she could stop it.

Slap.

His cheek barely moved. It was like hitting a warm rock. Her hand stung, pain bursting through her muscles. At the same time, something small and metallic fell on a rock, and judging from the sounds, rolled somewhere.

His black eyes darkened even more, and if she believed in magic, she'd say there was fire blazing in them. His eyebrows snapped together, his mouth curved downward, and his neck corded. Suddenly she knew, whatever he had in mind would be very, very bad for her.

She fled.

Through the darkness. Through the open door. Through the long space with the curved rock ceiling, which now, surprisingly, had several torches in the sconces on the walls rather than an electric light. The torches illuminated sacks, barrels, crates, swords, shields, and even firewood. She didn't have a second to think about how odd that was. If anything, it only spurred her fear and the urge to flee this space as quickly as possible. She heard his heavy steps pounding behind her and sped up.

Goddamn heels!

Up the curved stairs, and into a completely different space. There was no corridor that led into the Billeting Room. There was one large, square room with more torches on the walls and more casks, barrels, and the like.

She breathed heavily, not believing her eyes. Had she woken up into a nightmare? Had her single glass of champagne been spiked with LSD or something? That would have been a very, very mean joke on behalf of someone.

Behind her, the steps continued, and her adrenaline spiked to the next level.

"Karin! Anusua! Oh gosh, David!" she cried as she ran through the only door she'd seen and pushed it open.

She'd expected to see the small courtyard of Eilean Donan—rough, gray stone on all sides—the West Wing building, the tightly built small curtain wall where she'd stood and talked just a short time ago.

Instead, she ran out into a large bailey. The tall curtain wall was twenty or so feet away and ran in an uneven half circle from the left to the right. Built into the wall, two small towers—one to the left and one to the right. The courtyard was full of people walking, carrying things, rolling garden carts. The strangest thing was that they were all dressed in period clothes. Most of them were men, wearing similar tunics and breeches to the man downstairs, only in a worse condition. Must be thirteenth- or fourteenth-century clothes, the historian within her noted distantly. The men had shaggy hair and beards and linen coifs. The few women she'd seen wore caps on their heads and simple dresses with aprons. Several timber buildings with thatched roofs stood in the courtyard.

There were also warriors in heavily quilted coats called *leine croich*, the Scottish version of armor. They had mail coifs on their shoulders and sported swords on their belts.

Swords!

Heavy footsteps sounded somewhere behind her. Ground flashing by under her feet, she ran down the bailey, through the giant open gate, and onto a wooden jetty. Where the hell was the bridge? There was no bridge connecting the island to the mainland! She must be somewhere else, not in Eilean Donan. Had that Sìneag woman kidnapped her? Was the brute who called himself Angus Mackenzie in on it? What would he do if he caught her?

She saw an old man in a boat shoving off from the jetty. Without thinking, she sped up, giving it all she had in her legs, and jumped. She landed in the boat, her stomach connecting with something hard and sharp. The impact kicked all air out of her. The boat careened from her landing, and water splashed, soaking her already freezing skin.

"What, by God's blood, are ye doing, lass?" croaked a voice roughened by age.

She sat back, gasping for breath, but realized the tall man might still be after her and sank to the bottom of the ancient boat, her beautiful dress soaking up a puddle of pungent greenish-brown water.

"A man is after me," she said, looking at the old man. "Please, just get me as far away from here as possible."

The old man moved his lower jaw from left to right as though he had no teeth.

"I can only get ye as far as Dornie."

"Dornie is perfect," she said.

He nodded and started rowing.

Then it hit her. Dornie?

"Is that Eilean Donan Castle?" she asked.

And as she spoke, something else occurred to her.

She wasn't speaking English anymore—and neither had the old man...or the man down in the basement.

They all spoke Gaelic.

What?

She'd learned a little of Gaelic for her research, but she'd never spoken it. And never in her life had she understood it so well that she wouldn't have had to mentally translate each word.

"Aye," the old man said. "Ye're a strange one. Of course 'tis. Why? Why dinna ye ken where ye are?"

She peered from behind the side of the boat. With a sinking stomach, she saw that this Eilean Donan was not the same castle she'd been at for the wedding.

The castle on the island now had a long curtain wall around the perimeter, three towers, and a low keep—just three stories high—smaller and simpler than the keep where the wedding had taken place.

This looked so medieval! Actually, it looked like the archaeological drawing of the castle from the thirteenth to fourteenth centuries had come alive.

'Tis a Pictish carving that opens a tunnel through time... She remembered Sìneag's words. *Angus Mackenzie is the man for ye...*

The glowing rock.

The sensation of falling through something.

The sense of disappearing.

Time travel?

No. No, no, no, no! Impossible. Sìneag had probably drugged her or pushed her, and she was hallucinating or dreaming. Or maybe one of the rocks from the ceiling had fallen on her head and she was now unconscious, experiencing some sort of lucid dream.

As a little girl, she'd imagined so often traveling back in time. When she'd been a child and had gone to museums, castles, and historical ships, she'd often wished she could live in the past for a day. Taste the food, inhale the scents, talk to the people, see the villages and castles for herself, maybe even dance at a medieval feast.

Yes, that must be what it was. So if this were a dream, she wouldn't get into trouble or danger.

She sat up straight, although not as confidently as she would like, and looked around.

Dornie village, which had been behind the bridge over Loch Long, was bigger than the one she remembered. The white two- and three-story buildings were gone, replaced by stone houses with thatched roofs. Among them, a short, round tower was visible with a flat roof, likely a Romanesque style—the early medieval style that was popular between the sixth and the eleventh centuries. A church! There was no church in Dornie in the twenty-first century.

The old man kept staring at her with a frown.

"Lassie," he finally said. "Whatever happened to ye? Ye dinna strike me as a whore, and yet ye're dressed like one."

Heat crept into her cheeks and neck, and she tightened the bolero on her chest. Another person telling her she looked like a prostitute... Which, she supposed, must be pretty realistic in the Middle Ages, as women's outfits covered as much of their body as possible, and the lowest a woman's neckline would go was below the neck. Her dress's neckline plunged down between her breasts. There wasn't much to look at, but still. She doubted even medieval prostitutes dressed so provocatively.

Cold wind grazed against her flaming cheeks. The oars splashed in the water, and waves rocked the boat. She was so cold in this dress. Was it possible she'd be this cold in a dream?

She doubted it.

"I'm not a whore," she said.

He pursed his lips as though he wanted to believe her, but

wasn't convinced and needed more of an explanation.

Ah! Darn it. She probably needed to come up with some sort of believable backstory. Her mind worked fast, thinking of something that would work.

"I was robbed," she said.

"Robbed of yer dress?"

"Yes." She straightened her back. "I'm on my way north to Caithness to my relatives, and robbers attacked me, my bodyguards, and my maid. I was able to get away...at a great cost."

"Ye poor lass," he said.

To her relief, he didn't ask any more questions until they arrived at a small port by Dornie. Several jetties stood there with plenty of fishing boats—or at least that's what Rogene thought they were, based on the reek of fish.

Men were unloading nets full of fish—herring, from what she could tell. And then she remembered reading somewhere that Loch Duich, one of the three lochs that Eilean Donan lay on, was a major herring loch. Could her dream really be that specific? Yes, she knew a lot about history, but would she dream in such detail?

A drop of sweat snaked down her spine and chilled her as an icy gust of wind slammed into her. The old man helped her get out, and, by a sheer habit, she opened her clutch to pay him. There was her phone, and a tiny, elegant wallet with a couple of banknotes and credit cards. She licked her lips.

He didn't look like he accepted credit cards.

She removed a twenty-pound banknote. That was probably much more than the fare was worth, but he had helped her get away from that would-be rapist. Besides, if generosity would make a difference in a dream, it was well worth it.

She held out the banknote, and he took it. He turned it in his hands as though he'd never seen anything like it in his life.

"Thank you," she said.

He blinked and nodded, still looking baffled. She made her way down the jetty towards the village.

"Didna ye say ye were robbed?" the man mumbled after her, but she didn't look back.

She wasn't a great liar, that was for sure.

Her heels, which now had clumps of mud sticking to them, knocked against the wood as she walked. Fishermen stared at her and followed her with puzzled expressions and frowns, and she had an urge to put on a burlap sack that would cover her head to toe.

As she entered the village, the ground was even muddier, and she now was sinking into cold, soft muck. Her dressed was torn and stained with dank water and covered in mud—completely ruined. She sighed.

What was she going to do? If this was a dream, she needed to will herself to wake up now.

Come on, Rogene, wake up!

But she still saw the same gray stone houses with thatched roofs, the same people dressed in tunics and long, baggy dresses. She looked back. The castle on the island was still the same, too, and now she saw several *birlinns*—boats from the Western Islands of Scotland—at the water gate on the other end of the island, too.

'Tis a Pictish carving that opens a tunnel through time.

Oh, puh-lease.

She'd never heard or read about any myths like that. And her mom would have known.

Rogene was making her way through the busy streets. The mostly windowless houses were separated by small fences. Everywhere, people followed her with heavy, puzzled, and even antagonistic gazes.

But despite her skepticism, the farther she went, the more this felt like reality and not like a dream. There were too many details, too many things happening at once. And things were logical, whereas her dreams were often pure emotion with little coherence.

She made her way towards the church and discovered that it

had a small marketplace. There stood carts and booths with vegetables; bread; candles; textiles; fresh, smoked, and salted fish; baked pastries; and even silver and iron jewelry. This must have been a rather big village, then. It did look bigger than the current Dornie.

Next to the church stood a priest dressed in a long black robe, with a simple rope belt around his waist and a coif of the same color. He was a man of fifty or so, with an almost bald head and a grayish beard. He was talking to a woman, but when his glance fell on Rogene, his eyes widened and he hurried to her.

"Child, my dear lass," he said. "Are ye well?"

Rogene felt a sudden sense of relief that someone was taking a more caring interest in her.

"I'm fine. A bit lost."

"Did someone harm ye? I ken the women of yer trade get harmed so often."

Her trade? Another reference to her clothes? That was enough. This dream had to end, but she didn't seem able to wake up.

"I was robbed on my way to Caithness," she said. "That's all."

His soft brown eyes widened in astonishment, and she almost swallowed her tongue, suddenly aware that robbery wasn't something one referred to as "that's all."

Part of her knew that—as crazy as it sounded—if she had indeed traveled in time, she had to be very careful and come up with something believable.

She knew she needed to present herself as a noble lady to be taken seriously. She heard that she had an accent when she spoke Gaelic, and she wondered if she could pass as a Lowlander.

Yes, maybe she could be a lady of middle gentry or something from one of the Borderland clans. If, as Sìneag had said, she was destined for Angus Mackenzie—and the man she'd met in the basement was who he claimed to be—he'd lived during the Wars of Scottish Independence, so that must be the era in which she'd arrived. The south was pretty much occupied by the English, so she could say she was from one of the clans that had been hit hard.

And one of them was Douglas.

Yes. Douglas was perfect. Not only was Black Douglas one of Robert the Bruce's most important lieutenants, but also his father had been beheaded by the English, and his home had been taken from him. Yes, that was before 1306, so before the Bruce had made his comeback, but James Douglas had ransacked a lot of his own lands that had been taken away from him.

The idea began forming in her head.

"I'm James Douglas's cousin and there's been much unrest down in South Lanarkshire. My home has been burned and I'm on my way up north to clan Sinclair, who are my mother's family. I was robbed on my way here. All my bodyguards were killed as well as my maid. I barely escaped with my life."

The priest's eyes clouded with pity. "Ah. Did they take yer clothes, too, child?"

"Yes. They did."

He sighed. "Come with me, I'll give ye shelter. If nae Holy Church, then who? My name is Father Nicholas. Mayhap Lord Laomann could spare a few men to escort ye. I'll send him word."

Lord Laomann?

Father Nicholas gestured to the church, and she went to where he pointed. She was a little stunned as she moved.

"Uhm. Do you mean Laomann, chief of clan Mackenzie?" she asked.

She passed through the doors and into the church where it was as cold as it was outside and dark.

"Aye, aye, of course I do."

Laomann Mackenzie had lived between 1275 and 1330. Was it really possible that she had indeed traveled back in time?

"Father, forgive me," she said. "All this stress is playing tricks with my tired mind. What year is it?"

"Nae matter at all, child. 'Tis the year of our Lord 1310."

CHAPTER 3

T *wo days later...*

"WHAT DO YE THINK, BROTHER?" ANGUS SAID. "THIS?"

Raghnall sighed. "By God's arse, Angus, I am nae the person to ask. Why didna ye take Catrìona with ye?"

Angus studied the red cloth lying on a market booth. It was decent-looking cloth, well made and, he supposed, beautiful; though, he didn't see the need to spend silver or any other resources on his wedding attire.

But he had to. To show his respect and appreciation for the bride and her clan.

He sighed and turned to his younger brother, who stared at the cloth with the same puzzled expression.

"She has enough to do in the castle. And I didna ask ye to meet me here to pick the fabrics. I merely heard that ye were in the village and wanted to see ye."

Raghnall looked at the stand with swords, shields, and daggers.

"If ye ask my advice on weapons, I'm happy to help."

"I dinna need anyone's advice on weapons."

Raghnall hemmed and moved to the stall with smoked fish. He stared at it with hunger. Angus followed him and gave the seller a penny. Raghnall took a smoked herring and a piece of bread and bit into it.

"Thanks, man," he said through a full mouth. "Is it nae a wee bit late to get yer wedding attire done? Two sennights till the wedding, is it nae?"

They walked away from the booth and towards the church.

"Aye. They're due to arrive soon to negotiate the contract, so I must ask Father Nicholas if he needs anything prepared for that. Will ye come to talk to Laomann soon?"

Raghnall sighed and looked around. "Aye. I must, hey?"

"Aye. Ye still want him to give ye yer lands back?"

"I do."

"Mayhap the wedding would be a good point to do that. All goes well, God willing, and we will have a powerful family ally in the Rosses. He may feel forgiving."

Raghnall chewed the herring as they walked. "Aye. But 'tis nae his place to forgive me. My disagreement was with our father, who disinherited me and chased me away from the clan. Nae Laomann."

Angus's fists clenched. He wanted to help his brother. He did think that he'd redeemed himself and deserved the land. He'd fought greatly for Robert the Bruce and had grown since his rebellious youth. All the siblings had dealt with their father's terrible wrath in different ways.

And that would be what he'd do for Raghnall. "I'll back ye up when ye talk to Laomann. Make sure to call me for the talk."

Raghnall squeezed Angus's shoulder. "Thanks, brother. I must take my leave now. Someone is looking for a sword for hire, and I'm meeting them to talk."

"Aye. God be with ye, brother."

As Raghnall's tall and muscled figure walked away, Angus

wondered at how much his brother reminded him of a lean wolf, used to running and hunting long distances.

He entered the church, the scent of dust and incense reaching his nostrils. How many times had he been here for the communion and service? He looked around the dark building, illuminated dimly by the light coming from the small windows near the ceiling. The floor before the altar was swept and clean, the space feeling empty without the usual crowd who came to Mass.

And then, in the shadows by the altar, he noticed a female figure leaning over the wooden pulpit with the open Bible on it. Behind her, a large wooden cross hung on the wall, and between her and the cross was a simple stone altar with candles on both sides. Carved wooden icons hung on the wall.

It was strange to see a female leaning over the Bible in this familiar, calming room. Was she reading? Or just looking?

He'd rarely seen a woman interested in letters and science, apart from Catrìona. Mostly, they were busy with the womanly tasks of weaving, embroidering, rearing the children, and running the household.

His own father hadn't cared about teaching his children to read, calculate, and write. And as a result, only Laomann, who'd always been an arse-licker, got some sort of education. He could write a letter or read slowly, but he wasn't a great scribe, either.

Angus, Catrìona, and Raghnall had never learned letters. Something Angus had always deeply regretted, as he did have interest towards the written word and wished he could read the Holy Bible for himself, as well as the important letters and messages that came from the king, allies, and others.

But the task of recording the chronicles of events and wars, births and deaths and marriages, as well as writing letters, was most often given to priests and monks anyway, as the most educated people.

So seeing a woman studying the book with such concentration was surprising. Something told him she didn't want to be disturbed, but he wanted to find out who she was. Perhaps she knew where Father Nicholas could be. Soundlessly, he moved through the empty space towards her.

Lord, she was pretty. The light from the window high above fell on her profile, leaving her dark hair in the shadows. He admired her high cheekbones and straight nose, her lips, with her lower lip fuller than the upper one. Her dark eyelashes concealed the color of her eyes... Her hair was done in a simple style, with the upper part held with a leather string and the long, wavy strands cascading over her shoulders and back. She wore an old wool dress with patches and seams. It didna exactly fit her slender frame, which was obvious from the baggy parts that hung around the belt.

She looked familiar, he thought distantly.

And then it struck him. It was her! The woman he'd found in the cellar of the keep.

The woman who—as her slap had taught him—was not a whore, even though her attire showed more than any decent woman would want to show in public.

The woman, thanks to whom he'd lost his grandmother's wedding ring, which he wanted to give to Euphemia.

He'd lost his grip on it, thanks to her slap, and it had rolled away into the darkness. He hadn't been able to find it despite a careful search with a torch.

He was now so close to her, her scent reached him. Yes, that was her. Even through the slightly sweet scent of old clothes, undoubtedly coming from the dress, he could still smell her own aroma of exotic fruit and herbs—something like meadowsweet, and perhaps, lilac.

He yearned to reach out, take a lock of her hair, and inhale her scent...

As if sensing this desire, she went completely still, whirled, and bumped into him. She seemed to lose her balance for a moment, and he took her by the shoulders to steady her.

Brown, he realized. Her eyes were brown. So dark, they

seemed the color of twilight when a warm summer day changed into night, and it was time to let go of his worries and sit by the fire with his family.

Her lips were close to his, so pretty and pink and inviting.

She stared at him, their eyes connecting, and he saw her lips part just a little, and a tint of color brush over her cheeks.

The feel of her, warm and strong, and so feminine against him, in his arms, set a fire seething deep within him.

But her eyes widened in recognition, and the moment of heat between them was replaced by fear.

"Get off me!" she said through gritted teeth as she pushed him away. He let her go.

She breathed heavily, her chest rising and falling. He knew she was trapped between him and the pulpit, but he didn't want her to run off before he could talk to her.

"Who are ye?" he asked.

She lifted her chin. "*Not* a prostitute."

He frowned. "Who?"

She pursed her lips for a moment in an expression of a suppressed anger. "Not a whore," she said through gritted teeth.

He remembered the sting of her slap and rubbed his cheek with a smile.

"Aye. Ye made that clear. But then, again, who are ye?"

She straightened her shoulders even more and clutched the base of her throat in a nervous gesture.

"My name is Rogene Douglas," she said after she glanced down. "I am James Douglas's distant cousin."

He raised his brows. "James 'Black' Douglas?"

She nodded.

"I fought with him several times for the king, just last year, in the Battle of the Pass of Brander."

Her eyes burned. "The Pass of Brander? That must have been quite a battle..."

Something was so different about her. "Why would a woman be so interested in a battle?" he asked.

She made her face appear impartial again. "You're mistaken," she said. "I was merely being polite."

And that accent... He'd never heard anything like that.

"Do ye come from the Lowlands, then?"

She nodded. "Yes. My home was raided in the war, and I fled to clan Sinclair, who are my relatives on my mother's side. On our way, we were robbed, and my bodyguards were killed as well as my maid."

"I'm sorry to hear that," he said. "How did ye end up in my cellar, then?"

She swallowed, and the blush deepened on her cheeks. "I don't know. I was knocked unconscious. The next thing I knew, I opened my eyes and there you were, with a torch, staring at me."

He narrowed his eyes, studying her face. She was knocked unconscious? Was it a band of Mackenzie men who attacked them? Surely not.

"And then you called me a whore," she said. "I thought you wanted to rape me."

He blinked. The woman certainly must be a highborn, talking to him like that.

"Suppose I believe ye, Lady Douglas. And I dinna say that I do. But suppose I do, why were ye so interested in the Bible? Can ye read?" He glanced at the book. There were no pictures, just letters. "Or were ye merely fascinated?"

Her face twitched, as though in uncertainty, then she cocked her head. "I can read. I know it's unusual for a woman, at least in this day and age, but I can. I also can write and calculate."

"Do ye understand Latin, then?" he said.

"Yes."

He sighed. "'Tis most unusual."

Most unusual and most interesting. She fascinated him. Beautiful, educated, clearly having her own will.

"But there's one problem with yer story," he said. "I ken James Douglas. I ken other Lowlanders. Ye sound nothing like any of them. Ye talk very differently than anyone I've ever met.

And that story of yers, implying that some of my men would attack a woman for robbery, then take her to my cellar—for what? 'Tis just very amusing to me."

She fell speechless.

"So I wilna let ye go until ye tell me the truth," he pressed.

"Or what?" she said.

"Or ye'll get back into that cellar and wilna leave it until ye give me an answer I'll be satisfied with."

She folded her arms over her chest. "Then I'll prove to you that no matter how strange I sound and no matter how strange it seems you found me in your cellar, I'm telling the truth. I'll tell you things only Douglas would know." She swallowed. "And you."

He folded his arms over his chest, as well. "All right, lass. Try."

She released a long breath. "James told me he'd heard from Robert the Bruce that he'd harbored in Eilean Donan to seek protection."

How did she know that? He supposed people knew things or heard things four years after—rumors spread—but that was strangely specific.

"Oh, aye?"

"Aye. Yes."

He watched her, stunned. Aye, she was probably telling the truth, but there was something about her that was strange in the most beautiful way.

"Father Nicholas offered me shelter and clothes until I can resume my way north," she said.

He hemmed and, reluctantly, stepped back, showing her that she was free to go. But as she gave him a curt nod and walked past him and out of the church, he felt a pinch of regret that he wouldn't be spending more time in her company.

CHAPTER 4

Angus knocked at the door to Father Nicholas's chamber. When no one answered, he knocked again.

The image of the beautiful Lady Rogene was still bright in his mind, her scent still in his nostrils. By God's bones, she was a delight. And if she was on her way north, she'd be gone soon.

The images of her half-naked chest, which he'd seen in the cellar, haunted him.

Aye, he'd seen breasts many times, but something about her allured him beyond words.

With his blood beginning to burn just from the thought of her, he shook his head to shake off the images and repeated the knock.

A low grunt came from behind the door.

Alarmed, he pushed the door open. Father Nicholas lay on his modest bed with his back to Angus. The room smelled of vomit. The tiny windows let a little light in, and under it stood his desk with a piece of vellum, a jar of ink, and a quill. Three small books lay on one of the chests along the wall.

"Father Nicholas?" Angus said.

Worry pinched Angus sharply in the gut.

"Are ye unwell, Father?" Angus insisted.

Father Nicholas turned his head to him. He was pale and had bloodshot eyes.

"Aye, son. I'm afraid some sort of pestilence is upon me."

Angus looked around. "Do ye want some water? Mayhap, a stew?"

"Thank ye, son. Lady Rogene has attended to me, though I must confess, I couldna hold anything in my stomach."

Lady Rogene... The thought of her warmed his whole body like sunlight.

"Aye, 'tis good..."

He shifted his weight, unsure if he should ask about her. He did want to know the priest's opinion of her, if he believed her and why, but he thought he must believe her since he let her stay. On the other hand, Angus didn't want to strain the priest any more than he needed to. Clearly, the man was very unwell.

"I'll go and fetch the healer from the village, aye?"

"Ah, dinna ye fash, Lord Angus," he said, but his voice was weak. "God wouldna have sent me anything I couldna take."

But even though he'd said it, he didn't sound very convinced. His voice was raspy and the area under his nose wet.

He sniffed.

"Do ye have fever?" Angus said.

"Ah, dinna matter. I'll stay like this for a day or two and will be all right."

As he said that, he shuddered.

"I will go and fetch the healer, and I dinna want to hear anything about ye fighting it off on yer own. The village needs ye strong and healthy. Now turn around and try to sleep. I will come back soon, aye?"

Father Nicholas nodded weakly and turned back to face the wall.

Angus shook his head once and left the building.

Poor Father Nicholas. As a priest, he'd always been the one

who healed people, but he was also a human being and needed help.

As he passed by the market, he heard a hubbub by one of the booths. A small crowd of people had made a circle and were shouting something angrily.

"Who let ye speak—"

"How dare ye—"

"Ye need to be punished—"

As he elbowed past the people to see what was going on, he was surprised to see Lady Rogene in the middle of the circle. She was standing, shielding a woman from a man. Her arm was stretched out in front of her in a protective manner as she held the woman behind her. The man was as red as a crimson sunset, yelling, saliva flying, his shaggy beard wet with spittle.

"How dare ye!" he yelled. "She is my wife. I have the right to discipline her as I wish."

"No! You can't just beat a woman publicly like that... No, you cannot beat a woman, period."

The woman in question was hiding her face in her hands and sobbing. The surrounding crowd was getting angrier. Food started flying at Rogene: pieces of bread, a few apple cores, fish bones.

Angus felt rooted to the spot as he watched the scene. Suddenly, he didn't see Rogene shielding a woman from a man.

He saw himself.

He'd been the eternal shield to his siblings ever since he was twelve. Always a big, sturdy lad, even for his age, he knew he could take it better than any of his siblings or his ma.

Except, for him, it had always been just one opponent—his father.

For Rogene, a mob was quickly forming. There must be about two dozen people around her now, plus an angry husband, and if folk had already started throwing things at her, they were out for blood.

"Calm down, everyone!" he said loudly, but his words were swallowed by the screams and shouts.

Goddamn it.

He stood in front of Rogene, shielding her. Bones and peels and even a stone landed on his chest, his shoulders, and his face. But folk knew him.

He was one of their lords, and very quickly, the shouts died out. Nothing flew, and only a few angry yells sounded around him.

"There will be nae more disturbance," he said. "'Tis enough."

"Lord, this woman, whoever she is, interfered in my business with my wife."

Angus nodded. "Aye, so I hear. What is yer name, good man?"

"Gill-Eathain, Lord," the man said. "My wife's name is Sorcha."

"Gill-Eathain, are ye nae one of the guards in the castle?"

"I am, Lord."

"Good. Then ye ken 'tis nae a matter for public uproar. 'Tis for the lord to judge upon and decide. Take the matter to Laomann if ye wish during a regular gathering. But Lady Rogene is guest of the clan." He looked back at her and she met his gaze with wide eyes, breathing heavily. "So ye shouldna offend any member of clan Douglas, who are loyal friends of the King of Scotland. For now, I do understand yer wrath, but it must wait. Please take yer wife home and do with her as ye please, as any good husband would."

Rogene gasped in indignation. "Take her home? He'll beat her! Just as he did—"

"Lady Rogene, while I am protecting ye, this man is right. 'Tis his right to do as he pleases with his wife. I must insist that ye shut yer mouth and dinna say another word until I get ye into the church."

Lady Rogene stared at him with indignation. Did she not know how much danger she was in? Even he might not be able to shield her from the wrath of the crowd. And what in the world had possessed her to rise up against a man like that, as though it was wrong that a man punished his wife? He hated it, personally, and would never raise a hand against a woman or a child, but he was one of the rare ones. And it was certainly accepted that if a woman did something wrong or behaved badly—which women sometimes did, nothing to do about that—then a man would need to show her what is wrong and what is right.

The angry husband shook his head, clearly dissatisfied. But there was something else that stopped Angus cold. The man eyed Rogene with some sort of lust.

"I say, Lord, she needs to be punished, too. If her da failed to teach her nae to get into other peoples' business, then 'tis another man's task to do so. If other women see her going unpunished, they will get ideas. And what then?"

Rogene shook her head and muttered something. Angus thought it might have been "Damned Middle Ages…" though he didn't know what that meant. Some sort of curse?

"Look, Gill-Eathain," he said, "nae harm has been done. Ye still get to go and teach Sorcha a lesson at home. I canna allow ye to do anything about a noblewoman as she's under my protection. And if she's under my protection, she's under the chief's. So I suggest we all go home."

The man folded his arms over his chest. "She's nae noblewoman. Look at her."

A murmur went through the crowd.

"All right, all right, everyone…" Angus said and stretched out his hand with an open palm to Rogene.

But she still refused to look at him or follow him. "I can't leave her, Angus," she whispered, panting.

"Ye dinna have a choice," he said. "Ye must come with me to the castle, 'tis the safest place."

"Ah Jesus Christ," she said.

He stared at her, horrified that she would use the Lord's name so.

"Lord…" The man still wasn't giving up.

"'Tis enough. If ye try to assault a woman of clan Douglas, ye may as well leave clan Mackenzie because James Douglas fights for yer freedom and for yer king, as well as I did and my brother Raghnall."

Gill-Eathain gave Angus a long, heavy stare, then walked to his wife, took her by the elbow, and dragged her, whimpering, away.

Despite the people staring, Angus took Lady Rogene by her elbow, too, and led her away towards the small port where his boat waited for him.

He saw a wee lad playing and stopped him, gave him a coin, and told him to ask the healer to go look in on Father Nicholas.

"Where are you taking me?" Rogene said as they stood on the jetty and he offered her his hand to help her get into the boat.

"To the castle."

"But—"

He sighed. "Look, Lady Rogene, if I say ye're a guest of the clan, then ye're a guest of the clan and should be in the castle. People in the village will remember ye, so 'tisna safe for ye to walk around the village alone, anyway. Besides"—he eyed her—"my betrothed may arrive at any moment." A small feeling of satisfaction warmed up his chest as an unhappy frown crossed her face. "If Father Nicholas is so ill that he canna write..." He shrugged. "We need a scribe who can write down the contract that we negotiate with the Earl of Ross."

Suddenly, her face went limp and expressionless. "The Earl of Ross? Right! You're marrying Euphemia of Ross, aren't you?"

He cocked his head. "How do ye ken?"

She glanced back at the village and licked her lips. "I heard in the village. They're baking pies and cleaning houses to accommodate the Ross men if needed, and washing the bed linens, and there's more ale that's been brewed."

"Aye."

He looked her over as she shook her head. "What?" he asked.

"Nothing. Well..." She cleared her throat. "Angus Mackenzie would marry Euphemia of Ross. I was just thinking how funny it is that a Highland faerie can be both right and wrong at the same time."

He frowned. "What?"

"Nothing. Just a story I heard in the village. Turns out, the time-travel legend is real. But the matchmaking is wrong."

CHAPTER 5

T *he next day...*

"BA-BA-BA-BA!" ANNOUNCED A BABY SOMEWHERE BEHIND
Rogene, and she turned her head.

She was leaning over the Bible that Catrìona had given her,
which lay on one of the tables in the great hall. Barely touching
the smooth parchment, she trailed her finger over a line. Even in
the little light coming from the slit windows and the tallow
candles—which smelled like old, burning fat—she could see the
indents of the thin lines the letters were written on.

Once she'd accepted that there was no other explanation
than time travel for the medieval world around her, it had
occurred to her that this was the opportunity she shouldn't miss.
Books like the one she was studying, documents, letters that
didn't make it to the twenty-first century, lost church registries...
somewhere here must be the proof for her thesis. She just had to
find it. There must be something in the castle, and she could ask

Angus, Laomann, or Catrìona. She had her phone, so she could take pictures, and she had switched it off to save the battery.

The baby's voice brought her back to the gray walls of rough stone, the scent of stale beer coming from the tabletops, and the quiet crackling of wood burning in the fireplace.

A male servant carried a heap of wood towards the hearth, but she could see no baby. Something about an infant in these harsh times sounded wrong—which was ridiculous, of course.

"Da-da-da-da!" The voice was closer now.

A female voice cooed at the baby, and Rogene's stomach squeezed. She liked babies. Back in her aunt and uncle's house, she'd helped with her youngest cousin, Deborah, who was born a month after Rogene and David had moved in with them. And although she didn't have many friends with children, something ached in Rogene's heart every time she saw a baby. Perhaps it was the realization she might never have one of her own—she couldn't imagine ever being able to trust someone and be happy in a committed relationship.

Angus came through the arched doorway, and her heart leaped. Big, tall, and broad-shouldered, he held a bundle in his arms...

A baby.

The baby was probably eight or nine months old and was happily sitting on Angus's hip, nestled in the crease of his elbow. Wearing a coif-style hat with ties under his chin and a long, straight shirt, the baby waved one chubby little arm excitedly and kept blabbering. Angus was cooing to it with the most love-struck expression on his face.

Rogene didn't know what was cuter—the baby or the giant, battle-clad warrior who was carrying it like it was the dearest treasure in the world.

She went completely still.

Was that... That couldn't be his baby, could it?

But then a woman Rogene's age walked from behind him, smiling and babbling together with the baby. Dark-haired and curvy, she was short and sweet, in a yellow dress. Judging by the air of a mother hen around her, she must be the baby's mom.

"Go, Mairead," Angus said. "My nephew and I will be all right. Isna it true, my lad?"

This must be Laomann's wife. Mairead glanced at Rogene and her face relaxed with relief. "Ah. I see ye have a woman here who might help ye. Good."

Angus's eyes met Rogene's, and suddenly her lungs were robbed of air. His gaze darkened and his Adam's apple bobbed under his short beard. Gosh, he had such a handsome face. Thick, black eyebrows, long, curled eyelashes, high cheekbones, and a strong jaw. He had that rough beauty with an aura of masculine power that accelerated every woman's breath.

"I can take care of Ualan by myself," he said without looking away from Rogene.

Her heart beat in her throat.

"I suppose ye can," Mairead said. "Ye're so good with him. Better than his own da sometimes. Ye'll be a wonderful father one day."

Father to Paul Mackenzie, Rogene thought.

Mairead threw her hands in the air. "All right, then, I will go to get my dress altered in peace. Ye call for me if ye need something, aye?"

"Aye."

She disappeared back through the doorway, and Angus walked with the babbling baby to the fireplace. There was a large, wooden cradle, where he set Ualan, arranging him among the pillows and linens. The boy grabbed a clay rattle shaped like a pig and began shaking it, his eyes widening and his smile broadening from the clanking he was making.

"Aye," Angus cooed. "Good lad."

Rogene came to sit on the bench by his side. It was warmer here, by the fireplace, but she was acutely aware of Angus's strong body, as though he was the source of the heat. He was leaning over the cradle, and Ualan stopped shaking the rattle and reached to Angus's face with his little hand. He grabbed his uncle by the nose and squeezed. He probably had sharp fingernails because Angus grimaced, his nose reddening.

"Strong lad," he said, slowly twisting out of the grasp.

The baby squealed in delight as Angus escaped him, and went on with his business of shaking his toy, filling the room with loud, echoey clanking. Watching Angus massage his nose with an exaggerated frown, Rogene giggled.

"Are you all right?" she asked.

"Didna think the lad had nails like wee daggers."

He caught Ualan's hand and looked at his nails. They were long, though some of them were broken and had sharp edges. Glancing at the boy, Rogene noticed small scratches around his eyes and nose. He was probably hurting himself.

"Ye dinna give yer mother a chance to get rid of those, dinna ye, lad?" Angus said. "Lady Rogene, can ye please distract him? I'll take care of this."

Rogene frowned. She didn't remember any baby nail clippers in the Middle Ages, and scissors were too rough for such small fingers. "Distract him? How?"

He chuckled in his beard. "Sing to him, make faces, I dinna ken. Arenae women supposed to ken what to do with babies?"

Uneasiness churned in her stomach.

What if he hurt the boy? What if the child screamed? Did Angus know what he was doing?

"Come on, Lady Rogene!" he urged as Ualan was trying to free his little hand from Angus's giant fist with whiny grunts.

"What are you going to do?" she said doubtfully.

"Why does every woman think I'm going to eat the baby?" he growled. "I'm going to bite his nails off, of course. How else do ye expect me to shorten them?"

She blinked. She was in the Middle Ages, she reminded herself. She looked at his lips and at the tiny pink fingers of Ualan. Could this giant be so gentle he was ready to give a baby a manicure without hurting him?

And if so, what else was his mouth capable of?

Heat rushed through her core and she felt her cheeks and neck burn.

"Um..." she said, looking down and wiping her suddenly sweaty palms on her knees. "Yes, of course."

Baby books... In the twenty-first century, she'd pick a colorful baby book. The only book she had here was the Bible. She took it and found a big icon made with golden-and-red inks and showed it to Ualan.

"Here, Ualan, see, this is..."

The boy's mouth fell open as he studied the picture with wide eyes, completely forgetting about Angus. Using the boy's distraction, and with a concentrated look, Angus took Ualan's fingers in his mouth. This was both disgusting and cute.

"Um...Virgin Mary with our Lord Jesus Christ," she said as she watched Angus with horror.

To her surprise, the boy was watching her and the book with his jaw open in that sweet way very young children do.

Then, as if he realized something was going on with his hand, Ualan jerked it out of Angus's mouth with an unhappy grunt.

"Can ye do something else, please?" Angus said. "I managed three fingers."

Rogene cleared her throat. Good grief. It was one thing to like babies. It was another to know how to be a mom and how to take care of them. It seemed Angus would be a better parent than she.

"Um," she said again. Then she remembered babies liked singing. What could she sing? "Are you sleeping, are you sleeping," she howled, and smiled as Ualan's eyes widened. He stilled, mesmerized by her bad singing. Angus didn't waste any time and put Ualan's fingers back in his mouth, continuing his medieval manicure. "Brother John, Brother John..."

Angus grasped the other hand and worked quickly.

"Morning bells are ringing, morning bells are ringing..."

Rogene kept singing and gave a small giggle as Ualan's pink lips spread in a broad smile.

"Ding, dang, dong. Ding, dang, dong," she finished.

"Ba-ba-ba!" echoed Ualan, sporting four teeth as he grinned.

Seeing that Angus was still working on the boy's fingers, Rogene started from the top. "Are you sleeping, are you sleeping..."

By the time Angus let go of his nephew's hand, the boy grasped the rattle and was shaking it, staring at Rogene with a broad smile.

Angus spat the small nails on the floor and grinned. She finished singing and smiled back to him.

"Your sister-in-law is right," she said. "You're going to be a wonderful father."

To Paul Mackenzie—the son he would have with another woman.

He inhaled sharply. "I surely want to be a better father than my da was for me. Though, it takes the right woman, too."

Their eyes locked and heat ran between them.

She swallowed hard.

Quick steps approached.

"My lord! They're here. The Ross clan. They're in Dornie."

Angus looked at the servant, and Rogene felt a stab of disappointment as the heat between them vanished.

"Thanks," Angus said, and the servant left.

Rogene stood up, and he followed her. They were so close, she had to tilt her head up to look at him. She felt drawn to him as through some magnetic force.

He chuckled. "My bride arrived, but thanks to ye, the betrothal ring I was supposed to give her is lost."

He eyed Rogene up and down, and she had a sense that he was undressing her with his gaze. Suddenly, she was acutely aware of the warmth of his body that she could feel standing one step away from him.

She swallowed. "It's not like I made you lose it on purpose."

Though, in truth, if the lost ring would make them postpone the wedding, it wouldn't be the worst thing of all.

He shook his head once. "Aye. True enough." Suddenly, he reached out and tucked a loose strand of her hair behind her ear. "But something makes me wish it would never be found."

Her lips parted, and she suppressed an urge to lean into his hand. His palm, so close to her face, emanated slow, warm electrical charges that went through her skin.

But before she melted into a puddle like a snowman under the sun, he withdrew his hand. He went to Ualan and picked him up, making her heart melt all over again.

"Enough. Now, come, I need to greet the Earl of Ross and his sister, and announce to everyone that a woman shall be writing our marriage contract."

CHAPTER 6

A ngus stood with his legs wide apart and his arms folded over his chest, watching the boat with Euphemia and William, as well as their servants, approach the shore. On either side of him stood Laomann and Catrìona. Somewhere behind was Lady Rogene, whose presence he felt because of the slow, warm burning of his cock.

God's bones, how could he be aroused even now, still thinking of her milky skin and that small, feminine frame under the proper lady's dress that Catrìona had given her.

His brother had accepted Lady Rogene yesterday and was glad to give a Douglas woman in peril shelter and protection. But he still didn't know that she'd be the one writing the contract.

Earlier this morning, Angus had sent a lad to check on Father Nicholas's health, and he'd returned with the news that the old man was worse. It was some sort of flu, and Father Nicholas was coughing much. The healer was with him, so he'd been taken care of. But there was no chance he'd be well enough to write the marriage contract.

It was a beautiful morning to greet their guests. Birds chirped, the sun shone, and there was almost no wind, so the loch stood still and waiting. Water splashed softly as the oars rose and fell, drawing the boat closer to shore.

Her hair reflected gold in the sun. Euphemia was still pretty, and was probably able to bear a child. But with every inch that the boat approached, dread grew heavier in his gut. He glanced at Rogene over his shoulder and found that she was staring right at him. She quickly lowered her eyes.

So it was not just him thinking of her. She was affected, too. Her lips reddened ever so slightly, her cheeks blushed. And if he wasn't mistaken, her nipples hardened and protruded through the material of her dress.

God Almighty, help him. He didn't remember ever desiring a woman as he desired her. Why would God send him a temptation like this right before he was bound to marry another?

He sighed and turned his attention to the boat again. This was just infatuation, nothing but a craving of his flesh. He had a duty before him—the duty to his clan—and he'd be damned if he didn't meet it.

The first boat with the honorable guests arrived and bumped softly into the wooden jetty. The rest of the boats followed. The servants helped their masters to climb out of the boats and step onto the jetty. Euphemia was dressed in a beautiful red woolen cloak with white fox-fur trimmings. With her golden hair, bright-blue eyes, and pleasant features, she was a sight.

For any other man.

Not for Angus. As she climbed out and straightened, looking at him, the heavy stone of dread sank deeper into his gut.

Behind her, her mousy daughter came onto the shore, also, and Angus felt for the lass. It couldn't be easy to have a mother like Euphemia.

It wouldn't be easy to have a wife like her.

"Welcome," Laomann said, and clasped the Earl of Ross's arm in a handshake till the elbow. William greeted Angus in the same way and passed farther into the castle. Euphemia stopped in front of Angus and smiled, slowly looking him up and down.

She licked her lower lip, and Angus had the unsettling sensation that she'd been undressing him in her head.

By God, this must be flattering for any man, that a noble-woman would behave like a harlot for him. Angus wanted to shake her off and never see her again. He wanted another to look at him like that. And, by God's blood, if she did, he wouldn't be able to resist her. Out of the corner of his eye, he saw Rogene walk the path leading towards the castle, and stop, watching him. The thought made his shoulders clench. Then she kept walking.

"Welcome, my lady," he said.

"Good day to ye, Angus," Euphemia said. "And thank ye. I was looking forward to this."

He cocked his head and held her gaze. She offered a small, sly smile, and walked up the path and into the castle.

When everyone was settled to feast in the great hall, Euphemia was placed next to him. Servants brought plates of bread, cheese, smoked and dried fish, bowls with butter, platters with dried apples and plums, as well as savory and sweet pastries baked yesterday. The great hall was filled with scents of food and ale. There were about a hundred men, both Ross and Mackenzie, sitting around the long tables of the great hall, filling the room with a murmur of voices and occasional bursts of laughter.

Angus asked Euphemia politely how the journey went. He didn't need to ask many more questions, as she was happy to keep talking about the journey, and how they'd been stopped by a storm on the way, and that they'd have arrived five days before, and that she was quite tired... He only offered her "hmm"s and "aye"s, and his eyes kept going back to Rogene.

She sat with his sister, watching everyone and every detail of the great hall as though she'd entered a land of elves and faeries. She ate a bit, but Angus had a sense that she wasn't used to or wasn't comfortable eating with her hands, and her left hand kept reaching out to a space next to her tray. She also kept wiping her hands against a cloth, and he found that odd, as one cleansed the fingers sometimes after the meal but not during. He always kept clean and hygienic and washed in the loch at least every other day. But he was not the rule.

She must like keeping clean, too.

Suddenly, he realized Euphemia had stopped talking. She narrowed her eyes at Rogene, too.

"Who is that that ye keep ogling, my dear betrothed?" she asked.

Angus cleared his throat. Ah, to hell and back. "Lady Rogene of clan Douglas, my lady. She is a guest of our clan and will be writing down our contract."

Euphemia sat silent, and he turned to see her face. She looked stunned, speechless, then burst out in a small laugh.

"She? Our scribe?"

"Aye. Father Nicholas is ill."

"Canna ye send for another priest?"

"Aye. But this will be faster. We already have someone."

"I can read and write, too."

"But ye will be negotiating alongside yer brother, I believe?"

She folded her arms over her chest and leaned back in her chair. "Just ken this, Lord Angus." Her lips flattened. "My brother didna tell ye, but besides my unfaithful husband, I also had the whore he'd slept with beheaded."

Angus cursed under his breath. "I gave ye my word, Lady Euphemia. And I will hold to it."

She raised an eyebrow. "I ken. I'm just mentioning it." Then she leaned forward and looked at Laomann, who was sitting in his lord's chair. "Lord Laomann! How could ye allow a woman to be writing down our contract?"

His face fell, and he frowned. "A woman?"

God's arse! He hadn't yet talked with Laomann about this, precisely because he was sure his brother would hate the idea. "Lady Rogene can read and write," Angus said. "Father Nicholas being sick, we have no one else who can fulfill the role."

"I can write," Laomann said.

"But ye canna both write and negotiate," Angus argued. "And until we find a priest who can spare the time..."

Laomann shook his head. "Nae. A woman... 'Tis wrong. 'Tis nae a woman's job to do that. Surely a woman dinna have the brains to write down a marriage contract."

Lady Euphemia's lips tightened even further. Her stare was so cold, it could freeze a man to death. "A woman dinna have the brains to write?" she said.

Laomann's nostrils flared. Then—as he often did when a higher authority contradicted him—he swallowed his anger, just as he had with their father. Every time.

"I didna mean ye, Lady Euphemia," he said.

She raised her eyebrows in an annoyed expression. "Oh, ye didna." She scoffed. "Ye men think women are so beneath ye, dinna ye? That women should stay home, and do embroidery, and weave, and bear ye children, and wipe everyone's arses." She looked at her brother, who was scowling at her. This looked like a conversation they may have had many times. "And yet, some of ye are too good at licking arses when ye need to be strong and fight for what is right for ye. Had I had a cock, trust me, the situation in Scotland would have been very different."

"Ye still wouldna be the earl," William mumbled. "I'm older."

She rolled her eyes and put the cup with wine to her mouth. "Ye wouldna be here." Angus thought she said into her cup.

Laomann cleared his throat and glanced at William. But judging by his sad demeanor as he chewed on a piece of meat, the man was not going to put his sister in her place. She'd just undermined his authority, showed the disagreement in their clan, and scolded a man who was responsible for her.

Angus looked at Rogene, who stared at Euphemia with surprise and respect. He had no doubt Rogene had enjoyed that, remembering how she'd protected a woman yesterday in the market, risking her own life.

Laomann, seeing that William wasn't going to do anything,

sighed and gestured with his fingers. "Lady Rogene, please, do come closer."

She sat stunned for a mere moment, then rose to her feet and walked to the table of honor. As if not sure how to behave, she bent her knees for a moment and gave a curt bow. What did she mean by that, Angus wondered? A common sign of respect was a bowed head. The lower the bow, the lower the position of the person. Why did she need to do that knee-bending movement?

Her dress hugged her slender figure, her arms delicate under the broad sleeves that almost reached the ground. She blushed, and was so pretty in that moment. Her eyes shone as she looked at him briefly.

Like an adolescent, he had a sudden image of her blushing as he'd traced his finger down her elegant neck.

"My brother told me ye will be our scribe for the contract?" Laomann said.

"Yes," she said. "That's what he asked me. I'm happy to help."

Everyone at the table stared at her briefly, probably at the oddness of her speech. Though everyone understood her words, no one talked like that. "Happy to help..." That was an odd expression.

"I thank ye." Laomann nodded. "I believe we start tomorrow, if the Earl of Ross and Lady Euphemia dinna object."

They both shook their heads no.

"And, Lady Rogene," Euphemia said, and Angus saw that cold glare again. "I will carefully check if yer writing is satisfactory. Though I think 'tis nae surprising that a woman can read and write, as I am able to do so myself, nae everyone's quality of writing is the same."

Rogene cocked her head. "Of course. Check as much as you want." She looked at Angus. "Perhaps, in preparation, I could look over the marriage contract of your father and mother? Just to be sure what I write is similar in style. I've never worked on a marriage contract before."

"Aye, Lady Rogene," Angus said. "I can show ye."

He should have checked with Laomann, but he didn't. Although the meal was not yet finished, he stood up and, not even waiting for anyone's approval, gestured for her to follow him. He thought he heard Euphemia's teeth cracking, but he didn't care.

CHAPTER 7

She didn't dare to touch the vellum. Even though it was already thirty-eight years old, it was so fresh and so new, and there were barely any signs of aging—well, not compared to seven-hundred-year-old documents that were in the museums and archives, preserved in pristine conditions, guarded from direct sunlight and kept under the right temperature.

And here it was, the contract written in Medieval Latin between Kenneth Og Mackenzie and Alexander MacDougall, who was the father of Morna MacDougall.

"This indentur made at Eilean Donan, the fifth day of the moneth of Marche, the yheir of our Lord a thousand twohundreth and LXXV, betuyx Kenneth Og Mackenzie and Alexander MacDougall."

The letters were written in black ink in medieval calligraphy. Carefully, feeling like she was touching history itself, she brushed against them with her thumb, noting the tiniest indents and bumps formed by ink under her finger.

She would need to write like this. She'd be the one who'd seal the fate of Angus and Euphemia through that contract.

She both loved and hated that knowledge.

Angus's gaze burned her skin. She looked up. He was so

handsome in the semidarkness of Laomann's lord's hall. It was one story up from the great hall in the castle keep. The room was like an office with a table, probably to discuss clan matters, she guessed. There was a fireplace and small slit windows with a foot-thick windowsill. The table was situated by the window so that the daylight fell on it. In the chest by its side were documents. That was where Angus had taken the contract from. Unable to read, he'd shown her the documents one by one, and she'd read aloud their titles until they'd found this one. There weren't many things at all in the chest—mostly letters to Laomann and the previous chief, Kenneth Og, registrations of land deeds, rent collections, and such. She itched for her phone, in the purse that was right there with her. She'd need to sneak in here alone somehow and photograph all the documents.

And yet, that didn't mean she'd be any closer to proving that Bruce did come here to give up and not to gather forces.

And time was ticking. She had to get back to finish and defend her thesis soon.

"What does it say?" Angus said.

She pursed her lips. Thankfully, she'd had to study Medieval Latin for her PhD. However, her modern mind recognized that what she was reading was strange, foreign. It was the weirdest thing. Like speaking a foreign language, she supposed. Her mind understood everything, and was able to reproduce it, but at the same time recognized it as foreign.

She smiled. Angus was dashing in his rough, masculine handsomeness, leaning on the table, his hand pressed against the edge right next to hers. If she'd only moved her pinkie an inch, it would touch his thumb. She swallowed. The room was full of crackling electricity again, and the air seemed to have disappeared from it. Heat radiated from him, and perspiration covered her forehead.

"It says, your mother's tocher, or dowry, includes a few islands south of Skye, and fifty marks. Your father paid two hundred marks to conclude the deal."

Angus nodded and frowned. He let go of the table and straightened up, turned away, and stared out the window. "Aye. Those islands belong to me. I am to move there with my future wife."

With his future wife... The thought stung, and to distract herself, she consulted the contract. The land, indeed, was to be given to one of the male heirs. Studying marriage contracts wasn't one of her fields, so she didn't know if that was typical. But she had read somewhere that a marriage contract could, in essence, have any conditions that the clans wanted to put there.

"How did ye learn to read and write?" Angus turned around, his tone suddenly different—light, curious, and...did she hear a tad of envy?

"Um. My father considered it important and insisted that I learn."

He looked out the window again, nodded, and chuckled. "Yer father must have been a good man. Since ye fled north to yer mother's family, I assume he's passed away."

Rogene swallowed a hard knot and blinked to will the burning in her eyes away. "He has. My mother has, too. She, too, insisted that I always learn and always improve myself."

He looked at her, and a pain in his eyes made her chest tighten. "Ye were lucky to have a da and a ma like that."

She looked at the contract in front of her. Kenneth Og Mackenzie was his father, and this document, essentially, was the beginning of his life.

"What was your father like?" she asked.

His mouth curved downwards within his beard. "'Tis nae good to talk badly of those who are deceased," he said. "So I wilna say anything."

His voice rasped, and she heard suppressed anger underneath. "What did he do?" she asked.

He turned to her completely, cold and distant. Pain raged in his dark eyes as he tucked his fingers between his torso and his arms.

"He did what he did, and I"—he gritted his teeth—"did what I did."

"That sounds ominous," Rogene said.

He frowned. "Dinna matter how it sounds." He looked at the contract. "Did ye finish here?"

With a pinch of regret, she rolled the vellum and handed it to him. As she did, their fingers touched briefly, and their eyes met. She held her breath, unable to move, chained to the captivity in his eyes.

"Do you love her?" she asked, surprising herself.

He frowned briefly. "Nae."

She didn't think a single syllable could make anyone happier than it made her. He took the parchment from her and put it into the chest. When he closed it and straightened, his eyes were sad. "But it doesna matter. My life has always been about duty to this clan. And it always will be."

He swallowed and looked her over with such longing that her cheeks burned.

"My own desires will never matter. Because clan comes first."

CHAPTER 8

T he next day...

ROGENE DIPPED THE QUILL INTO THE JAR OF INK. AS SHE brought it over the parchment to start writing, a drop fell from the tip of her reed pen and a giant black blot spread on the surface. *No!*

"...aye, and I want the islands to be included in yer clan's payment," Euphemia said.

"Damn it," Rogene muttered under her breath.

Laomann was staring at Euphemia helplessly, Angus was pacing the room, holding his elbows as though he was restricting himself from lunging at Euphemia and strangling her, and the Earl of Ross was rubbing the tip of his chin with an amused half smile.

Laomann's lord's hall was cold despite the bright morning sunlight that fell from the slit window. They had just eaten a breakfast of oatmeal and had been here for maybe ten minutes.

And already, they were at each other's throats.

Euphemia glanced sharply at Rogene. "What are ye doing?" she asked.

"Uhm." Rogene looked around. "What do I wipe this with?"

Euphemia narrowed her eyes, jumped up from the chair, and marched towards her. "Have ye never written a text before?" she demanded. She opened a small chest standing by the base of the reclining table, retrieved a linen cloth, a penknife, and something like a wooden ruler. She crossed her arms and scowled at Rogene.

"Here ye go, Lady Rogene. Have forgotten how to use the writing tools? Or have ye been lying to us and ye actually canna write?"

Rogene bit the inside of her cheek and took the cloth. "Thanks," she said and straightened her back. Forgotten? She'd been writing since she was old enough to hold a pen, sitting on her mother's lap. "I will write your contract, don't you worry."

She returned the woman's angry stare. How could she have thought yesterday that Euphemia was a feminist? That she was standing up for women's rights centuries earlier than what had been recorded? If this were high school, Euphemia would have been one of the mean girls, and Rogene refused to be bullied.

Euphemia scoffed and returned to her chair. Rogene wiped the blot, took the penknife, and scraped the dark spot away. It worked almost like an elastic eraser, except the pen took out a layer of the parchment completely and left a creamy white surface again. It was a bit rougher than the untouched rest, but Rogene was sure it would work just the same.

Great job ruining a historic document before she'd even started on it. She glanced at Angus, feeling her cheeks redden, and saw him hiding a smile.

Now what? She looked at the ruler and remembered that in medieval books, there were often lines. Monks drew thin lines before starting writing. That was what she did, using the ruler and the penknife.

Euphemia sighed with exasperation and returned her attention to Angus. "The islands are to be included in yer clan's payment," she repeated.

Then, just like in the contract between Angus's father and mother, Rogene wrote the date and the place and the parties involved. She tried her best to imitate the calligraphy, but her words were blotchy and uneven and...well...horrible.

But, thankfully, while she was doing her best at imitating the writing style of the fourteenth century, the negotiators were too busy arguing and didn't pay any attention to her.

"Over my dead body!" Angus boomed. "Those islands belong to me and to Mackenzie clan. They are where ye and I are supposed to live, Lady Euphemia."

"And we shall live there, if ye wish, my lord. And, therefore, they will remain in the family."

"Oh, they will remain in the family? Whose?"

"Ours."

"Ours." Angus scoffed. "And what if I die, just like yer two husbands before? What happens to my land then?"

"The islands go to clan Ross, of course." She stood up and walked to the other side of the room.

She thumbed one of the swords along its edge, gasped, and drew her thumb into her mouth.

Laomann fidgeted in his seat. "Clan Ross?" He drummed his fingers briefly, then covered his mouth with his hand as though stopping himself from speaking. "Those islands belonged to our mother, and they were her tocher," he said with his hand still over his mouth.

"And they will be tocher for our daughter." Hiding her thumb in her fist, Euphemia leisurely walked to Angus and stopped before him.

With her stomach flipping, Rogene watched a playful, flirtatious expression flourish on Euphemia's face as she looked up at Angus, standing so close, her breasts almost brushed his chest.

"Or son," she added.

He held her gaze. "Those islands will go to our daughter or son," he said slowly, "but as part of the Mackenzie lands."

Hyear... Rogene wrote. Hearing Euphemia's teeth screech, Rogene glanced at her quickly, and her pen did an uneven lurch. Damn it! She didn't remember reading how they would agree in the end, but this didn't sound like a great start. She knew she was just an observer, but she secretly rooted for Angus.

The Earl of Ross waved his hand. "Frankly, sister, I dinna understand why ye insist so much on having these small islands. The Earldom of Ross is many folds bigger."

Without touching her, Angus walked towards Rogene. As he approached, he locked his eyes with her.

"Speaking of the Earldom of Ross..." He turned to Euphemia. "Dinna ye have land, my lady?"

She pursed her lips like a duck's bill and put her hands on the back of the giant, wooden chair. "Aye. 'Tis so."

"'Tis customary that the bride brings lands with her to the marriage. And the groom offers a monetary retribution. 'Tis what we want. Land."

She looked around with her eyebrows raised. "Monetary retribution?" She scoffed. "Ye dinna have enough, Lord Angus, quite frankly. Ye couldna even pay full tribute, and we all ken that a bride of my status and wealth would normally nae marry a small landowner like yerself. Ye have already been unable to pay yer full tribute."

Swallowing, Rogene looked up at Angus, who stood by her side. Even under his beard, she saw his jaw muscles working. "By God's blood, Lady Euphemia, we need to find a solution, or this marriage wilna take place."

Somehow, they would, Rogene knew, though her heart drummed against her rib cage. Paul Mackenzie would be born. She hadn't seen their marriage contract, but she did remember seeing the registration of the marriage, which had been held in Dornie church. Next year, Paul would be born and registered in Dornie, too.

Everyone stilled. Rogene froze with her pen and heard a drop of ink fall onto the parchment with a soft *plop*.

"Lord Angus," Euphemia said. "Cursing like that, profaning God's body like that... Oh, ye're a bad lad, are ye nae? Tell ye what, I do have a proposition that ye may find acceptable."

She walked to him and took him by the shoulder, leading him into the corner of the room and away from everyone. She stood on her toes and whispered something in his ear. By the way she brushed up and down his right biceps, Rogene could guess what she was proposing, and she hated every bit of it. She looked at William, who stared at the table with an expression of "Oh boy, here we go again." Laomann sat with his mouth covered with his hand and fingered a small indent in the table, a deep frown on his brow. Rogene hated that her heart beat so quickly, and her stomach squeezed so painfully from the jealousy and hatred she felt towards Euphemia.

She was just an observer, she reminded herself. She wasn't even sure if her being here might have some sort of drastic butterfly effect and change everything. She shouldn't involve herself emotionally. Not to mention wishing that Angus wasn't marrying a woman like Euphemia. Any woman, actually.

She took the penknife and started scrubbing away the blotch she'd made.

Finally, Lady Euphemia stepped away from Angus and studied him expectantly. "What do ye say, Lord Angus? If ye agree, ye may keep yer islands, and I will put part of my lands at yer disposal."

Angus stared at her as one stares at a snake, and something lightened up in Rogene's chest, knowing that he wasn't impressed by this beautiful, strong, but clearly evil woman.

"I see that these negotiations are leading nowhere," he said. "Lords and Ladies, I do suggest we stop for now and come back to the table tomorrow." He looked at Euphemia. "I think we all need to have a clear head, as 'tis dangerous nae to be thinking with it."

He walked out of the room, his heavy footsteps pounding against the staircase as he descended. Lady Euphemia turned to look at her brother. And for the first time, Rogene realized that not only was this woman evil.

She was also very dangerous.

Because on her tense face and in her chilly eyes, the pain of rejection mixed with the power of a deadly storm.

CHAPTER 9

After a swim in the icy loch later that evening, Angus sat on the wooden jetty by the water gate of the castle. The sun was setting over Loch Alsh, sinking behind the hills to the west. The waters were still, reflecting the frenzy of orange, pink, and gold, and the colors spilled against the blue and indigo in the east. His feet hung from the jetty and dangled. He had his fresh clothes on and felt clean, and dry, and like himself. His hair was still wet.

God Almighty, it had been so good to dip into the cool waters and forget what had happened in the negotiation room. He didn't know how he'd marry Euphemia. Under her beautiful exterior was a woman of similar character to his father—selfish, cold, and ready to do anything to get what she wanted. Having a father like that had been bad enough. And although Angus had regretted his death, as he hadn't wished the man harm, he did feel like a new stage of his life had begun, a free one.

And now, tying himself to Euphemia, it felt like he'd be chaining himself up once again.

Light footsteps sounded on the jetty and he turned. Lady Rogene was coming to him. He stopped breathing for a moment. She was the epitome of beauty: slender, with small breasts and fair skin, her long hair falling over her shoulders and chest. Her figure under the dress moved in the elegant ways of a highborn woman. To be the ideal, she only needed to be blond, but he'd been recently appalled by a blond woman, and he wasn't someone who wanted an ideal, anyway.

But he wanted her.

God forgive him, he wanted her. He imagined her naked legs kicking that dress as she walked, the thin waist with a soft belly, the small breasts with bare nipples—would they be rosy like her lips or darker? he wondered. His cock began rousing again. Goddamn it! He'd just been in the lake where he'd taken care of his appetite for her behind some bushes—and now again? What was he, a goddamn bull?

But it was more than just her body, he knew. Something about her was so different from anyone he'd ever met, and as soon as she entered the surrounding space, he breathed easier, and colors gained vividness and brightness, and sounds became louder.

She came to stand next to him, and he continued looking up at her. He could just reach out, pull her by her legs, and catch her as she fell into his arms.

"Um, Angus," she said. "Sorry. Lord Angus..."

"Ye may call me Angus," he said, his voice rasping. He cleared his throat.

She smiled. "Well, then you can stop calling me Lady. Rogene's fine."

"Aye," he said and patted the jetty by his side.

"I only came to say supper is served. Your sister wanted to go look for you, but she's a little under the weather, so I volunteered."

Voluntee— What was that word? It probably meant she said she'd go find him.

"Supper can wait," he said, turning to look at the sky. The first stars were already shining in the east. "I'm nae particularly eager to get back to our guests."

She didn't reply, but he heard the rustle of her dress as she sat down by his side. Out of the corner of his eye, he stared at her sharp knees and slender thighs under the fabric of her dress. She sat so close, her dress was touching his hand where he held the edge of the jetty.

"But the guests are eager for you to get back." She chuckled.

"Are they," he said and sighed. "They can wait. I'll have my whole life to attend to their whims."

He saw her turn to him. "What did she suggest?"

He picked up a small piece of dry dirt and threw it into the loch. A single soft gurgle came from the spot where it went under, and the surface rippled around it.

"I'm nae sure 'tis a proper thing to tell to unmarrit ladies," he said.

She chuckled. "Ah, come on. I'm not a—" She stopped herself suddenly, and he looked at her sharply. She kept searching for a word as her cheeks blushed, and she looked guilty, as though she'd been caught in a lie.

"Virgin?" he asked, surprised. Then his stomach fell. "Were ye raped while ye were robbed?"

She widened her eyes. "No! No. I wasn't raped. But..." She straightened her back. "What the hell. Yes, I'm not a virgin, though I'm not sure that's any of your business, frankly. So, anyway, you can tell me whatever it was you hesitated to tell me."

He eyed her, and although, being raised Catholic, he expected previously unmarried young women to be virgins, he didn't think she was a whore as he'd previously accused her of being. Jealousy stung him as he thought of the man who'd made her a woman, and he suddenly wanted to punch someone.

He turned away, cleared his throat—more to distract himself from another frenzy of dirty thoughts about her—and said, "She wants me to lie with her before the wedding. She wants a son. Soon."

"Oh."

"She's nae young nae more, and she's always wanted a boy.

Her daughter is frail, poor thing, so 'tis unlikely she'll get marrit. I suppose, I'm Euphemia's last chance to have a legitimate heir."

She nodded. "And you don't want to lie with her before the wedding?"

"I have to marry her," he said. "'Tis the only way to protect my clan."

She frowned. "Protect? From whom?"

"From her. She wants Kintail because we failed to pay the tribute in full. It used to be part of Ross territory, but was claimed by my ancestors and then approved by the king. My clan won a skirmish with the chief of clan Ross a long time ago, but Euphemia thinks that battle needs to happen again. God kens my clan isna in a position to fight a large force."

"Right. Especially not during the Wars of Scottish Independence."

He glanced at her. "I've never heard anyone call them that. But aye, 'tis a good name. We do fight for our independence."

He leaned back, supporting himself with his arms. Why did he have this feeling of lightness in his chest around her? Like she'd understand anything he'd tell her, like she'd make it better.

"I've always been the one protecting them, taking on the load, anything that would harm them. And it wasna like I had anyone I loved to marry, so...I thought if I marrit anyone, it should be for the well-being of my clan."

She eyed him with something that resembled wonder. "Really?"

Ah nae, dinna look at me like that...

Too late. He was already drowning in her magic, in the depths of those beautiful sparkling eyes. He let out a long breath. "Truth be told, Lady Rogene..." He chuckled. "Rogene, I mean. I dinna want to lie with her at all." He looked at her. Her eyes shone in the dying light of the day, reflecting the brilliant, intense sunset. Her lips looked so soft, and her skin was radiant with the golden glow. Her dark hair was like a veil of silk around her face. "I want another."

She blinked and swallowed. "Who?"

It was as though someone had punched his logical mind, and it lay unmoving, allowing his feelings and emotions to do whatever they wanted.

"You."

She opened her mouth, her eyes widening in surprise. She bit her full lower lip, and he wanted to be the one biting it. Her eyes darkened, and he knew she wanted him, too. The soft blue vein in her neck pulsed faster.

His logical mind was still out cold when he reached for her, dragged her to himself by the waist, and kissed her. For a moment, he expected her to push him away and slap him again, but, thank heavens, she didn't.

Her lips met his with a soft, warm delight, a thousand times more delicious than Christmas pastry and as intoxicating as a cask of uisge. He pressed his lips to hers, softly at first, gently. And when that caused a burst of small lightning bolts to run through his senses, he knew he was lost. He kissed her again, stronger, hungrier, then licked that sweet lower lip and gently dipped his tongue into her mouth, meeting hers.

Stop, ye simpleton. Ye are betrothed to another.

God Almighty, she was like a succulent, forbidden fruit he didn't have the strength to stop tasting. He brushed her tongue with his, drinking her in. Her warm, slim body was pressed against him, and he wanted to undress her, and dissolve with her, and make her his.

But coldness rushed over him as she suddenly broke the kiss and leaned back, staring at him with horror.

CHAPTER 10

"Oh, no, no, no!" Rogene whispered. "What the hell did I just do?"

"Nothing we both didna want to, sweet," Angus said.

Oh, shoot, why did he need to be such a great kisser? A gorgeous Highland god—tall, with arms like columns, handsome and responsible and kind and so, so hot...

And now a good kisser.

Well, not so responsible, she realized. He did have a fiancée, and he was kissing her with no remorse, seemingly, whatsoever.

But she! Kissing a guy from history, goddamn it. Yes, she liked him... More than that. She was clearly developing a crush on him, but he was getting married and would soon produce an important heir. What was she thinking? Could she not get a hold of herself?

Her body warm and fuzzy from the kiss, she realized she was still in his arms. His naked torso was as hard against her as a rock, and as hot as furnace despite the chilly evening air. And God help her if she allowed herself another glance at his hard abs and broad chest covered in soft, dark hair. Before she could allow her self-control to fall apart and get back to kissing him, she pushed herself away and out of his embrace, then jumped to her feet.

"It's not right," she said. "You're about to get married. You cannot run around kissing girls. You have a duty."

A duty to history, she meant. A duty to Scotland, not just to his clan. A duty the meaning of which he couldn't even imagine.

His eyes darkened and his shoulders slumped, as though she'd kicked him where it hurt the most. And Rogene felt a stab of guilt.

"Dinna ye berate me about duty," he spat. "And I dinna run around kissing lasses." He picked up his wet clothes. "One lass. Ye."

With that he walked past her, leaving a whiff of lake water and something woody, and earthy, and so masculine her insides began sizzling and begging for him to stay.

She forced herself to turn back towards the water, not watching as he walked away. The best thing for her to do now would be to go down into the basement and just get the hell out. David must be going crazy back in her own time, and she was clearly stirring up things here that she wasn't supposed to.

But her dissertation... She had to prove her mother's theory right. She missed her mom so much, and if she could prove that the Bruce had almost given himself up to the enemies, she'd be able to defend her dissertation and publish her results—and show everyone that Mom had been right. If she could find something that would help her prove her hypothesis, she'd leave right away. She just needed to dig a bit more. She should ask around... and see if she could sneak into the lord's hall when it was empty.

Then she'd leave this time, where she wasn't supposed to be, anyway.

She just needed to become more proactive, see if she could find some records or letters.

And avoid Angus like the plague, because, clearly, her self-control took a vacation anytime he was near. And if she wasn't careful, he would not just steal her breath.

He would also steal her heart.

~

WHEN THE DOOR TO HIS BEDCHAMBER CLOSED WITH A LOW *thump* behind Angus, he knew he wasn't alone. With the fireplace dead, his bedchamber was dark. The sun had set, and little light came from the slit window. A shadow moved to his right, and he sensed a sweet breath. His hand shot to his belt only to brush against empty air.

Something sharp and cold pierced into the flesh under his chin. A knife.

"Dinna move, Lord Angus," a woman said.

Euphemia.

"Kindly remove yer blade from my neck, Lady Euphemia," he said through gritted teeth.

She didn't. Still holding it to his throat, she moved to stand before him. She was gray in the dim twilight, her hair ashen, her skin silver. She stared at him with her eyes narrowed, like she wanted to dig under his skin and find what made his heart beat faster.

A corner of her mouth crawled up. "Ah, a wee bit of excitement 'tis all, Lord. Ye just had a bit of that of yer own, didna ye?"

Angus's skin chilled. By God's blood—had she seen him kiss Lady Rogene?

What a goddamn idiot he was. Even though it had felt so good—like touching the sun—and Rogene had clearly enjoyed it, he knew he was putting her and himself in danger. Euphemia wasn't a woman to be jesting with.

"Whatever do ye mean?" he asked, hoping it was something else.

"I mean, 'tis a shame yer fun didna include me."

The edge of the knife dug deeper into his skin. Something was seriously wrong with this woman.

"Ye told me ye'd be faithful," she said. "Ye told me ye're a man of yer word."

Aye, he had. And, although he'd fully intended to keep his word, it was so hard to do that with Rogene.

"Whatever ye saw"—he grasped her hand and pressed it harder into his throat. His skin broke under the blade and a warm drop of liquid crawled down his neck. Euphemia's eyes widened in excitement and seemed to sparkle—"it doesna matter. It wilna be repeated."

She arched one elegant eyebrow.

"Kill me now if ye wish," he said, his fingers tightening around her wrist. "But I wilna betray my clan. I will stay true to my duty. I will stay true to ye."

She raised her head, and a small, satisfied smile spread on her lips. "Oh? Prove it."

"How?"

She removed the knife and took a step towards him, so close she pressed herself against him. Angus tensed, his stomach squeezing in revulsion. She leaned forward and licked the drop of blood from his neck. Her flowery, almost sickening scent reached him. That must be what rose water smelled like, he realized. The expensive rose water imported from the south.

"Ye ken how, Lord. Make me yers. Right now."

He suppressed a cringe. How was it possible that he was ready to take Lady Rogene with no regard to the consequences, but couldn't even imagine consummating the marriage with Euphemia? How would he live with her for the rest of his life?

The same way he'd endured his father, he supposed. He'd lived for his family, to protect his loved ones from a selfish, violent man. He thought of wee Ualan. Angus had to protect him and the rest of his family and clan from this woman.

He had to find some way to reason with her.

She looked at him from below, her eyes like pools of muddy blue water, peering at him dreamily and with hunger. He had to be careful. He knew he'd wounded her pride, and his father's wrath had taught what that could do. Angus's broken ribs that hadn't healed well and his broken nose, which had left a permanent bump, weren't even the worst of it.

He was pretty sure that his mother had been pregnant with another child at some point but had lost it. She had died soon after from an unknown sickness, too. Angus had always suspected she'd been weakened by internal injuries his father's fists had inflicted on her.

Besides wounding his children physically, Kenneth Og Mackenzie had possessed an uncanny ability to wound their hearts and souls, as well. Laomann had grown into a weak man who lived by licking arses. Raghnall had grown from a strong-willed boy with his own mind into a scoundrel. Catrìona couldn't imagine marrying at all, after seeing that a woman's role was to be a dirty rug under the man of the house's shoes. She'd found the release of her worries as a child in prayer and meditation, and now felt that her calling was to serve God—and, most definitely—not a husband.

And Angus... Angus felt that his life was not his own, and if he didn't protect his clan, then no one would. He couldn't imagine wee Ualan among blood and destruction. He believed love and happiness were a lie. His father had taught him that wanting something for himself was selfish. That he had to put others first no matter what.

And he could take it. He was big and strong, and others—like Catrìona and his mother and Laomann—weren't.

He cupped Euphemia's jaw, marveling at her beautiful mouth. Her full lips parted, waiting for him to kiss her.

But instead of her mouth, he saw Lady Rogene's. Her upper lip slightly thin, her lower lip full. He remembered how she'd tasted—sweet, fruity, succulent.

And he just couldn't bring himself to kiss Euphemia. Quite surprisingly, it felt that he'd be betraying Rogene if he did.

By God's blood, what was wrong with him?

Euphemia was still waiting, her eyes growing cold and angry

the longer he stood still. Finally, he planted a kiss on her forehead. With a sigh, he let go of her and went to his bed. He removed his shoes and lay down, gazing up at the canopy attached to the ceiling above him. The curtains hanging from the bed's four corners almost blocked Euphemia from view.

"Forgive me," he said. "I'm exhausted and dinna think I can perform."

All true. He couldn't perform *with her*.

He stared at the dark wooden paneling of the canopy and saw the raven hair and dark eyes of the woman he really wanted to be with.

He heard quiet footsteps approach, and the mattress sank a little as Euphemia sat on the edge of the bed. She lit a tallow candle that stood on the chest by the bed, and golden-orange light illuminated her stone-cold face. The scent of burning fat reached his nostrils.

"If ye want to rest, Lord, let me tell ye a story to help ye go to sleep."

He briefly closed his eyes. He really, really didn't want to go to sleep next to a woman who would hide in the darkness and threaten him with a knife. He put his hands behind his head, willing his tight muscles to soften, but his senses were on edge.

"Please," he said through gritted teeth.

Fire from the candle played against her face, casting dark shadows from her nose and lips, and making her look devilish, evil.

She smiled. "A long time ago," she said in a singsong voice, as though telling a good-night story to a child, "there was a young lass so beautiful that all the lads in the village wanted to marry her. One day, a king was passing by the village and stopped to give his horses a rest. He came to her house, wanting a jug of milk to satisfy his thirst. But once he saw her, he was stricken by her beauty. The king was good, and handsome, and brave, and strong, and a great warrior. His people loved him, his neighbor kings feared him, and all was well in his life...until he met the beautiful lass."

She paused and angled her head to look at him. He kept silent, waiting for her to continue.

"Dinna ye want to ken why he got in trouble, Lord?" she asked.

Angus really didn't want to know. Her voice was too soft, too soothing. "Why did he get in trouble?" he asked.

"Because he had a wife, see," she said as though she were explaining how to build with wooden blocks to a child. "A queen."

Angus didn't like where this was going, didn't like it at all.

"Aye, I see," he said.

"But the king fell in love with the village lass, and she fell in love with him. So, all he could offer her was to become his mistress. But she was so in love that she rejected all her suitors and went with him, like a whore, and lived in his castle. Do ye see a problem here?"

Angus released a long sigh. "Lady Euphemia, I get yer meaning, and I already assured ye, I wilna have mistresses."

"Oh, aye, ye did. But there are many bonnie lasses out there in the villages, and one is right under yer nose. So, let me finish to tell ye how the story ended."

Angus rubbed his eyes. "Please, do."

"So." Euphemia leaned over the candle and circled the small flame with her index finger several times, her eyes thoughtful. "So, of course, his queen noticed things. He stopped making love to her, stopped being playful with her, even stopped looking into her eyes." Her eyes watered and her tears glistened in the light of the candle. "And so the queen knew. She loved him, see. She really loved him." Her voice shook as she said the word "loved."

Angus ignored a cold knot that was forming in the pit of his stomach.

She continued, "And it hurt her so much, that he betrayed her, that she—" She broke off and pressed a fist to her mouth.

A tear fell down her cheek, and she wiped it away.

"That her heart cracked and broke," she said. "And even though she'd guarded it before, now that she'd opened up to the king, and knew happiness, she felt betrayed. She knew that had the king not met the bonnie lass, he'd still love the queen. And she was the queen, oh, aye."

Her eyes blazed with the fire from the candle. "She could make her go away. And so, she did. The bonnie lass, as beautiful and innocent and kind as she was, hankered after another woman's man. And she had to be punished." She smiled a wild, mad smile that brought a chill to Angus from head to toe. "And so, one dark night, guards came to her bedchamber. The queen watched as they dragged her screaming and kicking, then as the hangman stripped her and whipped her in front of the whole castle. And finally, when the king came to see what the uproar was, the queen watched the reflection in his eyes of the beautiful head rolling away from the lass's flayed body."

Silence hung between them as her meaning spread through the room like darkness. He wasn't afraid of Euphemia—not for himself, anyway.

But if she did hurt Rogene, it would be his fault. Who was he marrying? he wondered. Was his wife any better than his father had been?

God Almighty, if she was as self-absorbed and evil as his father, there'd be no way he could get a grip on her. He could reason with a normal woman. Even if he didn't love her or want her, he could still live in peace with her and take care of her. Have children. This was the way of things.

But why did he have a feeling he was about to marry a viper? And if he was, he needed to show the viper his own fangs.

He leaned towards her on his elbow and met her eyes. "Lady Euphemia, I understand ye were hurt in the past, but I wilna let ye behead or kill innocent people because of yer suspicions. I dinna ken what kind of husbands ye had in the past, but ye will be my wife and ye will obey yer husband. Me. And if ye do any kind of injustice or evil deed, it wilna go unpunished as it did in the past."

He noted with satisfaction that her eyes widened and she blinked in surprise. Her lips parted, her cheeks reddened, and her pupils dilated... Her chest rose and fell quickly. Had she just become aroused?

She stood up and hid the knife in the folds of her dress. "I hear ye, Lord," she said. "I will be only too happy to obey my husband. I thought I was marrying a handsome giant, a stallion. But I'm marrying a man who is so much more—a lion." She walked to the door, and Angus sighed with relief, but she paused and looked back at him, her eyes glimmering white in the darkness. "And trust me when I say that ye just became the best man I've even kent."

When the door closed behind her, and Angus was left alone, he thought that instead of making this situation better, he'd just caused her to dig her claws even deeper into him.

And if he ever wanted to break things off with her, she wouldn't let him go without spilling blood.

CHAPTER 11

T *he next day...*

"MAY I ASK YE, WHAT DO YE THINK OF LADY EUPHEMIA?" Catrìona said to Rogene.

Sitting at the table in the middle of the lord's hall, Rogene stopped writing and looked up at Catrìona, surprised. Besides the two of them, the only other person in the great hall was a male servant who was cleaning out coals from the fireplace. He didn't give any sign that he'd heard them. Catrìona pulled the handle of the warp-weighted loom and created a new layer of white woolen fabric. Rogene was practicing writing. She'd told Catrìona, who couldn't read or write, that she was preparing the contract. It was a lie. Rogene *had* to practice her calligraphy or she'd not only risk being exposed as an impostor, but she would also create a potentially unreadable document for the people of today and generations to come.

As a historian, she just couldn't have that.

Rogene studied Catrìona's pretty face. Unlike her brothers,

she was blond, and Rogene wondered if the young woman resembled her father or her mother more. Her wavy hair was the color of wheat, her eyelashes and eyebrows a bit darker. She was a beautiful young woman, and Rogene wondered how she'd look in colors that would suit her and a more fitted style, not this baggy, dirty-brown dress. Catrìona was preparing to go into the monastery, Rogene knew, and she should do what she wanted to do, but somehow, Rogene just couldn't see her being a nun. She sensed the girl had way too much passion and character to be an obedient nun. She'd seen her stick out her chin stubbornly if her brothers told her to do something she didn't want to do.

Catrìona was a wonderful roommate and very considerate. Rogene didn't mind sharing the bed with her, and through their conversations, Rogene had learned some fascinating details about everyday life, beliefs, and customs of the Middle Ages.

Rogene thought about Catrìona's question. "What do I think of Lady Euphemia?" she said slowly. "I'm not the person you should be asking that."

Wood crackled cheerfully as a servant added more logs to the fire.

What else could she say? Euphemia would be the mother of Angus's child, no matter how much Rogene wished Angus wouldn't marry her. The kiss yesterday hadn't helped. Actually, it had made her crave more. Even thinking of Angus's hard body pressed against hers made her head spin and caused a thin layer of sweat to break through her skin.

"Please, I want to ken..." Catrìona spread a single thread between the woolen cords lined vertically. The stones tied to the ends of the cords clunked softly against each other as she worked. "Ye're a guest, an outsider. Mayhap ye see something I dinna."

Watching the servant leave from the room, Rogene bit her lip and returned to her writing. She dipped the pen into the jar and touched the edge of the vessel to remove the extra ink. She dragged the pen against the parchment and drew an *A*.

"Um," she said. She had to be careful. "She's beautiful."

Catrìona sighed. "Aye, she's bonnie, isna she? But do ye think she suits Angus?"

Rogene's pen slipped and fell out of her fingers, and the tail of the *A* jumped too high.

"I didn't think that was the point of their marriage." She looked at Catrìona, who met her gaze.

Catrìona winced thoughtfully as she considered her words. "Aye. I suppose nae. I ken I'll never get marrit. Nae after I lost Taog."

Catrìona's voice jumped as she said the name, and Rogene frowned. She considered asking who that was and what had happened, but the pain in Catrìona's eyes made her swallow her words.

Catrìona put the giant spindle on her lap. "But I do think that people should be at least compatible, should they nae? Or, at least, decent people. I grew up seeing my da being terrible to my ma and to us. Angus was always protecting us from him—he took our beatings. He even provoked Father sometimes so that he'd snap on him. And she..."

Rogene's stomach churned. Angus, the protector. Angus, who looked as dependable and strong as a mountain to her. Angus, who'd made her steam inside and want to curl up on his lap and purr against him like a kitten.

Catrìona shook her head and pressed out a smile. Then she returned to her work and pulled the horizontal thread between the two rows of taut thread. "Please, tell me, what do ye think of her? I'm asking ye as a friend."

"I..." Rogene returned to her writing. "I don't think she's right for him."

There, she'd said it, impartiality be damned.

Out of the corner of her eye, she saw Catrìona drop the spindle, on which the thread was twisted, and catch it again in midair.

Catrìona met her gaze, her face frowning. "I didna think ye'd say that. Why?"

Because a man like him doesn't deserve a rotten woman like her.

Because I like him.

Because hundreds of years between us be damned, I can't stop thinking about him.

"Because she won't make him happy," she said finally, suppressing the dark, burning feeling of jealousy that stabbed at her like a red-hot knife.

"Aye. I dinna think she would." Catrìona sighed and resumed weaving. "He does deserve to be happy. After all he's done for us. He fought and protected us with no regard for himself. And he's doing it again by marrying her..." She said "her" with the same intonation as "that awful woman." "If there's another way to resolve our debt and at least marry him to someone decent, nae someone who wants to either kill him or his family, that would make me very happy."

Rogene stopped writing. Yes, there were so many things she wished were different. Like her parents being alive. Like not having grown up with an aunt and uncle who didn't want to be bothered with her or her brother. Like her developing feelings for a man who could never be hers.

But history was cruel and unforgiving. Angus was supposed to marry a sociopath who would give birth to someone important. Someone who'd help protect the line of Scottish kings and queens for the next several hundred years.

Catrìona kept chatting about marriage, and how she didn't see the use for herself, and Rogene kept thinking of Angus as she wrote. God, she'd already learned so much about medieval times —enough to start three more PhD dissertations.

She glanced at the chest that held all the letters and contracts with longing. Her purse was securely inside a leather pouch that the priest had given her, and she kept it on her belt. There, in the purse, was her phone. She hoped there was enough power left. Once she had photos of something useful, she'd be on her way.

Though she knew she'd never meet a man like Angus in the twenty-first century.

And even if she did, it wouldn't change the fact that love didn't exist for her. Marriage and love were about trust, about relying on someone. She did wish she could bring herself to trust someone and rely on them. But she couldn't bring herself to, even though she knew this problem was messing up her life.

She dipped the pen in the jar only to discover that there was no ink left. She still had so much more she could practice. She stood up and rummaged in the chest by the writing table where she'd written the contract yesterday, but the jars there were empty and dry.

"Oh, shoot," she said. "I think I'm out of ink."

Catrìona glanced at her. "Ye have such strange expressions, Lady Rogene. Shoot... Why would you say that? Is that how ye Lowlanders speak in Lanarkshire?"

Rogene hid a smile. Catrìona would probably have a meltdown if she learned what "shoot" really stood for.

"Yes, sweetie," she said, "we do speak very strangely in Lanarkshire, I'm so sorry for confusing you."

"Ah, 'tis all right. I'd like to travel more once I become a nun, help people around Scotland. So I'd like to learn different manners of speech."

Aw, she was a sweetheart. "Do you know where I can get more ink?"

"Aye, ye need to look downstairs in the storeroom."

"Thanks," she said.

She descended the stairs and was looking through the boxes and jars of stuff. She heard some noise coming out the door to the left of the one she knew led to the time-travel rock. It was Angus's voice, and he sounded like he was swearing. Something within her squeezed at the sound of his low boom. She should just find the ink and go back up. She had promised herself yesterday she would step away.

Something exploded from behind the door, and before she could stop herself, Rogene rushed to the door and opened it.

Illuminated by the fire of the torches, Angus stood surrounded by a giant puddle that reeked like fermented bread and stared at her with a face distorted by anger.

CHATPER 12

"Goddamn it," Angus growled.

"Let me help." Rogene hurried, picking up heaps of rushes and hay that lay in one of the sacks in the storeroom she'd entered from.

The uisge brewery smelled strongly like alcohol and hops. It was as hot as the depths of hell here. He'd just been brewing the malt and had accidentally hit the cauldron as he thought about Euphemia. The uisge was supposed to be ready for the wedding. The heavy, sharp spirits of alcohol hung in the small cave-like room, and as he inhaled them, he felt drunk.

Nae.

That must be the sight of Rogene, who stood in the doorway like an apparition. Her cheeks were flushed, and her big, dark eyes rested on him in an amused yet serious expression.

There was no one bonnier than Lady Rogene.

His head spun and his body was light as he grabbed a cloth and began wiping malt from the ground.

"Too bad I destroyed a cask."

Again they were alone, and that was very bad for him, though he couldn't remember why at the moment.

She grabbed a cloth and began wiping the stone floor, as well. "Do you brew the moonshine yourself?"

"Aye. I do. One of the only useful things my father taught me is the recipe for good uisge."

He suddenly became aware of a very delicious, round behind that was stuck in the air as she bent down. God's arse, he thought with his breeches suddenly too tight for his cock and his balls aching.

"What else did your father teach you?" she asked.

Angus crouched on his heels, still watching her move despite his very logical reasoning not to.

"Um," he mumbled, his mind swimming. Good Lord, why did he have to be alone with her again? "To fight well."

She straightened and turned to him with a cloth in her hands. A few locks of dark hair had come loose from the single braid that circled her head like a halo. Her lips were as flushed and red as her cheeks, and her eyes shone.

"Did you spend a lot of time fighting for the Bruce?"

"I fought for him since he came here in early 1307."

At the mention of this, she completely changed. Gone was the sweet, relaxed lass. Her eyes sharpened, her mouth opened as though she wanted to absorb his every word.

"Robert the Bruce?" she said. "He was here in 1307?"

Angus frowned. "Aye. Dinna ye ken all that from yer cousin James Douglas?"

"James wasn't with him yet, and you know it."

He stood up and threw the cloth in the remaining puddle. "And why does that seem so important to ye?"

"I'm just curious," she said. "I admire King Robert, and I wish I could meet him one day. I truly believe he's good for Scotland, and I admire those who fought for him. Without him, without you and men like you, Scotland wouldn't be independent."

Something bloomed in Angus's chest. She understood him. He fought not just for an ambitious nobleman, but for something bigger than himself, than Robert, and than even the King of England. He fought for Scotland and for freedom.

"So, he was here, right?" she pressed.

Angus's throat suddenly went as dry as sand. The walls of the brewery pressed in on him, the vaulted ceiling like that of a tomb. He remembered Robert the Bruce right there, in that cold, bitter winter when everything seemed to be lost.

"Aye," he said as memories took him. "He was."

Angus remembered how the king had arrived in a *birlinn* with barely enough sailors to man it. The loch wasn't yet frozen. He'd come from the Isle of Skye and clan Ruaidhrí, which had given him shelter from the English troops that were still on his tail. He'd arrived with his mighty shoulders lowered and his eyes sunken and shadowed. His beard had been shaggy, his dark hair dirty and smelly, his *leine croich* almost torn to pieces. Angus remembered Bruce's red face, weathered from months spent outside. He hadn't looked like a king, merely a beggar too proud to ask for alms.

"Laomann didn't want to take him in," Angus said. "He was afraid the Earl of Ross would find out."

Angus knew his brother wanted to be a stronger leader, but it was hard to unlearn the coping strategies he'd developed to survive their father.

"Raghnall was gone," Angus continued. "Had been ever since Father had cast him out of the clan. So it was me and Catrìona against Laomann. We swore to him Bruce wouldna be discovered. We hid him here, actually, because 'tis always warm here."

"Was he recruiting men?" she asked. "Even though he was so distressed?"

Angus eyed her for a while. "No one kens this, Rogene, and ye must promise ye wilna tell a soul."

He was probably drunk from the fumes, the way he always became if he spent too much time here, but he didn't care. He trusted her. He looked into her big doe eyes, so pretty, surrounded by thick, curly eyelashes. And they seemed to drink in every single word.

And he wanted to tell her. And he knew he may be a little tipsy, but it wasn't just that. He'd felt that *something* towards her from the moment he'd seen her. That pull. That connection that went deeper than the body.

"I promise," she whispered.

"He'd just found out that the Earl of Ross had ambushed his wife, his daughters, and his sister. William had broken the sacred law of sanctuary and taken them from an abbey in Tain and held them prisoner in his castle at first, then sent them down to England. So his family were in enemy hands."

She licked her fuller, lower lip and bit it in anticipation. Oh, how he wanted her to bite it from pleasure, from the sweet bliss he'd give her. How he wanted to let that raven hair spill on top of him, over his chest and stomach as he'd kiss the top of her head and inhale her magical scent that promised worlds and places he'd never known existed.

"Right," Rogene said. "So he was upset?"

"He wasna just upset," he said, and rose to his feet to distract himself from his blood boiling for her. "He was finished, Lady Rogene." Angus took a big ladle and stirred the boiling liquid in a giant cauldron. "He'd written a letter to Edward I that he was surrendering and begging for him to release his women. As brave and strong a warrior as he was, he couldna risk the lives of his wife and his daughter. He gave up."

Rogene's skin prickled. Her mom had been right! Her mom had had this hypothesis that after his devastating defeat in 1306, Bruce had fled for his life and had no intention of coming back. Her mom couldn't find evidence for that, but she'd gotten this idea based on the letter of Peter Ruaidhrí, a priest from the Isle of Skye, dated January 2, 1307, where he'd mentioned that hope for Scotland had died and would never shine again. That could be in reference to Bruce's general defeat, but her mom had thought that Ruaidhrí referred to something more concrete. To Bruce giving up completely.

Unfortunately, the records of Bruce's whereabouts around the winter of 1306–1307 were quite vague, and sources for that information were few, so it was very hard to prove.

Her mom had been right. Not only could Rogene prove that, but also defend her PhD dissertation. She could make a breakthrough in the field by supplying academic knowledge with the vast amount of information she now had about the Middle Ages.

"He did?" she said, her heart racing.

"Aye. He didna think he had it in him to resume the fight. He was devastated. All his forces, almost all his allies, were destroyed and forced to join the English side. He had very few friends left. The Cambels and us were among them. He came here to hide from the English."

"Not to gather forces?"

Angus chuckled. "Nae." He eyed her, clearly considering something. "He was so done, he was prepared to resign his crown to the English."

The words slashed like a whip.

"Resign?" she said.

Her fingers tingled as though she were touching something alive. A mystery she couldn't fathom.

History.

Time slowed down, seconds stretching into lifetimes. There was a whiff of air, the bubbling of the barley that smelled sharp and yeasty, and she thought that perhaps she heard the whisper of changing destinies.

Angus's eyes shone in the semidarkness. He left the large ladle and put a cover over the huge cauldron. He came to her and stood right in front of her, just one step away. A few fine hairs showed from the edge of his dark-gray tunic, at the base of his neck. Heat radiated from him, and on top of the scent of fermented barley, she noted the earthy scent of a man: iron, leather, and polished wood.

Her body was filling with helium and about to float up and away. How strange, she thought. Here he was telling her the story that showed her mother was right. If there was any physical evidence, that would ensure the success of her PhD dissertation—and possibly her whole future. And yet, all that paled in comparison to how simply being in one room with Angus made her feel—all wobbly, and warm, and as light as a feather.

"Aye," he said, his gaze taking in every detail of her face. "He wrote a letter to King Edward I where he was giving up the Scottish crown."

The words registered weakly in the back of her mind, her senses overwhelmed by his sheer presence. Her heart pounded out a staccato beat, and heat crept to her cheeks. She swayed an inch, hopelessly drawn to him.

Oh, he was bad for her cognitive ability. She couldn't think clearly. Had he really said Bruce wrote a letter?

A letter!

She blinked as her mind and body fought. Her body demanded she throw herself into his arms and kiss him, while her mind screamed for her to wake up and ask him more about that letter. If she found that letter, that would be her answer to everything.

As if hypnotized from his deep stare, she swallowed. "Why didn't he send it?" she asked.

He licked his lower lip. "Because I convinced him to change his mind."

Tingles ran through her. "You convinced him?"

"Aye. It was right here. If ye kent him, ye wouldna have believed yer eyes. Such a strong, capable man, a mighty warrior, and he was ashen, sunken, like his soul was sucked out of him."

Somehow, Angus looked even bigger—like the vaulted ceiling of the underground was too low for him, like the space was not wide enough for his strong shoulders. A man who'd convinced the king to change his mind, to keep fighting.

"What did you tell him?" she asked.

"I said that if he gave up, Scotland would never again get a chance to become free."

He looked down at his shoes and then at her. There was steel in his voice. "I said to him, if he wouldna rise, no one would. And if no one would, it would be the end of Scotland. The end of dignity, and honor, and freedom. And I swore that if he could find it in him to stand and fight, clan Mackenzie would fight with him till our dying breath.

"'But ye're nae laird to make such promises,' Bruce said.

"'And yet, I swear to ye that if I call on them, they will listen to me and nae to Laomann,' I told him."

Angus paused as he took in a deep breath of air. Rogene ached to stretch her hand to him, to place it on his broad chest, to feel his heartbeat against her palm. Would it beat in the same violent rhythm as her own?

"Is Laomann not loved?" she asked.

Angus's expression turned somber, and he went to sit on the bench by the wall. As Rogene walked to him, he watched her move with the eyes of a man who wanted a woman, and heat washed through her. Her skin became sensitive and her clothes scratchy.

"They ken that if worse comes to worst, 'tis me who'd die for them. So who do ye think they would follow?"

He was a natural leader. She could see that. Respect for him bloomed in her chest.

"What did Bruce say?" she asked.

Angus licked his lips and stared into the space between two cauldrons.

"He didn't say anything. I left him and said that I would take the letter and would send it tomorrow if he wished. The next day, he came out a different man. He slept and ate here, see. I was hiding him from Laomann." Angus chuckled. "So I do think it may have been my magical uisge that made him change his mind. In either case, he came out, without fearing Laomann, or anyone, and asked me to gather men so he might speak to them. Laomann was furious and scared as shite, but Bruce didna care. Neither did I. After speaking to our most trusted men, you should have seen their eyes. They were burning." A triumphant smile spread in his beard. "Burning. So we said we were on his side. Then I went around our lands and introduced him to tacksmen. We talked to more men, and although not everyone agreed, many did. Then we got him safely back to clan Ruaidhrí, who together with the Cambels and us, helped him win one castle after another as the spring of 1307 came. Inverlochy was the big breakthrough that changed everything. I fought there with him and the Cambels."

Rogene's hands shook with excitement. But why hadn't the letter been found in the twenty-first century? Why wasn't it known to modern scholars?

"You must have destroyed the letter?" she said. "I mean, it would be pretty bad if it landed in the hands of King Edward now, or became public knowledge."

He chuckled. "It would be. But since I ken ye're on Bruce's side, I can trust ye. I didna destroy it. It was the symbol of a comeback. It reminds me that even in the deepest despair, there's hope and light. And even the smallest man can change the destiny of the whole kingdom."

She swallowed hard as she clasped her cold fingers. "So you still have it?"

He looked at her in such a way that her legs went weak. "I do, Lady Rogene. 'Tis hidden in my bedchamber. But I must destroy it. Lady Euphemia can never ken about it."

Oh, yes, he was right. If the letter got into her hands, she'd show it to everyone and use it as a reason to usurp Bruce, altering the course of history. Rogene really needed to find the letter before he destroyed it and take a picture. But how would she prove that her photo was of the original, that she hadn't faked the letter? Could she hide it somewhere, bury it so deep that she could find it again in the twenty-first century, whole and untouched?

Or would she be playing with destiny and risk changing everything?

CHAPTER 12

T*hree days later...*

ROGENE STOOD BEFORE THE DOOR INTO ANGUS'S BEDROOM. Her phone was in her hand with only 3 percent battery life left. Her feet were weak, her heart beat hard against her ribs. The last three days had flown past in preparations for the wedding, and though Rogene had been scouting for every opportunity to get into Angus's room to find the letter, there was always someone next to her.

Then, finally, this afternoon a merchant ship had arrived with silks and perfumes and soaps from the Kingdom of Galicia, or Spain, and now, it seemed, the whole castle—including the servants and even the warriors—had gone to the sea gate to take a look and buy stuff for the wedding feast.

She glanced over her shoulder, down the dark flight of stairs that led to the landing in front of his room. No movement, no noise. With her hand trembling, she pushed the cold wood of the door and stepped in.

Angus's scent enveloped her—leather and iron and something musky and woody and dark. She also smelled some herbs with a sharp aroma she didn't recognize. The room was modest and straightforward, like him. The simple canopy bed of dark wood, the swords and shields on the wall, the chests under them —massive and dark. There was a dummy with armor on it—*leine croich* and his chain mail coif. The room was simple, and tidy, and sturdy. Rogene suppressed an urge to climb onto the tidily made bed and inhale the scent of Angus's pillow, imagining that he'd wrap his arm around her and pull her to him.

A noise came from behind her. She looked back, her blood chilling.

The landing was empty.

She shut the door and listened for a moment. Quiet. She should hurry. If Angus saw her here, he might think she'd come to offer herself to him... Or he might realize what she was really after and never trust her again.

In the fireplace, ambers glowed under the white ash that lay like snow. She was so nervous and so cold, she itched to stretch her hands to the warmth. She heard the excited voices and laughter coming from beyond the window, from the jetty by the sea gate where Angus had kissed her a few days ago.

The memory burned her, brought heat to her cheeks. How was it possible that the two serious boyfriends she'd had in the past had never caused this reaction from her, yet after knowing Angus for such a short time, she was set ablaze at the very thought of him?

Ridiculous.

Get yourself together, she told herself, looking around. Where could the letter be? Surely, he'd hidden it. Perhaps in one of the chests? With guilt heavy as a stone in her stomach, she opened the first chest by the fireplace. Clothes. Clean tunics and breeches—or rather medieval hose, which were essentially two long woolen stockings that covered the entire leg—and braies, which were knee-length linen breeches that looked like loose-fitting pajama bottoms. There were also several braiels, which were thin leather belts that fastened on the waist and held braies and the hose.

She bit her lip, feeling blood rush to her face and neck at the thought that she was rummaging in Angus's underwear...

No letter.

She opened the next chest. Woolen socks and several shoes, all in the medieval fashion—pointy—some made of rough leather, others made of thin, soft leather. The next chest held heavy clothes: cloaks and caps and coifs.

Ah, damn it. She opened several others, but there was nothing like a letter. She found some leather pouches with a few coins, a couple of boxes with herbs and clean pieces of cloth— probably the medieval version of a first aid kit. He had few possessions and no books, and she thought how different this simple life was compared to the twenty-first century. She, a struggling PhD student, owned so many things, and he owned so little, though he was wealthy for a man of the Middle Ages.

She straightened and looked around. Maybe under the mattress? She went to the bed and lifted the heavy mattress, filled with sheep wool, but there was nothing under it. Nothing under the pillow.

Ugh. Where could it be? She carefully looked around the walls, searching for holes in the mortar between the rough stones. Above the chimney? No. Under the windowsill?

And then she saw it... A small stone that protruded a bit more than the others and looked loose. With her stomach flipping, she moved to the window and touched the small rock. It was cool under her fingertips. Wiggling it up and down, she managed to pry it out...

And there it was, a leather roll. With her breath held, she pulled it out of the hole. She sat down on the bed and undid the roll with shaky hands...

Her heart drummed. There it was, on the parchment, written

in medieval calligraphy that she was already used to seeing. It was written in Old English.

JANUARY SIXTEENTH IN THE YEAR OF OUR LORD THIRTEEN *hundred and seven.*

ROBERT THE BRUCE TO KING EDWARD I, GREETINGS.

I received news that your lordship has my wife, my daughter, and my sister in captivity. I hereby resign my crown and become a humble servant and compel you to release my women. I am no longer King of Scots. May God bless you.

Your servant.

ROGENE STARED AT THE LETTER. HER HEART ACHED TO SEE that the legendary king, who was the symbol of independence and strength, could be so defeated. The parchment was smooth, though a bit dusty in her fingers. Her mind racing, she reread it. She retrieved her phone and took a couple of pictures.

She put the phone back in her pouch and read it again.

"What are ye doing?" said a cold female voice.

Rogene looked up.

Her pulse leaped. A pair of angry eyes bore into her. In the doorway, looking like a snake coiled to attack, stood Lady Euphemia.

CHAPTER 13

Without thinking, Rogene hid the letter behind her back. Her heart thumped against her rib cage.

"Um..." she said.

Euphemia marched towards her. "What is that?" She angled her head to see behind Rogene's back.

Rogene stood. "Nothing."

With her eyes as sharp as dagger tips, Euphemia came closer. "Ye're spying on Lord Angus, are ye nae? I've seen ye lurking here, and now ye're reading something. Ye will show me what it is."

Rogene stepped back. "It doesn't concern you."

Euphemia went into the folds of her dress with one hand. "And why does it concern ye?"

Casually, she retrieved a dirk and pointed it at Rogene. The short blade glistened. Rogene's feet chilled. If Euphemia got the letter, she could very well use it against Bruce. She could send it to Edward II. This could change history.

All because of Rogene.

No. To hell with her PhD. She couldn't let her actions undo the progress that Bruce had achieved. Even if it meant that she would achieve nothing.

She darted to the fireplace and threw the parchment on the hot embers.

Euphemia sprang after her and grabbed her by the shoulder, pressing the sharp edge of the blade to her neck. As she saw the embers ignite the letter and flames start to consume it, she let Rogene go and sank to her knees. With her dagger, she pierced the edge of the parchment and threw it onto the floor. She stepped on the flames several times until they died, leaving only the blackened edge.

Euphemia bent and picked up the letter. Oh, hell, no! Rogene leaned forward and waved her hand, trying to grab the letter, but Euphemia pulled her arm away. She hid the letter behind her back and pressed the tip of the dagger against Rogene's stomach.

"One movement, and I'll spill yer guts on the floor," Euphemia said.

Euphemia's eyes were icy blue and dead cold, and Rogene knew the woman had every intention of killing her. Rogene's hand fell.

"Ye were spying on my betrothed, were ye nae?" Euphemia said.

Rogene didn't say anything, feeling her chest rising and falling quickly. Euphemia was standing so close, the sickly scent of roses reached Rogene's nostrils.

Euphemia pressed the knife harder into her stomach, and Rogene felt the tip ripping through the layers of the dress and the undershirt and stinging her skin. Sweat tickled down her spine.

"Aye, spying on him after ye slept with him, were ye nae?" Her voice took on a bitter undertone.

Rogene swallowed a hard knot. "I didn't sleep with him."

Euphemia scoffed. "Ye should be a better liar for a spy. I've seen ye two kiss. Ye wilna take him away from me. He's mine."

Rogene sighed. "I have no intention of taking him away from

you, Lady Euphemia. You two are supposed to be together and you will have a son."

Euphemia's eyelashes trembled, and she blinked, hope softening her features. *She must really love him...*

The thought stabbed Rogene in the gut as though the knife had sunk deep into her.

But then Euphemia's eyes regained their steely expression.

"Even if 'tis so, it doesna change that ye were either stealing something or spying on Angus. What is this?" She turned and brought the letter to her eyes.

Using the woman's distraction, Rogene stomped on her foot and grabbed her wrist to take the dagger, but Euphemia came to her senses. She snatched her wrist out of Rogene's grasp—damn it, the woman was strong!—and shoved the blade into Rogene's chest. Red-hot pain seared through her in a flash as the edge of the knife cut her dress and her flesh, but it didn't go deep between the ribs.

She gasped, watching the edges of the tear in her pale-blue woolen dress become saturated with blood around a dark gash in her chest just under the collarbone.

"Move," Euphemia said. "Ye will be punished. Thieves and spies are whipped."

She pressed the edge of the dagger into Rogene's throat. A tremor rushed through Rogene. Her heart raced as she walked, moving her icy cold feet. The cut burned and ached.

And now—was Rogene really about to get whipped?

They came out onto the landing, Euphemia's dagger pressed against Rogene's lower back, right where her kidney was. Step after step, she descended to her doom.

CHAPTER 14

"Gift for your wife, my lord?" the Galician merchant said
to Angus in a thick accent. The dark-haired man was
short and stout with bronzed, weathered skin. He
gestured with a muscular arm around the goods displayed on the
booths.

"I dinna have a wife," Angus said, looking over the rolls of
white and red silk, casks of expensive wine, small bottles of
perfume and rose water.

But he needed a gift for Euphemia. She surely had her
wedding dress with her already, but he wanted to do something
nice for her and make sure she felt special.

Around him, people were talking excitedly, touching the
goods, smelling the cakes of soap, brushing the silk that was so
rare here in Scotland. Catrìona picked up a small Bible with a
gold-and-silver icon on the leather cover and was leafing through
it. Angus wondered why she was doing this to herself if she
couldn't read.

"He has a bride, though," Iòna said as he smelled a very
yellow fruit that the merchant had called a lemon. Iòna was
Angus's friend and the warrior he had fought side by side with
ever since his first battle.

"Ah," said the merchant. "This?"

He retrieved a pearl necklace. The pearls were perfect: white and round, they were worth a fortune and were so bonnie, he could imagine only one woman wearing them.

Lady Rogene.

Angus's neck muscles stiffened. Pearls were so rare and so expensive that, undoubtedly, he couldn't afford the necklace.

"How about something simpler?" he said.

The merchant hid the necklace, disappointment masked under a polite smile on his face. He produced a golden cross on a golden chain. The cross was covered with thin, twisted golden patterns and had a small, round ruby in the middle.

Angus nodded. "Aye. This will do as a wedding gift. And some silk."

"Lord, Lady Euphemia will be pleased," said Iòna, rubbing his short, blond beard.

"Thank ye," Angus said and turned to the merchant. "Will ye accept my finest uisge-beatha as part of the payment?"

The merchant's mouth curved, and he nodded.

"Would ye bring three casks, Iòna?" Angus asked.

"Yes, Lord," Iòna said and turned to the castle.

When the warrior returned with the uisge and the trade was done, Angus felt like he'd just lost half of his fortune. He tucked the white roll of silk under his arm and the necklace in his pouch. He doubted she deserved his gifts. But still. If she was anything like his father, she must be starved from the lack of attention, and that would only make her more dangerous.

The atmosphere was cheerful. Men and women bought plenty of goods—small and large—and looked forward to surprising their loved ones or trying an exotic new food.

Catrìona stood by his side eyeing the crowd. Angus reached into his pocket and retrieved a small wrapped in oiled canvas parcel.

"For ye," he said and held it out to her.

"For me?" She beamed and took the gift.

He loved it when his sister became so carefree. Her smile could light up the whole room. Unfortunately, he didn't see it so often.

She opened the parcel. "Soap!"

She brought the yellow cake with petals encased in its depths to her nose and inhaled.

"Rose soap. Thank ye, brother. That must have cost a fortune."

He chuckled. "Dinna fash. I dinna get to spoil ye often."

She shook her head and gave it back to him. "Nae, please. Give it to yer betrothed. 'Tis sin to indulge in bodily pleasures. And soap that smells so lovely surely would be that."

"Nae, I do think that God likes it when people are clean, aye?"

"I suppose..."

"Besides, ye'll have yer whole life to take care of yer immortal soul. Mayhap, ye can enjoy the rosy scent of soap before ye become a nun."

She beamed. "Thank ye! I do like a good bath."

Warmth spread in Angus's chest. In moments like this, he wished their whole family were together. "Do ye ken that Raghnall is in the village?"

"Is he? Nae, I didna ken." She glanced around. "Does Laomann ken?"

"Nae. But I think I want him at the wedding—"

A distant, urgent yell made him stop and look towards the castle. A woman was running towards the jetty, waving her hand.

"Lord Angus!" she cried. "Lord Angus!"

Fear washed over him in an icy wave.

"Here!" He ran towards the woman.

As he reached her, he recognized Sorcha, the woman Lady Rogene had tried to save from her husband, Gill-Eathain. She was panting, her cheeks red and strands of hair sticking out from under her cap.

"Lady Rogene..." she said as she gasped for air. "Yer bride told my husband to whip her..."

Angus shoved the silk to Catrìona and ran. His feet heavy and cold, he heard his ragged breath in his ears and had just one thought. *Protect her.*

Through the sea gate he ran, then the empty outer bailey with workshops and barracks and stables, through the second gate and into the inner bailey.

What he saw there made his heart drop into his heels.

Attached to the whipping pole, with her dress torn and her back bare, was Lady Rogene. Euphemia stood next to Gill-Eathain, who had a horse whip in his hand, ready to let it fly. By Euphemia's side was pale Laomann, who watched everything with wide eyes. Around them was a small crowd of people who were talking with one another excitedly. Gill-Eathain brought the hand with the whip up.

"Stop!" Angus cried.

Gill-Eathain froze and everyone looked at Angus.

"What's the meaning of this?" Angus boomed as he made his way through the crowd.

Fury and fear for Lady Rogene whirled in him, setting his blood on fire.

As he drew closer, Gill-Eathain lowered the whip. Euphemia stared at Angus with a victorious half smile. Rogene turned to him over her shoulder. She was pale, her bare back graceful as she breathed in and out heavily, her shoulder blades moving up and down quickly.

"Ah, my betrothed," Euphemia said. "Thankfully, I saw this woman rummaging in yer bedchamber. She was reading this."

Euphemia retrieved something from a pocket in her dress and showed it to him.

A roll of a parchment.

He felt his face fall. He stopped before Euphemia and locked eyes with Rogene. Betrayal slashed at him, wrenching his heart. Nae, he thought, that cannot be. Euphemia was just spinning lies. Surely it was only her means of getting back at Rogene for kissing him, and it was his fault.

But, on the other hand, this couldn't be a coincidence after he'd told Rogene about the letter. By God's blood, he really wanted to believe Rogene was innocent.

"What do ye say, Lady Rogene?" he asked. "Do ye deny it? Surely, this canna be true?"

She lifted her head and closed her eyes tight. When she opened them, he saw a hard decision there. "I looked in your room, and I was reading that document that's in Lady Euphemia's hand."

The crowd gasped and murmured. "Thief," some people said. "Spy..." A clod of dirt flew towards Rogene but passed by, then another.

Angus's stomach dropped. No. No. Was she a traitor?

"But I did it for a different reason than you might think," she said.

"What reason?" he asked.

"Lord Angus, I think she's said enough," Euphemia said. "Whatever reason she had, she was sneaking around yer room. She must be punished."

To Angus's horror, she took the whip from Gill-Eathain's hand, lifted her arm, and made a swing. The whip flew through the air like a thin snake with a soft *whoosh*. Rogene paled, tensed, and closed her eyes.

As if the world had slowed, he watched the whip come closer. It was the painful type, one with a small wooden ball on the tip.

He dashed forward, shielding Lady Rogene with his body, and pain slashed across his hand and arm in a fiery, violent line of burning. He heard a *thump* and a *click* as the ball on the tip hit him right across the cheekbone. People around them gasped, and so did Euphemia. Warm liquid rolled down his face and the copper tang of blood reached his nostrils.

While Euphemia rushed to him, he turned to Rogene. With her hands still tied to the pole, she looked at him over her shoulder, her eyes wide, her mouth open. He quickly scanned her body—no signs or harm. Thank the Lord, she was whole.

Euphemia took him by the shoulder and turned him to herself. "Lord Angus!" She truly looked worried—her blue eyes wide in horror, her face pale. "Why are ye defending her?"

He looked her over and shook his head once, fury boiling within him anew. He grasped the letter that was still in her other hand.

"This is mine." As she stared at him in astonishment, he tucked it into a belt pouch, took out the necklace, and shoved it into her hands. "'Tis for ye, dear betrothed. A wedding gift."

Then he marched to the pole and undid the ties on Rogene's hands. "Cover yerself," he commanded.

"What are ye doing?" Euphemia cried, outraged.

As Rogene clasped her dress to her body, he shot a glare at Euphemia. "Ye were wrong to punish a guest of my clan with nae consent."

"I asked Laomann," she said, pointing at the laird.

Laomann opened and closed his mouth and shrugged his shoulders.

"Goddamn it to hell!" Angus roared. "She was in my room, and looked through my things, so 'tis up to me to decide what punishment she will or wilna have after I question her. I will deal with ye later, Lady Euphemia." He grasped Rogene's upper arm and marched with her to the tower.

"And I will deal with ye now."

CHAPTER 15

C old crept into Rogene's bones as Angus shut the caged door of the dungeon behind her with a heavy *clang*. It was dark here despite three torches that cast eerie shadows on the rough walls. It smelled like mold and fungus and very old, wet rock. It turned out, the castle had a dungeon. It was the door right next to Angus's distillery. There was only one cage, and Rogene was in it.

The room was about twenty square feet and had walls on three sides. The fourth side was a wooden grating with a door made of the same material. The torches illuminated the room dully. A bench was attached to one of the walls, and chains and shackles hung on the opposite one. It was quiet here, almost deafeningly so. Distantly, Rogene heard a soft scratching, and nausea rose to her throat at the thought of rats and mice somewhere nearby.

She stood in the middle of the room, shaking from cold and fear, staring at Angus, who stood on the other side of the grating. The dress was falling off her shoulders, and she kept pulling it up. It was unbearable to watch his somber glare as he studied her. Then his eyes fell to her chest.

"Are ye hurt?" he asked.

"Just a scratch," she said. "Don't worry. Lady Euphemia was very protective of your letter."

His face fell. "Does she ken?"

"No. She never read it."

He sighed and hit the grating with his palm. "How could ye betray me?"

Guilt the size of a boulder weighed on Rogene's shoulders. "I didn't mean any harm. I wanted to see the letter for myself."

"Why?"

Oh fudge! What could she say that he'd believe? She hated lying, but she was sure if she told him the truth, he'd think she was crazy. And yet, she really wanted to tell him everything. He had stopped the whip by sacrificing himself, and now he had that awful wound on his cheek... The surrounding flesh was already swelling and bruising with yellow, red, and purple.

He'd taken a hit for her.

No one had ever done anything like that.

Could that mean that she could trust him? Give up control and rely on him?

"I really want to tell you the truth," she said, "but I'm afraid you won't believe me."

She shivered. He sighed, undid his cloak, and held it out to her through the grating. As she took it, their fingers touched, sending an electric shock through her. She wanted to grasp his hand and just hold it, but he pulled away, and disappointment slashed her gut. She wrapped the cloak around herself. His scent enveloped her, as though he were hugging her, shielding her again...

"Tell me," he said, "and let me decide on my own."

This man... He was a shield, a protector, always ready to take the pain and take everything on himself. How much inner strength did he have? How much unbreakable spirit was in him? But even he had a vulnerability, and she hated to think that someone like Euphemia would find it and use it for her own advantage.

Hadn't Rogene used Angus, too? He'd trusted her with the information about the letter, and she'd sneaked behind his back and gotten him and herself into trouble.

But the cloak he'd given her—the weight of it, the feel of it against her bare skin—made her feel as though he supported her yet again.

Feeling enveloped by him, she felt stronger. More in control. But telling him the truth, trusting him, would mean giving up that control. No. She couldn't trust even him.

Could she? For God's sake, how much lower could she fall than landing in a medieval dungeon? She should tell him the truth and just deal with whatever his reaction would be.

She took in a deep breath.

This could be the end of her. He might condemn her as a witch or let Euphemia whip her. Or even chase her away from the castle—which would be really bad because how the hell would she be able to go back to the twenty-first century?

But, who else could she trust here if not him? She would deal with it as it came.

"I'm from the future," she said.

He frowned and shook his head as though he'd heard her wrong. "What?"

"I'm from the twenty-first century, seven hundred years into the future."

He blinked and kept frowning, studying her.

"There's a rock that serves as a time-travel portal in the base of your castle. You were there when I arrived, next to that rock. A Highland faerie called Sìneag opened it for me and told me about you. That is how I fell through time."

It was probably better not to mention that Sìneag had told her Angus was her soul mate. That information was useless, as nothing would be possible between them, anyway.

He narrowed his eyes at her and winced. "And do ye think I would believe ye?"

She sighed, took a step forward, and grasped the grating with both hands. She met his eyes and nodded. "I didn't think you'd believe me, Angus. I mean, I wouldn't have, in your place. But you do remember the rock that I'm talking about, right?"

"I do."

"And you remember the strange way I was dressed? You thought I was a..." She felt heat creep to her cheeks as she remembered how she'd slapped him. "A whore."

His short beard moved as his jaw muscles worked. "Aye."

She went into her leather pouch, hoping that the phone battery still wasn't dead. "And this." She retrieved her phone, switched it on, and showed it to him. Still 2 percent battery. The colorful wallpaper on her home screen glowed, looking foreign and strange in the medieval setting around her. He stared at it with wide eyes and a deep frown, like she were holding a devil's spawn in her hand, but he didn't step back.

He squinted and looked closer, then shifted and studied it from different angles.

"What the devil?" he said.

"It's a smartphone, you can call people with it and talk with them from long distances. Also, you can take photos." She opened the photo gallery and showed him the picture of Bruce's letter. She zoomed in, and Angus's nostrils flared as he watched her. He clearly looked like he wanted to run away, but, as a battle-clad warrior, he stood and faced his fear.

"I took a picture of the letter because it doesn't exist in the future. And it proves my hypothesis—I mean, my mother's hypothesis—that Bruce was ready to give up when he was defeated in 1306. Only she couldn't prove it. And without this, I can't prove it, either."

"Prove it? To whom?"

"To the world. I study history and analyze it, and well, I'm writing a book on Robert the Bruce and want to defend it to get a doctoral degree... It doesn't matter. The point is, if I show this letter in 2021, I have a chance to have a good career in science. My brother, who is seventeen, can move in with me and I can support him. Right now, he lives with our aunt and uncle. They're good people, but they don't really want him there, as they have five kids of their own. So...this letter will help me prove my mom's hypothesis. And that would be how I honor her legacy. You know?"

He didn't. He stared at her as though he had a toothache.

"'Tis the biggest pile of horseshite I've ever heard," he boomed.

Oh, dang. Of course he wouldn't believe her. But she could still show him one more trick, which would, perhaps, tip the scale to her side. "Wait! Look!" she said and opened the camera app. In the darkness, she had to switch on the flash, and Angus roared and retrieved a dagger and pointed it at her. Her vision went blank, too, from the power of the flash.

"Ye blinded me, witch!" he growled.

But she managed to snap a picture of him and turned the phone around, showing him the screen. "Look!" she said. "It's you, do you see?"

The photo was a little blurry from the movement he'd made, but it was still clearly him. His black hair shone with white from the flash, the blade of his dagger blinding. His face was a grimace of battle rage, his teeth bared and white against his black beard.

He was still pointing the dagger at her through the grating of the cage. He was panting and studying the photo with round eyes.

Then, suddenly, the screen went black. Without the artificial light, it was dark in the dungeon. Rogene saw stars from the flash.

"Darn," she said, staring at the useless phone. "The battery died."

He brought the dagger closer to her. "Who died?"

She chuckled. "Not who. What. The battery. The energy source that feeds the phone with the ability to show the pictures and to take them. That's what we have in the future—electricity that makes it all possible."

He shook his head. "I dinna ken what this is, Lady Rogene, and I dinna believe ye."

He put the dagger back in place. "And if I dinna believe ye, ye're in big trouble, because no one else will. I need to think what to do with ye, but ken this. Ye just lost the one person that was on yer side."

He walked out of the dungeon, leaving her alone, shivering, and hurt. Because although she was terrified to think what Angus would do to her now, even worse was knowing she had lost his trust.

Because, somehow, the trust and appreciation of this kind, strong man had started to feel like a greater treasure than any lost letter or proof of her thesis could be.

CHAPTER 16

T*he next day...*

"AND WHAT MAKES YE THINK 'TIS A GOOD IDEA THAT I COME to yer wedding, brother?" Raghnall asked.

The bright sun was warm on Angus's shoulders, the dirt dry under his feet as he walked through Dornie at his brother's side. He wanted to check on Father Nicholas and see if he was doing any better. It was also an opportunity to see Raghnall and, perhaps, to stop thinking of the beautiful prisoner he'd put in the dungeon yesterday.

"Because ye're my brother," Angus said.

Raghnall scoffed. "But nae part of clan."

"Ye are, as far as I'm concerned. When will ye go and talk to Laomann?"

Raghnall shrugged. "After yer wedding, I reckon."

"Aye. 'Tis why 'tis a good idea that ye come to the wedding so that he can already see ye and mayhap start changing his mind.

He can see ye changed. Ye're nae the rascal ye used to be nae more."

Raghnall gave out a loud burst of laughter, scaring a young woman who was churning butter while sitting on the bench outside her house.

"Forgive me, good woman!" he called to her, and she laughed.

He grinned. Why women loved him so, Angus would never understand. He looked like a scoundrel, with his long, ungroomed hair and his clothes that were always covered with dust and had patches on them. Aye, he was athletic, and he carried himself confidently. And he had that sense of humor that made everyone around him feel lighter—unlike Angus. And aye, he sang so well that even Robert the Bruce stopped to listen to him by a campfire.

Were those things that women valued? Not in a husband, surely. Thinking of being a husband reminded him of his current problem.

What in the world was he going to do with Rogene? Part of him wanted to believe her, no matter how ridiculous her story sounded. But he was a rational man, and he didn't even believe that God could do miracles like time travel. He'd seen many strange things, aye. And he did remember that Owen Cambel's betrothed—the dark-skinned warrior woman—had a similar accent to Rogene, now that he thought about it. She also had a similar manner of speech, and the way she carried herself... The words she used... But she was from the caliphate, supposedly—although she had appeared rather suddenly in Inverlochy Castle last year. Was there a similar rock with a carving there, too?

Nae. Nonsense.

But that object with lights Rogene had with her, the one that created images and that small flash of lightning...

Now *that* he couldn't explain. He had no idea what could make such things happen other than magic. And if he'd accept that this object was magical, he might as well accept the possibility of falling through time.

He glanced at his brother, contemplating. Should he tell him, ask his opinion?

Raghnall marched by his side, staring around and looking like a wolf who was hunting for pleasure.

No. Something told Angus not to say anything. He wasn't sure if he believed her or not, but chances were, Raghnall would consider her a madwoman, and Angus highly doubted that it would do anyone any good.

But he could ask him another thing.

"I do want ye to stay, even if Laomann would refuse you the land that belongs to ye. Ye can live with me. I ken ye want a home and ye're tired of living on the road."

Raghnall raised his brows at Angus. "With ye? And yer new bride? Isna it a wee bit strange?"

"It would have been if I was in love with her. I'm nae."

Raghnall shrugged. "That isna unusual."

"Nae. But I'm afraid she's someone who's capable of stabbing a man in the back or poisoning him for her own benefit. And she wants Kintail to belong to clan Ross again."

"Och, brother, what are ye getting yerself into?"

Angus didn't reply. Silence hung between them, and he knew that Raghnall was thinking of all the days and nights when Angus had taken Raghnall's, Catrìona's and Mother's beatings on himself, even Laomann's.

"Dinna ye want someone ye could love?" Raghnall asked.

Rogene's face came to mind, her long, raven hair, that delicious, full lower lip, those beautiful long-lashed eyes that seemed to look right into his soul. Her body, slender and strong and delicious, against him. He'd never met a woman as smart as her and with such an unbreakable spirit, based on how she'd defended Sorcha against her own husband, even though every law said he could punish his wife as he liked.

"Even if there was someone," he said hoarsely, "'tis out of the question. The deal is done. There's more at stake than love."

"Ye have someone, dinna ye?" Raghnall said. "Ye bastart! Who is she?"

"Dinna matter."

"Och, come on, man, tell me!"

Angus groaned. "God's blood, Raghnall..."

"Brother, dinna ye think ye've done enough duty for this clan? If ye love someone else and dinna want to marry the evil witch, mayhap there's another way to keep Kintail safe. Ye dinna have to sacrifice yerself all the time."

Angus hated that there was a seed of truth in Raghnall's words. And he would love nothing more than to marry Lady Rogene—had he not been betrothed to another, and had Rogene not betrayed his trust.

"There's a woman I fancy, but 'tisna possible. Ye ken that."

"Everything is possible."

"She may be a thief and a spy."

"I dinna think so."

"How do ye ken? Ye've never even met her."

"Ye wouldna fall in love with a thief or a spy."

Angus scoffed. "I'm nae in love with her."

Raghnall shook his head, smiling in his short beard. "Mayhap nae yet. But I've never seen ye so...so..." He waved his hand in search of a word.

"What?"

He sighed. "Like ye really want to grab a pastry and are ready to cut yer own hand off if ye do."

Angus rubbed his left brow. "To hell ye with yer quick sight-edness. I've never kent ye were so knowledgeable in love."

"I'm knowledgeable in ye. If ye're really so in love with that other woman, consider carefully if there might be another way to protect Kintail against clan Ross. I think ye've done yer duty enough for our family. 'Tis time to put yerself first. Because this time, 'tis for the rest of yer life."

They arrived at the church. And as Angus opened the door

to step inside, annoyingly, he thought that Raghnall may be right.

Before he could enter, a cry made him turn his head. "Lord Angus!" called Iòna. "Lord Angus!"

Angus froze. He'd asked Iòna to keep an eye on Rogene and come fetch him if she was in danger.

"What is it?"

With a tight knot in his gut, he watched Iòna run towards him. "'Tis Lady Rogene, Lord. Lady Euphemia came to take her."

CHAPTER 17

A ngus ran down the stairs into the dungeon, his fingers curling into a fist. About a dozen Ross warriors stood with somber faces, hands on the hilts of their swords. With his heart jumping as he heard angry screams and shouts from the dungeon cell, he shouldered his way into the fiery darkness.

God's feet, Euphemia was relentless. What did she want now?

Looming over the entrance into the prison cell, Euphemia held a rod with one arm and was shouting at Rogene. Rogene, although still huddling into his cloak, glared back at her like a queen with her head high.

"...ye bitch, ye goddamn whore, get out of there, now!" Euphemia thundered.

"What's going on?" Angus said as he came to the grating.

"I'm not going away with them," Rogene said.

"Are ye mad?" Euphemia screamed. "The laird decided that ye must be punished! The laird is the law here. If ye dinna come out, I have ten men here who will take ye."

Angus's blood chilled. Laomann was looking straight at the

floor in front of him with the air of someone who was trying to will himself to disappear.

"Laomann, what is she talking about?"

"I dinna ken, Angus," he said. "Lady Euphemia made a good argument that I must, as laird, do justice and nae wait for ye. And I think she's right. What's the whole reason to wait? Justice must be done, or other thieves and spies will think that they can steal and spy with no consequences."

It was as though a scalding wall of water hit Angus's blood. He looked at Euphemia and at Rogene, who was wounded and abandoned, and he just couldn't stand the thought of Rogene being hurt.

It wasn't rational. It wasn't anything he could explain. Mayhap it was his instinct as protector. Mayhap it was a part of him that finally believed her—against his logic and reason.

"Get away from her," he growled.

Euphemia turned to him. "Angus," she said in a voice that one uses with an unreasonable child who is about to hurt himself.

Angus drew his claymore and heard the *swoosh* of nearly a dozen swords being drawn from their sheaths. Laomann gaped at him. Euphemia paled and stared at him with her mouth open, then she grew livid. He'd never seen anyone with quite the same expression of pure menace on their face.

Pointing his sword at Euphemia, he cried, "Lady Rogene, come out of the chamber."

"Ye're nae serious," Euphemia said as she watched Rogene pass by her and stand by Angus's side.

He looked at Laomann. "I had already talked to her. She was looking for an example of a letter to find a good wording for the contract."

He drew his sword back, acutely aware of the ten blade tips still pointed at him.

"A misunderstanding. Lady Euphemia didn't believe her, but I do. I drop all charges and demand that ye do the same,

Laomann." He looked straight at Euphemia, who had bared her teeth. "'Tis nae yer business, Lady Euphemia, because ye were nae affected. It was my bedchamber and my belongings, so 'tis nae up to ye to demand any sort of punishment. Am I clear?"

She drew her head back and sucked in a breath. When she didn't say anything, Angus put his hand on Rogene's shoulder and led her out of the dungeon and up the stairs. He felt her shaking under his palm and ached to take her into his arms and calm her down.

While they climbed the stairs towards his bedchamber, his mind raced. What had he gotten himself into by so openly defying his future wife and his laird? He'd lied to them. He'd lied for her, for a madwoman who'd assured him she was from the future.

What was wrong with him? He should have just let Laomann do whatever Euphemia was insisting. But he knew he couldn't live with himself if he let them harm Rogene. Shutting the door to his chamber behind him, he looked at her standing in the middle of his room.

Her eyes were wide and shining from fear, no doubt, and yet she still held her head high as she met his eyes.

"Angus, you're going to be in big trouble," she said. "You shouldn't have done that. You shouldn't have lied for me."

He chuckled and walked farther into the room. He put more wood on the dying fire in the fireplace and warmed his hands. Looking over his shoulder, he studied her. Her hair was in disarray, her skin translucent, and dark circles shadowed her eyes. He couldn't see her wound, which was under his cloak.

"'Tis done now. Ye didna do what she's accusing ye of, so I couldna let her harm ye."

Her eyes warmed and glistened.

"Thank you," she said. "I know I didn't particularly deserve it, given that I broke your trust."

He stood up. "Let me take a look at yer wound."

She watched him approach, and their eyes locked. Desire

stirred in him, deep and hot and urgent. They were alone, and he was about to touch her. And he saw in the way her eyes darkened that she'd just realized that, too.

~

ANGUS STOOD BEFORE HER, AS BIG AS A MOUNTAIN. HE brought his hands to the base of her neck and slowly undid the brooch that fastened the sides of his cloak together. Her breath caught as the warmth of his fingers reached her chin. The cloak fell on the floor with a soft *thud*, and the chill of the cool air grasped her bare back. The wound on her chest throbbed and ached, although right now, she wasn't aware of much else besides the ragged beating of her heart against her ribs.

The night she'd spent in the dungeon had left her freezing cold and aching all over. Catrìona had brought her water and porridge last night, and another portion this morning. She hadn't slept last night at all, too anxious and worried and regretting she'd said a word to Angus about time travel. Of course he didn't believe her. He was a rational man.

She'd spent the night on a cold, hard bench—her only luxury being a night pot for her to relieve herself—thinking of how different the medieval reality was compared to what she'd read in the books. Or rather, it was one thing to read about flogging, and torture, and beheading in books. It was quite another to know they were a possibility in her own life.

What was so romantic about the Middle Ages? All her life she spent dreaming of the past, wishing she'd experienced it. And now that she had, she wished she hadn't.

Except for one thing.

Angus.

The man who made her heart ache and her body feel as if she were next to an electric field.

She met his gaze. His eyes were dark and penetrating, and he was looking at her the way a bomb disposal officer might look at an explosive device wrapped in the most beautiful packaging he'd ever seen.

"Why are you helping me?" she asked. "Do you believe me?"

"Mayhap," he said.

He lowered his gaze to her mouth and swallowed. Heat rushed through her, and she felt like her body swayed towards him once, as though he were a giant magnet and she were made of iron.

He drew in a slow, noisy breath and stepped away from her. He walked to one of his chests and sank to his knees in front of it.

"Do ye still insist ye traveled in time?" he asked while rummaging.

She let out a long exhale, her lungs feeling like they were on fire. What should she say? Should she change her story and lie? No. She hated being dishonest with him. She wanted to tell him the whole truth, and she wanted him to believe her.

Her legs felt weak and wobbly. "I don't insist," she said as she walked to the bed and sat on the edge. "It's the truth."

"'Tis the truth ye believe." He retrieved a clean cloth and a small clay jar of something, then put it on the bed by her side. Then he walked to the corner of the room where there was a jug of water and poured some into a clay bowl.

Watching him come closer again, she didn't say anything. It was now up to him to believe her or not.

He crouched in front of her, and his eyes were now on the same level as hers.

"Lower yer dress," he said.

Something squeezed in her, and blood rushed to the apex of her thighs. She knew he wanted to have access to her wound, but, dear Lord, she was ready to undress herself and let him do whatever he wanted.

His dark, penetrating glare was consuming her, commanding her. Her throat contracted and she gave a small whimper. She licked her suddenly dry lips, and as he watched her do that, his eyes darkened even more.

Get a grip of yourself, she commanded. *He'll never be yours.*

She reached to the shoulder of her dress and pulled it down. Despite the cool air, her exposed skin felt hot under his gaze.

Reaching for a clean cloth that lay next to her on the bed, he accidentally brushed against her thigh. A jolt of electricity went up her hip and straight into her core. He froze and clenched his teeth like she'd hurt him.

If that was what it felt like when he touched her by accident, how would it feel if he was buried deep inside her, with no clothes between them? The images of their entwined bodies, the sounds of their combined breathing invaded her mind.

He took the cloth and dipped it into the bowl of water, then brought it to her chest and pressed it against the crust of blood. The cut burned and she sucked in air. He didn't look up at her, all his concentration on the task.

"Suppose I believe ye," he said. "Suppose ye tell the truth and time travel does happen... Tell me everything. About ye, about yer life. Clearly, ye lied when ye said ye were of clan Douglas. What clan do ye belong to?"

He wiped her wound with short, careful strokes, the cloth cooling the hot skin of her cut. Dark-red water dripped down her chest and wetted the edges of her dress.

"My name is Rogene Wakeley. I'm American. The United States doesn't exist yet in your time, but my ancestors were Scottish, Irish, and English. Like I said, I study history and write articles and books. I'm conducting research about Robert the Bruce, and the letter that you have, it confirms my hypothesis, and it's pretty revolutionary. We see Robert the Bruce as a strong king, a great warrior, and an iron-willed man. But seeing this, this small moment of weakness, it makes him more human somehow...and also gives clan Mackenzie a much clearer and more interesting role in the Wars of Scottish Independence. We hear all about clan Cambel, and James Douglas, and Sir Gilbert de la Hay, and

Bruce's brother Edward...others, too, but very little of clan Mackenzie. It's wrong. And this letter would move your clan to a completely different position."

Putting the wet, brownish cloth aside, Angus hemmed and met her gaze. He looked like a myth, like a dream—a hero from the legends, who came alive in front of her. And this hero looked very skeptical. The worm of uneasiness wriggled in her gut.

"Aye. Well, so ye keep saying," he said. "I dinna give a shite about clan Mackenzie being important in the eyes of some historians from the future. There may nae be a clan Mackenzie or Scotland as a kingdom if Euphemia got a hold of this letter."

She nodded. "I never meant to mess with the events of history. All I want is to prove my mom's hypothesis. Besides, I do need to think of my brother. We have no one else."

He opened a small clay jar, scooped some white salve onto his fingers, and spread it on her wound. It smelled like animal fat mixed with herbs.

"Tell me about yer family," he said.

She swallowed. She almost never talked about the hardest day of her life, and she felt if she did now, she'd let him in...

Brushing against her wound through a thick layer of the salve, his fingers burned her. She had a sense they were digging deeper, deeper, under her skin, almost touching her heart.

"If I do, will you believe me?" she said, her voice coming out raspy and low.

He cocked his head a little. "I canna promise ye that."

She bit her lip and considered it. It would mean letting him in deeper than she'd ever wanted to let anyone. She barely even talked to David about it.

But if hard facts couldn't convince Angus, perhaps her raw and vulnerable heart could.

And so, she had to take the risk. For the first time in her life, she wanted to.

CHAPTER 18

"The day my parents died was the worst day of my whole life," she said.

Every word scorched her throat like hot embers. Angus froze and pulled his fingers away from her, looking at her intently.

"I was twelve," she said, her chest aching from the memories. "My brother, David, was only five, and we stayed with my aunt while our parents were away at a conference in Scotland."

"Conference?" he said.

"Yes. They were both university professors. My mom was a historian and my dad a biologist. They worked at the same university, and my mom was the vice dean. Do you know what a university is?"

"I ken what a university is," he said through gritted teeth. "If I canna read it doesna mean I'm a simpleton."

Right...she remembered something about the first university in the world being established in the eleventh century in Bologna, and her own alma mater was next, just a few years later...

"Have you heard of Oxford University?" she said.

"Aye."

"Right. So that's the one I study at."

He took another clean, dry cloth and covered her wound. It stuck to the fat salve and didn't fall away. He stood. "Ye may dress yerself again."

As she tugged the shoulder of her dress up, he walked around the post of the bed, then gathered his medical supplies and put them back into one of the chests. When he closed it, he sat on it, leaning with his elbows on his thighs.

"So, are ye saying Oxford University still exists in...what year?"

"Two thousand and twenty-one," she said. "Yes, it does, and it's one of the best schools in the world. There are thousands of universities in the twenty-first century."

His eyes widened in surprise. "If that is true, it must be a world of knowledge."

"It is."

He nodded. "I like the sound of that. And yer mother—a woman—was a teacher in one of them?"

"Yes...and one of the most renowned in the world. She was a smart woman."

"She has a smart daughter."

Rogene smiled. "Well, I'd like to think so. But I also want to keep her memory alive and honor it by proving one of the most outrageous theories that she had. And, thanks to you, I see that she was right."

"How did she die?" he asked. "Them both, how did they die?"

Rogene swallowed a hard knot and looked at her hands. She was clutching the fabric of her dress without realizing. The salve was working its magic, and her wound was now itching more than hurting. She took a long breath in and allowed the memory to take her, with all the pain and horror of that day.

"They were in Scotland. My mom was a keynote speaker at a conference. My dad went along, to be with her." She chuckled as tears burned her eyes. "They were so in love. I don't remember them fighting, ever. Though I'm sure they did. Kisses, hugs, those special smiles people give each other when they share more than just private jokes but private thoughts and private memories..."

She threw a quick glance at him as she wiped away a tear.

"Now, thinking about it, I don't know why I fought with David, you know, the way siblings do. Why I sometimes acted like my parents not letting me watch a late-night TV show was the worst thing in the world. Had I known that all those precious moments, those twelve years were everything we'd ever get, I'd—" Her voice broke and her vision blurred. "I would have never spent a minute arguing or acting out. I'd have kissed them and hugged them and asked them about their lives."

She shook her head. "We never know how much time we have with our loved ones." She looked at him. He was blurry, and she wiped her eyes. "Because they can be taken away at any moment."

He blinked, the muscles over his cheekbones tightening. He stared at her with grave intensity, as though stopping himself from covering the distance between them and taking her into his arms.

She sniffed and sighed. "My mom told me about history, about the Middle Ages, about Scotland. She made me fall in love with it, too. The books I read—*Ivanhoe* by Walter Scott, *Lancelot, Sir Gawain and the Green Knight*, and other historical fiction... I dreamed I'd walk the dirt-packed streets and go to a medieval market and see noble knights and ladies and dance at a feast... I suppose I'm living that dream now. Though it's not as romantic as I'd have thought."

He kept staring at her, and, if she was right, he seemed less skeptical. There was empathy in his eyes, and he seemed more relaxed.

"We were close," she said. "My mom was my idol, my hero, my best friend. Though my dad was an amazing man, too. A bit of a mad scientist type." She chuckled. Though she was sure

Angus didn't know what that meant, she offered no explanation as she wanted to keep telling the story.

She turned to him, putting her knee on the bed. "David and I were staying with my mom's sister, Aunt Lucy, and my uncle Bob. They had only three kids back then, and we felt very welcome for a couple of days. Then, on the way from Scotland to Atlanta..." Her memory pressed on her skull from all sides like a helmet made of cast iron. "Their plane had an accident and...it crashed."

She stopped talking and had to breathe for a moment as the grief, the loss tightened around her chest in a painful vise.

"I dinna ken what any of that means," he said softly. "Except crash."

"Planes are like huge carriages that can carry hundreds of people and fly from continent to continent. I know this all sounds completely insane to you, but basically all that means is people found a way, in the future, to fly. It requires a lot of resources, like iron and fuel—oil that burns and creates energy for the thing to fly."

His eyes widened. "I am sorry, Lady Rogene, but going into a thing made of iron that burns oil and can supposedly fly sounds like a death wish."

Despite herself, she grinned, and her pain lifted and lightened.

"Yeah, it is pretty crazy to think that those things can be safe, but generally, they are..."

She trailed off as a heavy silence hung between them. *Generally*, they were.

Only not always.

"Engine malfunction..." she said hoarsely, fighting another wall of despair. She pressed out a smile through tears. "Accidents happen. Horses stumble and fall, too, don't they?"

She knew she was beginning to ramble, to rationalize and evade her grief, which she often did in her own head.

"They do," Angus said.

Without breaking eye contact, he walked to her. The mattress sank as he sat on the side of the bed. As though someone had turned on a radiator, she began warming up. And it made the next words that she wanted to say easier.

"We got the news in the evening," she said. "David was already sleeping. I remember it vividly. That ancient clock above Aunt Lucy's fireplace showed nine thirty-seven when the phone rang. My cousins and I were watching a late-night program while Aunt Lucy was cleaning the kitchen."

He frowned, and Rogene shook her head, berating herself for not explaining what any of that meant. "Sorry. Imagine a large black object with a moving picture on it."

Angus blinked and winced. "All this sounds like a faerie land to me."

She grinned. Strangely, even the worst memory of her life began brightening and gaining colors as she was imagining what it sounded like from a medieval Highlander's perspective.

"A faerie land..." she said. "All those things sound like magic, don't they? But, funny enough, it's science that makes them possible. Not magic."

"Science..." His eyes were sharp and curious on her. "What is that?"

"Well...it's about how the world works. What air consists of, how fire burns, how to measure if it's warm or cold. In the future, there are fridges, machines that keep food cool so that it doesn't spoil."

He nodded. "Like root cellars."

"Yeah." She smiled. "Like root cellars."

He blinked. "I've always wondered how the world works. I ken 'tis the creation of God, but all those things... I've always suspected there must be a more logical, rational explanation. I'd like to ken how it all is explained."

Rogene smiled at him. She knew he was a smart man, naturally smart. He lacked education, couldn't read and write, but her brother struggled with reading and writing, and he was one of the smartest people she knew.

"I'd like to tell you everything I know," she whispered and covered his large, warm hand, lying on the bed, with hers.

As always, there was that jolt of electrical energy between them, only this one was softer, smoother.

"Thank ye," he said. "I've always wanted to be able to read and write."

"I'd love to teach you."

His eyes were black and shiny and intense under his long eyelashes and thick eyebrows. The side of his face where Euphemia had lashed the whip was swollen and bruised, and he had the start of a black eye, but it didn't make him look ugly—not at all. On the contrary, he looked even more masculine and sexy...a bit of a rogue. She wondered, if he had been born in her time would he have become a powerful businessman, or a great leader, maybe—reforming the political and legal system to protect the weak?

"What happened when the...phone...rang?" he asked.

The memory returned, but it wasn't as dark and as hard anymore. Somehow, she had more distance from it, more strength to deal with it. "My aunt picked it up and talked, and then she leaned against the wall and slid down on the floor. She was pregnant, and her belly was big and round. She stared at me with wide eyes full of pain and sadness and fear. And"—she choked a little—"even disdain, I think."

"Disdain?"

"My uncle and she were our only relatives, so she knew what my parents' deaths meant. She had three kids of her own, another on the way, and she'd just gotten two more mouths to feed."

Rogene sighed. There had always been this tension between her mom and Aunt Lucy. They were sisters, but her mom had always been "the smart one" or "the educated one."

"Over the years, she'd have another," she said. "So she eventually had seven children to take care of, to feed, to help with homework. And my uncle had to support all of us. Five is already a handful, and of course, their own kids came first. David and I were always second. Which meant, I took care of him this whole time."

His eyes warmed. "I ken what 'tis like."

"I'm sure you do...from what I heard."

"Were ye safe?"

"Safe? As in, was I abused? No, thankfully I was not. Ignored, mostly."

He stared into space for some time, thoughtful. A muscle under his eye twitched.

"That's how I learned to not rely on anyone but myself," she said. "David has a learning disability—it's called dyslexia, which means he has difficulty reading and writing."

"Oh."

"In the beginning, we didn't know, so he got bad grades and complaints from teachers. When he got diagnosed, he got assigned a special teacher who taught him ways to cope. I helped him do homework, learned all those exercises with him. He's still doing amazing, given he learns in a different way. But he's too smart for this disability, and he's suffering because of it, I know that."

Angus sighed and chuckled. "I can relate to the feeling, lass. And I think ye're right nae to rely on anyone but yerself."

"Well, it comes with difficulties. I have problems with my PhD because I don't trust people. Especially when it comes to my mom's research. My supervisor told me that because I won't let anyone work with me on my research, I'm failing. And I may not graduate. They may take away my scholarship, which would mean I wouldn't have any means to support myself and David."

Angus nodded. "Ye do have yer brother to go back to."

She bit her lip. "I do."

"Ye have yer duty," he said slowly. "I can relate to that more than ye ken."

Their eyes met again and something passed between them—heat, desire. There was also tenderness and regret in his steel-gray eyes.

And an understanding. A connection that ran deeper than lust and longing.

A feeling of being known.

CHAPTER 19

The beautiful lass by his side was a sight worthy of a lifetime. Her story woke up something he'd never realized he wanted.

To share about his worst experience, too.

His family had witnessed it for years, and yet they rarely talked about it. But he wanted to tell her.

Could he trust her with this? Could he tell her about the worst humiliation of his life?

As she was telling him about time travel—he felt it, the truth of her words. No one could come up with all those lies. No one could create all those stories of science and machines and phones. And he'd seen it with his own eyes, the thing that made those pictures, as she'd called them. It had shone in a way he'd never seen anything shine before. And if that wasn't magic, he didn't know what was.

So, no matter how strange and ludicrous it all sounded, he believed her. Hard facts—her clothes, her speech, her *phone*—and the connection to her that he felt in his heart made him trust her.

The thought brought him both relief and pain because it meant he was falling for a good woman, not a thief and a spy. But it also meant that their time together would soon come to an end. It meant she didn't belong in this time.

She didn't belong to him.

The thought was like a dagger that someone drove right into his heart.

She'd soon leave. She did have her own duty she had to attend to, and he understood duty all too well. He was about to make himself a prisoner of a hard choice, following his own duty.

"How so?" she asked. "How can you relate? Is it because of your father?"

He nodded. "Aye."

Gathering his thoughts, he lay back on the bed and put his hands behind his head.

"My father was someone who demanded a lot of attention," he started. He felt her shift and sit against the pillows next to him. The soft warmth of her hip brushed against his side. He stared at the dark wooden canopy above them. He remembered one particular night, after Raghnall had angered their father so much that Father had chased him away and banned him from the clan.

Raghnall was gone, and there was nothing Angus could have done. He remembered lying in this same bed, staring at the canopy boards with a grave intensity, feeling acutely that his brother's bed, which had been here, too, was empty. Despite his anger and distress, he'd breathed lightly as his cracked rib hurt him. Studying the dark paneling above his head, he'd wished that he'd had the strength in him to rebel against his father and chase him away from the clan instead of Raghnall. That he'd followed his heart and not his duty to his father and his laird, to be loyal no matter what.

He could have been the laird himself then. He could have spared his mother and his siblings the pain and grief and emotional suffering as deep as physical wounds.

"He'd always been a difficult man," Angus continued. "He liked to talk of himself a lot. He'd always been the best landowner, the best warrior, the best father... There was no one better than him. And if someone contradicted that... If Raghnall said that he'd shot an arrow right into the target three consecutive times, Father would say that it must have been a coincidence and that it was hard to be as good an archer as himself. If my mother said she admired the sermon of the priest in Dornie, he'd say that the priest had obviously missed the correct Latin pronunciation of this and that word. No one could be more perfect than he was, and if they tried..." He chuckled. "His fists, his knees, and his feet weren't the worst of what he could do. His words wounded more deeply."

Rogene blinked. "He sounds like a narcissist."

Angus frowned. Her head was above him, and her eyelashes looked especially long from this perspective. "A narcissist?"

"Yeah. People with a narcissistic personality disorder have a huge sense of self-importance. They don't feel empathy for others and demand attention and admiration."

He rose on his elbows and sat up, leaning on the headboard. "Disorder? Like a sickness?"

"Well...in a way, yes. Only a mental one. I'm not a psychologist, of course, but I know that usually people who suffer from it have very low self-esteem deep inside, and they guard it in their perverse ways."

Low self-esteem? It seemed that there was no one with a higher regard for himself than his father. Anger roared in Angus. How could this be possible? She couldn't be right. He shook his head once and ran his fingers through his hair to calm himself down.

"I doubt that, lass," he said as he leaned on his elbows, which rested against his knees. "And even if 'tis, it doesna change anything. It doesna give me back the years of living in a twisted family where there was just one rule: whatever Kenneth Og said was law. And that law changed every day like the wind."

He shook his head, the middle of his chest tightening as the memory clawed at his mind.

"The night I realized I had to stand up to him was deep winter, the time when the wind wails in the through the windows and the snow melts on their sills. I was thirteen then. Father sat in the warmest spot by the fireplace, and I remember a golden glow around his dark, graying hair like a crown. I thought if Father could see himself, he'd be very pleased. Despite the puffiness of his face and a belly as big as a barrel, he was a handsome and strong man."

Oh, so strong. Angus knew it well. The bump on his nose hadn't gone away after being broken twice. Once, he'd had a broken rib, but he'd still had to work in the smithy and train on swords.

"Mother sat by Father's side," he continued, "working on another embroidery, squinting and wincing as she brought the fabric closer to her eyes. If Father told you to do something, you did it, no matter how little light. It was so quiet in the great hall. In winter, and especially in such a storm, there's nothing to do except huddle by the fire. Father sat on a great chair, Mother on a small chair next to him. Laomann was carving something, sitting by his side. Ever Father's pleaser, he was always near, but Father found even that irritating from time to time.

"'Stop with yer constant arse-licking,' he'd boom. 'Ye will be the chief after me. Ye need to grow a spine.'

"Raghnall, who was eleven, was playing with a puppy in the other side of the hall. Six-year-old Catrìona was sitting by my mother's side and working on a small embroidery of her own—a cross. Mother prayed with Catrìona every morning and night, and my sister thought God was one of the family members—though invisible—but kind and protective.

"Sadly, God didn't manage to protect her from the wrath of Kenneth Og Mackenzie.

"And I...I eyed the chess table. I'd always wanted to play chess, but Father had called me stupid and said that all my huge body was good for would be to become the first meat in a battle. I was unworthy of knowledge, he'd said."

Rogene shook her head. "That's such an awful thing to say."

"He'd done worse. I was so lost in my own thoughts that I wasn't aware of a heavy glance that landed on me.

"'Tired of sitting like a log, Angus? Doing nothing?'

"No one looked directly at me or at Father, and yet everyone stilled

"'What do ye want me to do, Father?' I asked.

"Father's face lost its contemptuous-bored expression and went completely still. I realized I had been wrong to ask that. To ask anything. A question meant defiance.

"'How about going and scrubbing the stables, huh, lad?'

"'Nae in the storm, Father,' Raghnall said.

"I cringed. Raghnall, ever the rebel. No matter how many times Father had tried to beat it out of him, he never could. Even at eleven years old, Raghnall wasn't afraid to stand up to him. My father's gaze on Raghnall chilled me.

"'And whyever nae, lad?' he said. 'Are ye saying I dinna ken what one can do in a storm and what one canna?'

"I kent the evening wouldna end peacefully. Raghnall walked towards us, the stick he'd been throwing to the puppy still in his hand. With my stomach in knots, I realized it looked like a weapon. By God's blood, he didn't look eleven at all. My wee brother had more courage and spirit than an army of grown men.

"Father rose, casting a shadow from the fire that danced and distorted on the stone floor.

"'Ye wee shite,' he muttered, 'ye need to be taught a lesson.'

"Another beating? God's arse, Raghnall had just had one the day before. As I always tried to calm the situation down, I said, 'Father, please. He only meant—'

"'Shut up,' Father barked.

"Mother looked at us with worry. She'd aged so much in recent years. She was pregnant again, but she looked like an old woman with a big belly, nae like a glowing woman with child.

"'Ye ken what a punishment was from my own father, lad? Ye must think me cruel. In the old days, my da would have put yer sorry arse out in the cold and let ye freeze, lose a couple of toes to frostbite. How would ye like that?'

"'Better than being in a room with ye,' Raghnall said.

"Mother gasped. Catrìona's eyes were as wide as two full moons. Laomann paled.

"By God's bones, Raghnall was playing a dangerous game. He hadn't so openly challenged Father before.

"'Brother, take yer words back,' I whispered. 'Before 'tis too late.'

"''Tis already too late,' Father said as he marched towards Raghnall, harsh decision written on his face. A vein began throbbing in his temple. He came to my brother and tried to grab him by the collar, but the lad ran away. Father's cheeks reddened. His upper lip curled up in a soundless snarl. Even more determined, he marched towards the other end of the hall where Raghnall was.

"The puppy barked—worried barking, confused barking. Mother stood up from her seat, helpless whimpers coming out of her mouth. Worried, Catrìona rose to her feet as well and held the skirt of Mother's dress.

"My own heart drummed. I suppressed the urge to grasp Father's clothes and stop him."

He remembered thinking he could. Taller than most, and strong and solid, he often felt like a boulder, or a post for people to lean on. Being the middle child, he didn't react as strongly to Father's whims and mood swings. Where Laomann ran to satisfy Father's requests, and Raghnall did everything to defy him, Angus went for observation and trying to find the way to calm the situation down for everyone. Which was probably why Father had called him stupid—because he didn't have something to say every time. He also didn't want to make it worse, especially not for his siblings and his mother.

"But you didn't?" Rogene said.

Angus shook his head. His chest ached, hollowed out, scraped from inside, and only pain remained there. He studied his arms, his giant fists that knew battle, that knew death and violence.

"Raghnall darted away again, but this time, Father was faster," Angus continued. His chest ached but also itched, as though he was healing. "He grabbed Raghnall. God's blood, he was strong. He brought his arm back for a hard blow. The wall was right behind Raghnall, and an image flashed in my head: my brother's skull crushed against the rough rock, blood flowing from the gash. His skin deadly pale."

Angus's throat contracted.

"Something snapped within me," he said. "I was stronger than my younger brother. My skull was as hard as rock, as Father often said. Before Father's fist could slam into Raghnall's face, I launched myself and crashed into him with such force that we fell on the floor, dragging Raghnall after us. Father swore and pushed me away. His face was almost purple.

"'Ye son of a whore,' he roared. 'Ye dare to challenge me?'

"He stood and yanked me up, then slammed his fist into my face. Through the burst of pain, I saw his distorted face and bloodshot eyes. His teeth were bared, yellowish, and glistening with spit. He looked like an animal, emptiness and fear behind his eyes.

"*Fear?* I thought distantly as Father drew his fist back to throw another punch into my face. *What was he afraid of?*

"'Twas the man who ordered the priest to write a book of legends about him. The man who had a castle that had been built to protect Scotland from Viking invasions in the west and that controlled three lochs at once.

"An important man.

"Was he afraid of his own sons?

"The iron ring on his fist crashed into my cheekbone, and I stopped hearing for a moment.

"Then a thought came. While he was busy with me, he couldn't harm my siblings and my mother. As his fist slammed into my face over and over, I knew this wasn't so bad. I could take it. I could protect Ma, Raghnall, and Catrìona.

"Mayhap that was why I was so sturdy, so strong, so big.

"To be a protector.

"Because as long as there was danger out there for my family, my needs weren't important. I had to put them and their safety first."

Rogene laid her hand on his arm, and her tenderness picked him up and carried him away from the horror of that memory. She shifted closer, and her gaze was so warm and so full of compassion that his heart ached.

"I understand why Sìneag said we're destined for each other," she said. "We both do anything to protect our siblings." She squeezed his arm. "But your father is dead now, Angus. Don't you think you've sacrificed enough and fulfilled your duty?"

Jesu, hearing her say that was like a knife cutting open an infected wound. Painful, but he knew it would bring healing.

Raghnall had said the same thing: *I think ye've done yer duty enough for our family. 'Tis time to put yerself first. Because this time, 'tis for the rest of yer life.* Catrìona had never liked Euphemia, either, and she had asked him several times whether he was sure.

The rest of his life...

When his father had died six years ago, it had been sudden. Although Kenneth Og had been having pains in his stomach and chest for a few years, he'd seemed immortal. So when one of the servants had found him stiff and cold, sitting in the garderobe with his breeches down, it had seemed to Angus like it was one of Father's cries for attention.

But it wasn't. He was dead. As much as Angus had been grieving his death, part of him felt free. Laomann was the new laird, who wouldn't be violent or manipulative. He had other weaknesses—too many of them—but the castle had breathed in relief. Everyone had tiptoed for a while by the sheer power of habit, but, finally, they'd settled into their new life.

He had a strong suspicion that this narcissism, as Rogene

called it, might also be something Euphemia suffered from. How would he be able to live with a female version of his father for the rest of his days? Would he become another punching bag for his wife, a shield she'd use to gnaw her teeth on? Was there truly no other way to repay the tribute and stop her from attacking Kintail?

He'd wanted Rogene from the moment he'd seen her. His desire for her only grew the more he got to know her. And there she was—he could just reach out with his hand and touch her. And she wouldn't want to bend him to her will and make him submit. She was healing, and light, and she was putting him together, piece by piece...

Just look at those pink, rosy lips, the gentle curves, the feminine body, all warm, smooth, and soft. And he wanted not just her body, but also her heart, her compassion, courage, and strength. He wasn't married to Euphemia yet. He hadn't yet said his marriage vows.

He could still choose desire. He could still choose freedom. If his brother and Rogene were right, he'd fulfilled his duty to the clan. He'd sacrificed enough. Was it time for him to put himself first?

It was, he thought. He'd had enough of living under the weight and the curse of a man who was long dead. He'd wanted to rebel against him then, but he never had. It was time he rebelled against that legacy of fear now.

Making the decision felt as if he'd cracked open a shell he'd been living in for years.

"I wilna marry Euphemia," he said, his voice rough.

Rogene's eyes widened, and the brightest smile illuminated her face. She beamed like sunlight, her cheeks growing rosy, but then her face fell. "Wait, what?"

"I'll tell her now," he said, rising up, but Lady Rogene caught his arm and pulled him back.

"Wait..."

He sat down and lost his balance a bit and leaned into her.

Her face was so close now, her big eyes bright, and dark, and shiny. And those lips... Oh, dear Lord, those lips were so tender, and so beautiful his heart squeezed.

"I wilna marry her, Lady Rogene," he whispered against her lips and claimed her mouth, swallowing the words *I want to marry ye instead...*

CHAPTER 20

A ngus's lips were soft but firm, his beard tickling her face. Rogene melted against him as he wrapped his strong arms around her and drew her to himself. Her head spun, as though she were on a helicopter that was spiraling out of control.

What are you doing? a voice screamed in her head. *Did you just break off the marriage of Angus Mackenzie and Euphemia Ross? Did you just change history?*

No, she couldn't do it! She couldn't give in to her own desires. She'd come here and mixed everything up. If Angus didn't marry Euphemia, she wouldn't bear him Paul Mackenzie, who'd save Robert III, the founder of royal Stuart line. Hundreds of years of Scottish history would be erased and changed. All because of her.

She pushed herself away from him. "I need to tell you something," she said, breathing heavily, her body feeling like it were dissolving and melting into warm wax.

"What?" he asked, kissing her again.

Oh dear Lord, those lips... He kissed her gently once, teasing her. Then a second time, bringing her blood seething like a flow of lava.

"You need to marry her," she said through those kisses.

"Nae, I dinna," he said, dipping his tongue between her lips, invading her mouth. "Nae more."

As his tongue began a teasing, lashing, seductive dance against hers, all thoughts disappeared, and her head went blank. "Hmmmm," she moaned into his lips.

The electricity she'd always felt when he touched her came back a hundredfold. Meeting his skillful tongue, she felt that an electromagnetic field went through her body, charging her every cell with life and energy and light. She rubbed against him as he teased and licked her tongue like he couldn't get enough of her. Like he'd finally gotten his prize.

He buried his fingers in her hair and held her head like a precious gift. Probing, playing, his sleek tongue glided against hers, and her insides burned and squeezed.

He smoothed his hands down her neck and farther down her body. His fingers brushed against the naked skin of her back, the touch like a brush of heat. Even through the material of her sleeves, her skin tingled as his hands went down her arms. She realized she was wrapping her arms around his neck and pulling him closer. He grabbed the edges of her torn dress and began kissing down her jaw and her neck, spreading small bursts of pleasure through her.

He was so hot, as though he were running a fever, and smelled like the Highlands: woods and earth, thistle and heather, and something otherworldly and magical. He was a Highland warrior, making love to her, impairing her thoughts. She felt as if she were in a dream.

He leaned back a little as he dragged the edges of her dress down her chest and stared there.

Right...her wound.

"Doesna it hurt?" he asked.

There was no such thing as hurt in a world where he filled her whole body with endorphins. "No."

"Good."

With one swift movement, he drew her dress all the way down to her waist, exposing her breasts. He stared at them with awe and hunger, and her stomach squeezed in delicious anticipation.

"By God's body, lass, those are beautiful breasts," he whispered and leaned down.

He cupped one breast with his hand and took her nipple in his mouth, sucking it in. His mouth was warm and soft and wet around her flesh. He tugged and gently nibbled, and a shudder ran through her. She put her fingers through his silky hair, as he massaged her second breast. Her skin feeling flushed and burning, she tilted her head back and arched into him, allowing him the most access she could.

Growling like a wolf, he teased her breasts until she was breathless and so pliable he could knead her like Play-Doh. He leaned back and pulled his tunic over his shoulders, and she froze, mesmerized by the sight of mighty pecs and a hard stomach with six distinct bulges. His shoulders were broad, his biceps like those of a Viking who rowed daily. Fine dark hair covered his upper chest, and she put her palm on his chest to feel it. Soft...

On a whim, she leaned down and kissed him under the collarbone, inhaling his masculine tang, the musk of his skin that made her want to straddle and ride him. She put out her tongue and licked down towards one of his nipples, feeling with satisfaction how his muscles hardened and a shudder ran through him. She found the nipple, small and hard, and licked around it.

"Ah, God's arse, lass..." he spat. "What are ye—"

"Do you like it?" she whispered as she looked up at him.

"I like this more." He lifted her and put her on his lap so that her legs were on either side of his hips. Their naked stomachs flattened against each other—hers soft and squishy, his hard. His chest firm against hers, her breasts tingled and her nipples drew into two hard buds. She was suddenly aware that she didn't have any underwear on—medieval women didn't use them—and that her very wet sex was nestled against his very hard cock.

A fact that he became aware of, too, as he pushed his hips into hers. The pressure on her clit made her gasp as a burst of liquid pleasure spread through her core.

"Aye, lass," he growled against her neck. "Moan, groan, sing my name. I've wanted ye since the moment ye slapped me."

Undoing his leather belt, she giggled a little. But as she dragged his breeches down and revealed a triangle of hard muscle pointing towards a huge cock that was long, and looked as hard as marble, all her humor died. She gulped, imagining it buried inside her to the hilt.

His sex jolted.

"Lass..." he groaned. "Enough of waiting. Enough of looking. Enough. God knows, I've been waiting for ye all my life. Ye're my only desire."

He wrapped his arms around her and flipped her onto her back. She lost her breath for a moment and inhaled as his pleasant weight settled on top of her, pinning her to the bed.

"Damn it to hell, what are ye doing to me," he whispered and kissed her again.

This kiss was different. Demanding. Possessive. Taking.

Claiming. She was his, and he'd make sure everyone knew that—including her.

He brushed against the inner side of her thigh, his fingers warm and callused, and so sexy. His hand went up, higher and higher as he was still kissing her. Her inner folds throbbed as he got closer to her sex. Then he spread her folds and found the most sensitive part of her. She gasped into his mouth and felt moisture wetting her entrance. He rubbed her clit, massaging her wet lips, and she ground against him, letting the sweet bliss take her higher and higher.

Then he inserted one finger inside her. She moaned, and so did he. He looked down at her spread thighs. "God, lass, ye're so tight and wet and warm..."

He kept thrusting his finger into her, then inserted another one. She felt him eyeing her, his gaze heavy and attentive on her face.

"Yes. Yes. Yes," she kept saying, as every thrust found the right spot inside her.

But, again, just before she reached the edge of pleasure, he withdrew, and she panted, watching him with what was almost anger.

"Patience, lass," he purred with a satisfied smile. "I waited too long for ye to spoil this with a hurry. Ye're mine now, and I will enjoy every moment. And have ye see the stars on the way."

"You're killing me," she half whispered, half whimpered.

He positioned himself between her thighs.

His jutting erection was pressing against her entrance. She looked into his eyes—the eyes of a wolf on a hunt, the eyes of a king conquering new land, the eyes of a man who has tasted love and freedom for the first time. At that moment, she knew that Sìneag was right. This was the man for her. The man she could be happy with forever, every single day of her life. The man who was probably her soul mate, who was opening up the best in her, and she in him.

And at that moment, nothing else existed besides them, their bodies, and the pounding of their hearts.

She saw that he felt it, too. This connection that went deeper and further than anything that he'd felt before, that was more profound than a blood oath, more magical than crossing the borders of time.

Slowly, he sank into her. She stretched, feeling filled and complete. Involuntarily, she spasmed around him once, twice, and he groaned a half oath.

Then he moved back and forth, picking up speed. As the brightest, most amazing bliss of her life was spreading through her core, she dug her fingers into him, trying to hold on. He tilted his hips, and was grinding against her most sensitive spot, bringing her higher, to the point of no return, faster than she'd ever thought possible.

She hugged him with her hips, urging him deeper. He growled, making animal sounds of pleasure that spurred her own joy further.

And then she was right there—staring into the face of the sun, or of God, or whatever was pure joy and love and bliss and pleasure, and he was right there with her. She fell apart with a gasp, and she heard him call her name as he was emptying inside of her. The orgasm slammed through her in a scorching wave. She vibrated with elation as he delivered the last few slamming thrusts. She shuddered as he sagged against her. Breathing as one with the man who had just become more important and closer than anyone had ever been, she fought feelings towards Angus Mackenzie that resembled sheer happiness. It spread from her heart and through her whole body, and sated, boneless, heavy, and exhausted, she fell into sleep.

But a dark thought chased her through her dreams...

She couldn't be the one who'd change the history of Scotland forever, no matter how much she wanted to be with him, no matter how much she wanted to stay.

CHAPTER 21

A ngus got up from the warm bed, leaving the most beautiful woman he'd ever seen sleeping peacefully. He covered her with his blanket and marveled at the translucent perfection of her skin, of her beautiful breasts, of her thin waist and her full hips. She was tired, his fiery lass, and he didn't want to disturb her.

It was already night now, and he knew that the guests must be at supper. So he didn't need her with him to announce his decision.

As he was dressing, he realized now that he'd had her, he'd never be able to forget her. Having her, choosing his desire over duty, felt right, even though he still had that worm of guilt deep in his gut.

But he'd made a decision, and he'd stand to face the consequences of his action. Raghnall was right, there were other ways to achieve the safety of Kintail than tying himself to a woman he didn't love and didn't respect. To a woman who was dangerous for him.

He'd already put on his breeches and now that his tunic was on, he made his way downstairs to the great hall.

The scent of cooked meat and vegetables meant he was right.

He was surprised that Euphemia hadn't besieged his bedchamber or sent anyone to interrupt him and try to take Rogene again. He wasn't complaining, of course. But something told him there was more to that and he needed to be careful.

He entered the hall. It was quiet there, and only a murmur of voices came from the table of honor where Laomann and Catrìona sat together with their guests: Euphemia, William, and Malise. Mackenzie men greeted him as he came through the aisle between the rows of tables. The Ross warriors eyes him heavily.

Euphemia lifted her head as he approached the table. "Ah," she said with a raised brow. "My betrothed. The man who openly took a mistress."

She cocked her head and pressed out a smile that didn't reach her cold eyes.

"How was the whore?" She licked her fingers, which were slick with chicken fat from the drumstick she was holding.

Angus took in a deep breath. His jaws crunched together, and his teeth hurt from the force. He hated that she spoke so about Rogene. Rogene, for whom his heart ached and who'd occupied his mind and soul.

But he needed to set his anger aside and act rationally. The best thing he could do now was to give her a gracious way out. To set it up so that she could claim it had been her idea to break their engagement.

He looked at her from under his eyebrows.

"I wilna stop seeing her even after we're marrit."

The drumstick fell from her hand, the smug expression washed from her face. "What?"

The room fell completely silent, apart from the wind howling outside the slit windows.

Laomann shifted uncomfortably. "Angus..."

Angus ignored the shocked expression on Catrìona's face. *Forgive me, sister...* He was exposing her to crude things that her tender ears were nae ready to hear.

"Ye asked," he said, looking straight at Euphemia. "I'm telling ye. Ye need to ken. I wilna be faithful. I will have a concubine."

Her eyelashes trembled and hurt crossed her face. Her eyes filled with tears as she wiped her fingers on a cloth.

"Ye're a bastart, Angus Mackenzie," she whispered hotly.

He did feel like a cruel bastart, and he hated hurting anyone, even someone like Euphemia, but he needed to resolve this without bloodshed.

"We'll see about that." She threw the cloth on the trencher she was eating from and rose. Her hair glistened pure gold, reflecting the light from the fires of the braziers.

"Do ye still want to marry me?" he asked. "Knowing that?"

"I can just have her beheaded," she rasped.

"Nae. Ye will be my wife, and I wilna allow that on my land. Ye may do that on yer brother's land with his permission. As yer lord and yer husband, I wilna permit ye to harm anyone. And if ye do, I will throw ye in prison. Understood?"

She gasped and opened her mouth several times in a state he'd never imagined: confused, lost, alarmed.

He held her gaze for a long time, feeling like a cliff standing strong against a raging sea. Finally, her face relaxed, and she straightened her shoulders. Something like a decision passed across her face. She licked her lips.

"Understood," she said.

William stood, enraged. "What?" he said, glaring at her in indignation.

Hope flickered in Angus's chest. Hope for freedom. Hope for happiness. Hope to spend time with Lady Rogene and persuade her to stay longer—mayhap even forever? He hadn't thought of any solutions or planned out their future, but he knew that if he was free from Lady Euphemia, he had a chance to be with Lady Rogene.

Euphemia slowly turned to William and bestowed a freezing glare upon him. "I said, aye," she said, punctuating every word as if he were a child.

"But what about the rest of the tribute? What about Kintail?" William growled.

"Aye," Angus said. "What about it? Will ye attack?"

Wearing a cooler expression than a stone statue, she turned to him. If her blue eyes could cut flesh, he'd be dead. "Nae."

The word released tension in his stomach. He felt lighter, the ground shifting under his feet.

"Truly?" he said.

She crossed her arms over her chest. "Truly. I wilna attack. I also wilna marry another cheater."

He sighed out audibly. Both Laomann and Catrìona stared at him, huge-eyed. Catrìona, he knew, was relieved, only not sure if she could be happy for him just yet.

"I am sorry this didna work as ye wanted it to," Angus said.

He knew he'd given her a way out that saved her pride, and though he felt like he'd gotten out of this too easily, he didn't want to question it.

She kept staring at him as though wanting to pin him to the wall with her gaze. She cocked her head in acknowledgment. "My clan will be on our way tomorrow."

Angus nodded. "Of course, my lady."

Then, free and relieved and happy, he turned and went to his bedchamber. There, he undressed, slid into his bed, scooped Rogene into his arms, and slept the first restful sleep in as long as he could remember.

Strong arms enveloping her, a hard, solid body pressing against her back...

Angus, she knew immediately from the way her whole body tingled and sang from the mere touch of his skin. She'd felt his erection against her thigh and rubbed against him, but he'd only grunted and pressed against her and let out a long, satisfied, happy sigh. Then he'd muttered something that she couldn't distinguish, and stilled, breathing deeply and evenly against her.

She'd fallen back to sleep, too, in the warmth and comfort of his arms.

Something awoke Rogene, and she stirred. A sound.

Go back to sleep...

There was a grunt, and a thud, and a sound like a sword being drawn from a sheath. When the warm body that lay next to her disappeared from her side, she opened her eyes. In the darkness, with only dim light coming through one slit window, she saw shadows of several people looming over her. She opened her mouth to scream, but a firm hand covered her mouth.

The hand smelled of blood and dirt, the filthy skin salty against her lips.

Still screaming into the hand, she saw two warriors holding Angus's limp body. Horror struck her. She went as cold as ice. They were dragging him away, through the doorway. In the dim light, his body almost glowed white against the inky darkness of the walls.

Men held her against the bed as she thrashed and screamed, her muffled cries coming out in whimpers.

And then she saw her. The thin, willowy silhouette of a woman standing next to the door. She was staring right at Rogene. Her eyeballs were white, and her long, straight hair as silvery as a spiderweb.

Then Euphemia made a gesture with her hand and turned to walk to the door. One of the men drew back his fist, and pain burst in Rogene's skull just before everything went black.

CHAPTER 22

For a moment, before she opened her eyes, Rogene had a sense that she was a little girl again, and that she slept in her bed in Atlanta. Her parents were still alive, and Mom was making crepes downstairs in the kitchen while Dad was probably feeding David, who was still a baby. If she opened her eyes, her window would be to her right, and her walk-in closet in front of the bed, and the door to her room would be open just a slit because she knew Mom had peeked in to check on her before she'd gone down to the kitchen.

But as her heavy eyelids lifted, and her head splintered into a thousand aching pieces, she knew she wasn't a child anymore. Staring at the dark-wood canopy above her and the rough stone walls around her, she remembered right away where she was.

And when she was.

Then the image of Angus's limp body being dragged away through the darkness slammed into her mind. Euphemia staring at her. She felt as if her heart had been pierced with a knife.

She sat up with a jolt, and a stab of pain went through her head. She was naked, with her dress gathered around her waist. With her hands shaking, she pushed her arms through the sleeves and pulled the edges of the dress up and over her shoulders. She found her shoes—the soft leather, pointy-toed medieval shoes Catrìona had lent her—and ran out of the room.

With her heart drumming, she flew into the great hall, panting. It was morning, and the Mackenzies and their men were eating their porridge. Catrìona looked up from her bowl, a frown on her face. Laomann glanced at her and kept eating. There was not a single person of clan Ross.

"Angus was kidnapped!" Rogene cried.

Every single face turned to her. Catrìona jumped up, spilling her porridge on the table. Laomann gave out a grunt.

"What?" he said.

Rogene hurried to their table that stood at the farther end of the hall. "Euphemia kidnapped Angus!" she cried as she ran. "We have to get him back..."

But even as she said that, she trailed off as realization dawned on her.

"Wait...why did she kidnap her own betrothed?" she said as she stopped in front of them. "Did something happen?"

"Ye dinna ken?" Catrìona said. "He broke off the engagement."

Rogene had to grasp the edge of the table to steady herself. He broke off the engagement! The thought brought happiness to her heart, like a tired sail finally getting some wind to play with. But at the same time, dread for Angus filled her whole being.

"So he broke off the engagement," Rogene said, "and in response, she kidnapped him and took him...back to Ross, I suppose?"

"Aye, they're all gone," Catrìona said. "But are ye sure he was kidnapped?"

"I'm sure. I saw them with my own eyes. They knocked me out."

Catrìona turned to Laomann. "So, brother? Come on, command the men to get on their horses. We have to get him back."

Laomann stared at her as though he had a toothache. "But they're clan Ross. Our overlords."

Catrìona widened her eyes. "Laomann, our brother's in the hands of a woman who has a habit of beheading men."

Laomann looked at Mairead, who was holding Ualan close, her face in a deep frown.

"Laomann," she said quietly, "I ken ye had to make hard decisions to avoid conflict for my and Ualan's sakes..."

Rogene watched in astonishment how Laomann's face lit up with love. The deep lines on his forehead smoothed; his dark eyes stopped jumping from object to object, face to face. They sparkled as he watched his wife and son.

"Mairead, dear," he said, his voice deep and confident. Rogene wondered for a moment if this was his usual manner when he was alone with Mairead and Ualan. No judging eyes on him, no pressure, no decisions to make.

"But ye also have to protect yer brother," Mairead finished.

Rogene was thinking hard. All her being was screaming at herself to demand the same as Catrìona, that they get the men, get the horses, and go save Angus. But then again, she would be interfering with the flow of history. Maybe this was how Angus was supposed to fall in love with Euphemia. Maybe he needed to see her strength and decisiveness to really open up to her, and then they'd get married and have Paul... She'd seen the marriage registration—it was in the museum in Edinburgh.

But her heart was screaming something else entirely. He was in danger. A deranged woman who wanted him but couldn't have him had kidnapped him. Euphemia had a huge ego and she tended to get people killed when she was offended.

She could torture him for sport, keep him in her dungeon forever, even force herself on him...

Her whole body went cold.

To hell with history. If history was about making people she cared for suffer, she wanted none of that. To hell with the Stuart line. To hell with everything. She couldn't allow Angus to get hurt.

"Yes, Lord," she said. "Your wife is right. Please, command your men to go, and I'll go, as well. Let's get him back."

Laomann swallowed hard but kept staring at her.

Was he really such a coward? Was he truly not going to stand up and protect the brother who'd taken beatings for him?

"Lord," she said, "you can't leave Angus in peril now, after everything he's done for you. After he's been a shield and a protector for you and your clan his whole life, how can you let him down now that he needs *you* to be his protector?"

Laomann swallowed and paled. Then he stood up and nodded, slamming his fist against the table. "Aye. Ye're right, Lady Rogene. 'Tis time I had his back, too. I give ye a dozen of our best men. Go. Get Angus back."

Rogene nodded.

Catrìona looked at him. "I'll go, too."

She walked around the table, hooked her arm through Rogene's, and walked her towards the door. "My brother Raghnall is in Dornie, and he will want to go help Angus. Let's get him back."

As Rogene marched with Catrìona, she knew she'd do whatever it took. Even if she had to give up everything she loved or cared about, she would not let any harm come to Angus.

CHAPTER 23

D elny, Ross
   A week later...

THE DOOR TO THE BEDCHAMBER OPENED AND EUPHEMIA SLID into the room. *Damn it.* Angus jolted, and struggled to free himself from the handcuffs that were attached to the bed's headboard. He was naked under the soft furs. It would have been better had she thrown him into a dungeon with no windows and with water dripping down ancient walls.

Instead, this was a rich bedchamber for the most important guests. Warm, thanks to the large fireplace, with two slit windows allowing plenty of light and even fur rugs by the foot of the large canopy bed. The mattress was filled with goose down, the bed linens clean, and the blanket warm. He'd never been so comfortable in his life, goddamn it.

He was drowsy and had slept for most of the journey, and he had a strong suspicion that he'd been given some sort of potion. Since yesterday, when they'd arrived, he'd been offered grilled boar, exquisite and rare French wine, and bread, the scent of which made his stomach growl. He'd refused everything, of course. He didn't want to give the woman any sign that he was enjoying or accepting what she'd done.

She proceeded into the room with an angelic smile on her face. She wore a beautiful red dress with sophisticated embroidered patterns of flowers and leaves in golden thread. Her shiny hair cascaded down her shoulders and over her chest, and she'd done something to her lips and cheeks so that they appeared red.

She could be a beautiful sight—for another man. He knew what a selfish soul lay under that pretty appearance.

He wanted one woman. One woman who had been sent to him from the future by destiny.

Euphemia stood before the bed and her smile grew wider. "Lord, did ye rest?" she asked.

He glared at her. "What have ye done to Lady Rogene?"

Euphemia could beat and humiliate and try whatever she wanted with him. But all he really cared about was what she had done with Rogene, who'd been in the bedchamber when he was taken. Had they kidnapped her, too?

Euphemia's smug smile fell. "If ye say her name one more time—"

"I'm nae afraid of ye," he said.

"Oh. I ken. But ye will be."

He swallowed hard. There was only one way she could scare him—by endangering his clan or the woman he was falling in love with...

In love? Was he mad? He hadn't known her very long. How could she take such a big piece of his heart? Wasn't he just desiring her? And what was the big issue with wanting a woman?

But he'd never wanted anyone as much as he wanted her. Indeed, he wanted her so much that he'd betrayed everything he stood for: duty, honor, and clan. Had he truly let his cock guide him and endanger hundreds of people of his clan? Nae, he told himself. He wanted to be selfish—didn't he deserve that? Couldn't he put himself first just for once in his life?

Well. Look what it had led him to.

Euphemia had outsmarted him, and he was now paying for his selfishness. His father was right—all he was good for was fighting in battles.

As she sat on the edge of the mattress, he sucked in a breath and shifted away from her on an instinct. She reached out and gently pulled the edge of the blanket down, exposing his chest. Wanting to smack her hands away, he jerked, but the handcuffs rattled and cut angrily into his wrists.

"Get yer hands off me," he said.

She cocked one brow as she studied his pecs. "Aw, Lord Angus," she singsonged, and as her eyes met his, there was hurt in them—no doubt from his rejection and anger. "I'm nae playing by yer rules nae more. I've given ye everything ye wanted. I agreed to yer conditions. I came to Eilean Donan to be yer wife. I agreed nae to attack Kintail—for ye. All I wanted in return was a husband. A husband who'd make love to me. Who'd give me a son. How hard is it?"

She slowly traced a finger down his chest, her pupils dilating as she followed it with her gaze.

"Ye're a strong, capable man," she continued. "In yer prime. Clearly, ye're able to perform since ye've taken a lover to yer bed. Why is it that ye canna lie with me?"

Nails bit into Angus's own palm. *Because ye're nae her...* He couldn't even think of any other woman than Rogene.

Euphemia took the blanket and threw it off him, exposing his body. He suppressed a low growl. As she lazily, slowly looked him over, his mouth curled in a snarl. Her eyes stopped and widened at his cock, and the smile on her face chilled his blood.

"Oh, I kent ye'd be worth every trouble I'm going through for ye," she said, and when she looked into his eyes, there was nothing but triumph. "Ye'll give me a wonderful son."

She undid the brooch at the base of her neck and the cloak fell. She was completely naked underneath. Although, no doubt, she was beautiful, Angus turned his face away and closed his eyes. He didn't want to see her. The sight of her made him sick because he saw her for who she truly was inside.

"Angus, ye may resist this all ye want." Settling herself so that she was straddling him, she purred. He felt her warm thighs around his and shifted up in a futile attempt to get away from her. "But ye will marry me."

He looked at her. "What?"

Her eyes were half closed—a cat that had caught her mouse and wasn't going to let it go.

Gliding her palms over his chest and stomach, she said, "Aye. I give ye a sennight to come to terms with this. But I do have a priest who, nae matter what ye say, will only hear 'aye.' So either ye agree on yer own, or the priest will agree for ye. Either way, we will get marrit."

Sweat dripped down his neck. Suddenly the room wasn't warm anymore but cold. The place where her thighs touched his stung, as if many small needles were stabbing him.

"'Tis nae a real marriage," he said.

She bit her lip and watched her hands as they massaged and brushed against him. "Oh, it will be. In everyone's eyes."

"Nae in mine." Angus thrust his hips to the side, attempting to throw her off.

She chuckled excitedly and dug her nails like a cat dug its claws. "Oh, struggle all ye want. Men think they can rape women whenever they want. Well. I canna be a laird. But I am as powerful as a man in all other ways. I will make ye mine, Angus Mackenzie. Oh, I will."

Helplessness weighed on him, injecting weakness into his arms and legs like venom. He thrust, and tried to throw her off, but she held on, as excited as a lass on a wild horse. He wanted to scream, but he knew it would be futile. He had not a single friend in this castle. And no one would dare to go against their mistress, even if they pitied him. He felt like a piece of meat, nothing but a bull that was expected to inseminate a herd of cows.

He wouldn't give her the satisfaction. She'd imprisoned his body. But she didn't own his mind. She never would. With coldness creeping into his soul, he stilled and met her eyes.

"And what happens after the wedding, Euphemia?" he said. "Will ye keep me locked up forever?"

She leaned down and began planting wet kisses on his body. They felt chilly and slurpy. "Aye. Till ye submit to me."

When her lips reached the lower part of his stomach, he stilled and clenched his fists. Her face came close to his cock, and he felt her warm breath on his skin. He cringed and pressed himself back into the mattress, as though it would help to escape her. With a featherlight brush of her fingers, she stroked his cock once, then twice.

"If ye think this will arouse me, ye're wrong. I can never want a woman like ye."

"A woman like me?" she purred as she wrapped her hand around him and started moving her fist up and down.

By God's blood, he was still a man. He still felt things, and his treacherous body was enjoying this. Nae! Ashamed, hating himself, he felt his sex swell with the need for more. Aye, this was only physical, but he hated every inch of himself for reacting to her command.

"A woman who has nae soul," he spat.

She smiled. "Mayhap I have nae soul," she said with an undertone of bitterness. "But ye're wrong that ye canna want me. Look at yer gorgeous cock."

A low growl escaped his throat. *Stop*, he willed himself. *Stop! Ye canna show her she can win this.*

But as she moved her hand up and down, his body was still eager to respond, and more blood flowed to his member. *Goddamn it!*

"Dinna fight this, Angus," she said. "Ye already lost. Give me a son. Be my husband. Lie with me. Make me the happiest woman alive."

He moved his hips sharply away from her hands and to the

side and away from her. She lost her grip, and immediately his erection softened. *Good! Think of worms...* he thought. *Snakes... A latrine...*

With an angry grunt, she found him again, but his cock was completely flat now. She began pumping him faster, annoyed.

Latrine...

The pleasure didn't come anymore. He willed his body, and her movements felt disgusting. He didn't hate his body anymore. He hated her. She was abusing him, doing things against his will. He wouldn't let her.

She kept moving her fist, but her face lost the expression of satisfaction, the expression of victory. She looked angry, her lips pursed. He closed his eyes.

"Keep trying. I told ye I dinna want ye."

"Oh, ye will. Nae man has ever gone soft on me."

Angus chuckled. "Keep me here all ye want. Do whatever ye want. I ken who ye are inside. Rotten. Selfish."

She let go of him with a jerk. She jumped up and put on her cloak. With a furious snarl, she stood and looked down at him as though she was considering where to spit on him.

"Ye will regret this, Angus," she said. "Mayhap 'tis the pretty dark-haired girl that's clouding yer mind. Well, let me see if ye keep thinking of her once her head is nae attached to her body nae more."

She marched out of the room and slammed the door shut, the heavy iron handle knocking against the wood.

Horror dripped down his spine. "Nae!" he cried after her.

He was already regretting rejecting her—she was right. If he'd known that he would be protecting Rogene by mating with Euphemia, he wouldn't have resisted.

He was ready to sell his soul to the devil if it meant she would live.

CHAPTER 24

T*he next day...*

"So, how do we do this?" Rogene asked the band of rescuers who had come with her.

They sat about a hundred or so feet away from Delny Castle, hidden in the bushes and undergrowth. It stood on a hill, and about twenty feet down the slope was Cromarty Firth with its unruly water gray in the light of a cloudy evening. On the other side of the Firth were two long greenish-brown lines of land with a neck of water between them that connected directly to the North Sea. Strong wind, wailing in Rogene's ears, brought the salty scent of fish and algae. At the base of the slope below them, by the gravel beach, was a small jetty where three birlinns and a couple of fishing boats were docked. Two guards stood watch over the area.

Crouching to her left was Catrìona, the only one in the group wearing a dress, but armored with a dagger on her hip. Would-be nun or not, Catrìona looked like a woman not to mess with.

To Rogene's right was Raghnall. When Catrìona had brought her to meet him in Dornie, she would have never thought this man was a Mackenzie brother. With tears all around his *leine croich*, and holes and seams on his cloak, he didn't look like gentry—more like a rogue from a band of highwaymen. Although he seemed charming and at ease, there was something very dangerous about him.

On the way to Delny, he would sing and play his lute from time to time, and in his voice, she heard anger and sadness that he didn't show when he talked. Most of the things he said to her were questions masked as jokes. And from the way his penetrating dark eyes studied her, she knew he was assessing her, trying to dig under her skin.

They also had two dozen men with them: a dozen whom Laomann had commanded to go and a dozen volunteers. It seemed every Mackenzie warrior wanted to go and help Angus once they heard what had happened. Many of them blamed themselves that they noticed what was happening and failed to stop Euphemia's men. Laomann had been generous enough to allow the best warriors to go.

And now, after a week of hard riding where she'd spent most of the time clinging to Catrìona's back on her horse, they were finally looking at Delny Castle, seat of clan Ross. One of their men had casually asked some villagers if their lady had come with a prisoner, and they had said there was no prisoner, but one of the carts had held a man who was sleeping under many furs and blankets.

The men looked at her, frowning.

"Obviously, we can't take it by siege," she said. "We need to think of something else."

"Aye," Raghnall said, squinting as he studied the castle with an estimating look on his face. "We need to get in without anyone noticing. With Bruce, 'tis what we often did, when we took castles and burned them. Sometimes, we hid in the carts of tradespeople. Other times, we threw ladders with special hooks to climb the walls. We hid to ambush trading vessels that came to sea gates... And now..."

He rubbed his chin, which was covered with a short black beard.

"We could find someone who would allow us to get into their wagon..." Catrìona said.

"Or steal a wagon," Rogene said.

She shivered, looking at the impenetrable castle walls. Stone walls two stories high surrounded the big rectangular keep and a courtyard that looked like a perverse fairy-tale castle.

Catrìona frowned. Although she didn't say anything, Rogene thought she must disapprove of the idea of stealing.

"Nae likely in the bright daylight," Raghnall said as he peered at the village, which was to the left of the castle.

They exchanged worried glances. The only one who'd been in the castle before was Catrìona, and she didn't know of any weaknesses or any secret ways to get inside. This didn't look good, and they were losing precious time. Who knew what condition Angus was in? The orange sun came out from behind a cloud and reflected off the water in a fiery frenzy of light. And right in the middle of it was a dark spot—a big birlinn, its sail shielding a fair bit of the blinding surface.

"Look, guys!" Rogene pointed.

They all glanced in the direction she was pointing.

"A ship..." Raghnall muttered.

Catrìona shifted closer to Rogene and whispered, "Who did ye call just now?"

Rogene felt heat rushing to her cheeks. "Um...I said, guys... I meant all of you."

"Oh..." Catrìona said, still studying Rogene with a puzzled expression. "I dinna ken that word."

Rogene muttered an oath. Even after a couple of weeks here, she still couldn't make herself forget the modern expressions. She needed to be more careful.

She shifted her attention to the ship. "What kind of ship do you think it is?" she asked. "A trader?"

Raghnall shielded his eyes with his hand, studying the vessel. "'Tis hard to say. But it looks like 'tis loaded, based on how low it sits in the water. I say, aye. It must be a trader or mayhap a delivery. Food, weapons...who kens?"

That sounded oddly familiar to Rogene. She glanced down at the small harbor with the jetty, then back up at the castle. The shore broke sharply there, creating a cliff of sorts that shielded the small gravel beach from view of the castle. Yes, that could work!

She came to sit by Raghnall. "Guys!" she said, and bit her tongue as she cursed herself inwardly.

Everyone looked at her with puzzled expressions again.

"Uhm. I just thought of something that we can use. In February 1307, James 'Black' Douglas went with a small raiding party to the Isle of Arran where Brodick Castle was, occupied by the English, of course. The underwarden of the castle arrived with a couple of boats from the mainland with provisions, clothes, and arms. About twenty Englishmen came to unload the boat, and Douglas and his men killed them all. The men in the castle came to their rescue, but Douglas killed them all, too. Then they gathered everything from the boat and camped nearby, waiting for Robert the Bruce to arrive."

Raghnall winced. "How do ye ken all that?"

Oh, shoot! She knew from her research, of course. "My cousin James Douglas told me," she said.

Raghnall's smart, dark eyes bored into her. "Ye're a wry one, are ye nae? 'Tis a peculiar thing that a woman would ken such military details. I understand why Angus is in love with ye."

Her face fell. She went completely still. "In love?" she whispered. "Did he say that?"

"He didna need to. I ken him. And good for him for abandoning this evil bitch for ye. 'Tis long overdue he stopped protecting everyone and let others protect him."

She swallowed hard. He loved her... But no, just because

Raghnall said that didn't mean it was true, right? And even if it was, there would be no future between them, no matter how much she wished otherwise. But even if she couldn't be with him, she wouldn't let him be kidnapped and held against his will.

"Anyway," she said. "Could we do something like that?"

Oh God, she couldn't believe she was suggesting killing twenty men!

"Maybe not kill them but just knock them unconscious and tie them up?" she said.

Raghnall nodded slowly. "Aye. We could. We could take their clothes and provisions and get into the castle carrying all that."

"Wouldn't the guards from the castle see that? Or hear us?" Catrìona asked.

"I think the beach is shielded enough from the keep," Raghnall said. "But ye're right about the sound of battle. And we still dinna ken who and how many men are on the birlinn. But it might just work."

"So we wait for the ship to arrive and see who's there?" Rogene said.

"Aye."

When the ship arrived, it was already evening. The group went closer to the cliff and watched it dock. It wasn't a trader. The ship belonged to the castle, and the captain with a dozen men went there directly without unloading.

"They're leaving it for the next day," Raghnall murmured. "'Tis already late."

"So, what do you think happens next?" Rogene asked. "Do they unload it tomorrow?"

"Aye," Raghnall said, his slightly slanted eyes glistening in the twilight. Something about his face gave Rogene the impression of a hawk. "They must have come a long way, and the ship is well loaded, as far as I can see. They want to rest first." He looked at her. "I bet they'll start in the morn, Black Fox."

She frowned. "Black Fox?"

The men were settling around them to sleep on the ground,

huddling in their heavy woolen cloaks. Not wanting to light the fire, they made a simple meal of bannocks and dried meat and fish. Catrìona sat at the base of a bush and looked into the night sky while chewing absentmindedly.

Raghnall chuckled. "Aye. Black Fox. They're a myth. No one has actually seen one in Scotland. But folk claim that they exist, only disguised as faeries. They're especially smart and especially precious." He looked at her, his dark eyes piercing. "I've seen one, though. When my father chased me away, I traveled the world. Before I joined Robert the Bruce, I went to England, and France, and Flanders. Sleeping, just like now, on the forest floor isna new to me. Doing work both honest and...well...nae so honest."

He picked up a piece of grass and put it in the corner of his mouth, chewing on it slowly.

"I woke up one night because I heard a sound. It was summer, and I'd just left Edinburgh and was heading north where I'd heard Robert the Bruce was gathering men to fight the English. My purse was full of provisions for the road. Cheese. Bread. Bannocks. I even had a small jar of butter. The moon shone brightly. And there it was. Black, its fur glistening like silver in the moonlight, its muzzle in my travel purse. I lifted my head, staring at it. I didna want to harm it and didna mind if it ate my food—I could always get more. But if it was a faerie, I didna want to get on its bad side."

Rogene licked her lips. He was right about that. Contrary to all logic and reason, faeries existed, and her being here, talking to him, was proof.

"Then it finished and looked at me. Its muzzle glistened with fat—the wicked animal ate all my butter. I only chuckled and marveled at it. It was so bonnie, Lady Rogene. So...out of this world that I wondered for a moment if I was dreaming. Then, when it kent I wasna going to attack, the bonnie thing went into my purse again, grabbed a linen pouch with dried meat, and ran away." He shook his head and cackled. "It ate everything I had except for my old bannock, which was as hard as wood. Trust me, I regretted nae shooing it away."

He met her eyes and a corner of his mouth lifted. "Angus told me he wondered if ye were a thief or a spy, and I told him 'tis unlikely. But having met ye now, I dinna ken if I was too quick to come to that conclusion. Ye have a mystery or two of yer own, dinna ye? Ye're like the black fox, are ye nae, Lady Rogene? Clever. Bonnie. A thing of myths and legends and mayhap nae of this world. And mayhap stealing a thing or two while we're nae watching. The question is, will ye disappear in the darkness like that wee visitor, never to be seen again, and break Angus's heart?"

Rogene didn't dare to move, both shocked and mesmerized by his story. Raghnall, like Angus, was so much more inside than he let show on the outside. Raghnall wasn't a rogue or a bandit. Angus wasn't just a giant warrior. And her brother wasn't just a boy with a learning disability. The three had more brains and wit than many people she knew.

She swallowed hard. "I assure you, I have no intention of breaking anyone's heart. All I want is to free Angus."

Raghnall nodded. "We have that in common, lass. Get some sleep. I'll keep watch. We attack tomorrow."

Rogene nodded and went back to Catrìona. They made a sort of sleeping bag for the two of them out of two woolen cloaks. But she couldn't fall asleep, thinking of the black fox from Raghnall's story.

Foxes were lonely animals. She was lonely. She'd always relied on herself.

But she couldn't get inside the castle by herself.

She had to trust Raghnall, and Catrìona, and twenty-four warriors she didn't really know.

And she had to be able to entrust her life and Angus's life to them.

The thought made her stomach tighten, her gut twisting into a painful knot.

CHAPTER 25

T*he next day...*

"THIRTY-TWO, I THINK," ROGENE SAID AS SHE PEERED through the undergrowth at the jetty.

The morning was gray and dull, the freshly risen sun invisible behind leaden clouds. A storm was coming from the sea in a heavy black cloud with a wall of indigo rain. The wind threw misty drizzle that smelled of seaweed into their faces. Waves crashed into the beach beneath them. The ships and boats jumped up and down, knocking against one another.

"Thirty-seven," Raghnall said.

Worry stabbed Rogene in the gut. She had counted only thirty-two. While she was trying to find the five men she hadn't noticed, Raghnall turned to the warriors who gathered behind them.

Wait, Rogene wanted to scream, *we need to check how many there are...*

But she knew with her rational mind that it meant wasting

time. She just needed to trust Raghnall and the rest. And that was hard. How could she put her life in the hands of strangers when she didn't even trust her aunt and uncle?

Sweat misted her back under the man's tunic she wore.

"There are many more of them than of us," Raghnall said to the men. "And they're all warriors. Look at their swords and axes."

They scowled at him, attentive. Broad-shouldered and muscular, they all looked menacing and experienced enough to do their job right. But Rogene wished she could take a sword and wield it together with them.

"We must act fast," he said. "They'll be distracted by the rain and the storm, which will play out for us. It might even muffle the screams." His gaze darkened. "Remember. Nae honor. We slice through them like a scythe of death."

Rogene and Catrìona gasped. "We said nae deaths. Just knock them unconscious," Catrìona said.

Raghnall gave her a hard stare. "There are too many of them. We canna allow them to alert the rest of the castle."

"But—" Rogene said.

"Nae but, Black Fox," Raghnall said. "They took my brother. Kidnapped him. I dinna have time for mercy. 'Tis war."

"But—"

"'Tis final," he said, and she saw steel in his eyes. The steel of a killer. "If ye disagree, ye both"—he looked at Catrìona—"I suggest ye stay behind."

Her stomach flipped with panic and fear. She had no choice. She had to trust him. All of them. "I won't stay behind," she said.

"Neither will I," Catrìona said, her face pale. She clasped Rogene's hand. "'Tis one thing to hear about battles and death from my brothers," she said. "'Tis quite another to see people die...to kill them."

Rogene squeezed her hand back. She couldn't agree more. She'd read about medieval battles and clever Highlanders' tricks in warfare. Thousands died in this skirmish, hundreds in that.

This guy won, the other lost. Those had been just numbers on paper.

Now it was time to see people die. To watch those numbers come into existence.

And maybe become a number, too.

Rogene said, "Won't it interfere with you becoming a nun?"

Catrìona gave her a hard look, no less steel in her eyes than in her brother's. "I have only one chance to save my brother, who protected me my whole life."

Raghnall gave Rogene a dagger. "Use it if necessary," he said.

She took it with a shaking hand. While Raghnall turned back and led the men down the slope covered in grass and bush, Catrìona picked up two thick sticks. "I'd still like to spare lives and just knock them unconscious if I can." She handed one to Rogene and they began climbing down the slope.

As planned, they appeared silently and calmly, as though they belonged there. There were no battle cries, no commotion. Claymores and daggers were in the sheaths in the folds of their cloaks. Gravel crunched under Rogene's feet as she stepped onto the beach. The wind was fresh and brought the sharp, salty scent of the sea. Seagulls squawked, flying high above. The beach was filled with voices of the men throwing sacks and barrels and loading the cart.

Raghnall's men blended into the lines of those carrying and throwing things. They got a few surprised glances, but, as Raghnall said, the castle and the village were big enough so that not everyone knew each other and there were enough new warriors circulating around. Raghnall had said they would just assume more manpower had come to help.

Rogene's hair was done in a braid and hidden under her hood. She could pass as a boy or a young man, perhaps, at the first glance. Catrìona might attract attention with her dress, but so far, she talked to one of the workers by the cart without alerting anyone.

Rogene stepped onto the jetty and into the line of the warriors who passed sacks with clothes to one another.

Once everyone had blended in and was carrying and throwing things, they awaited Raghnall's signal. Rain hammered against Rogene's hood. Wet cold crept into her bones. She was shivering—no doubt as much from adrenaline as from the cold. Was she really about to kill someone? Take someone's life?

Was she ready to do it for the man she'd known for such a short time and only slept with once?

A cuckoo called. *Cu–ckoo, cu–ckoo. Cu–ckoo, cu–ckoo.*

Rogene's heart drummed against her rib cage. She caught a roll of cloth thrown to her and passed it, then laid her hand on the stick she had tucked into the belt of her tunic. A couple of men raised their heads, probably realizing that it was weird to hear the call of a cuckoo in the middle of a rainstorm.

Then, a moment later, came the third and final call.

Cu–ckoo, cu–ckoo.

She wished they were allowed a battle cry—one would really help her. But even without it, she turned and hit the warrior who stood with his back to her. Muffled moans of pain went through the jetty, and the sounds of bodies hitting the wooden surface. Waves splashed as sacks and men fell into water. The man Rogene had just hit slowly turned to her, his eyes wide in surprise and anger.

"Why did ye do that for?" he growled. Then, seeing the battle starting around him, his face fell and he reached for his sword. Fear hit Rogene in a cold wave. She grabbed the stick with both hands and hit him again right in the face. To her surprise, he lost his balance and fell into the river.

She gasped. But she had no time to ponder the man's fate, as another man swung his sword at her. She ducked, out of sheer luck, and felt the backsplash of raindrops in her face as the blade passed an inch away from her nose. She retrieved her dagger and ducked again as he swung his sword a second time. Someone was screaming for help, but the waves were crashing hard now, and the storm had hit the beach in earnest. Someone who was fighting behind Rogene's attacker fell and hit a barrel standing on the jetty. It rolled and tumbled the man off his feet, and he fell between two ships, hitting his head against one of them. The river swallowed him.

Surprisingly, the battle was dying out. Only a few enemy warriors were still wielding their weapons, and soon the last of the men had been thrown into the water or killed. Rogene stood panting and looking around. Raghnall came to her.

"Ye all right, wee Black Fox?" he said, touching her shoulder.

She swallowed through her contracting throat. "Yeah," she said. "I think so."

She knew she must be in shock. The realization that she'd just killed a man roamed somewhere in the back of her mind, ready to hit her like that black storm. But she didn't let it. She couldn't afford to yet, because she knew she might fall apart from guilt. And there was no time for that.

She had to save Angus. She had to focus.

"Good," Raghnall said. "These men dinna have special clothes, and the storm will cover us. No one will look at our faces under the hoods." He turned around and called louder, "Everyone grab something and let's go."

Breathing heavily, Rogene hid the dagger and the stick under her cloak and grabbed two rolls of wool. She passed by a few dead men who lay on the jetty. Pools of blood mixed with the heavy rain and poured into the river. She shuddered and kept looking before her, trying to ignore them. When she found Catrìona, surprisingly, the woman was much more together than she. Her dagger was bloodied, and her eyes shone with a fury that Rogene wouldn't have believed could exist in the sweet young woman.

"Are you all right?" Rogene asked.

With a shaking hand, Catrìona wiped her weapon against her skirt, nodded, and walked with the men up the narrow path towards the castle.

The cart wouldn't come up the path, the wheels struggling through the slippery mud, and the men simply left it on the beach. Everyone had packs, barrels, casks, and sacks in their hands. There were no cries of victory and no sense of it—not yet. They'd only gotten themselves an opportunity of a free pass into the castle.

"Did we lose anyone?" she asked Catriona.

The girl nodded solemnly. "We lost two good men. Another is wounded."

Rogene's heart dropped. "I'm sorry."

"So am I."

And as they turned the curve of the path and the castle rose before them, Rogene wondered how many they would lose and if she and Angus would get out of the castle alive at all.

CHAPTER 26

They passed through the gates with no problems, and Rogene looked up at the heavy portcullis with sharp iron edges. The courtyard was muddy, rain bubbling in the black puddles of the dirt-packed ground. The keep loomed tall against the leaden sky, gray and misty through the curtain of rain. Surrounded by four walls, they passed by two buildings. There was no one in the courtyard—everyone was probably inside, hiding from the rain...which wasn't great news if they had to fight.

But no one threw a second glance at them as they proceeded. Sentinels stood on the walls, huddling in their cloaks, no doubt just wishing rain would stop. No one expected an attack in such weather.

"Where do you think he is?" Rogene asked Raghnall, who carried a sack on his back.

"Catrìona?" he said.

His sister held a light chest under her armpit. "There's a dungeon," she said. "He could be there."

Raghnall nodded and turned to his men, who walked behind. "Follow me," he said. "To the dungeon."

They proceeded to the keep and once they'd entered through

a heavy, arched door, he leaned to Rogene. "If we encounter someone, I'll do the talking."

Again, a protest formed in her gut. Let him do the talking? What if he said something wrong?

But at the beach, allowing him to take the lead had worked well. The bloodshed had gone as seamlessly as possible given the advantage of the enemy in numbers. Raghnall had been right about everything so far. Was it so bad to work as a team? It wasn't about Rogene being the best at everything. She knew she wasn't, clearly. Raghnall was an experienced warrior and someone who one could entrust with their life, as he'd just proved.

It was about relying on others. About giving up control. About trusting life.

Back in the twenty-first century, she didn't trust others with her mom's research. She told herself she didn't want to share her mother's legacy. But it was just an excuse. The real reason was that Rogene feared trusting others.

Her parents had let her down when they died. It was irrational, but that was how a twelve-year-old Rogene had felt. Abandoned and betrayed and very, very afraid.

Her aunt and uncle had been the only two people left on whom she could rely.

But they'd showed her she couldn't count on them after all. They'd showed her she and David were on their own.

There was no team. There was no family. There were just people trying to survive.

But Raghnall had managed to win down there. He'd been right about every single thing. It was because he cared, she realized. Because he was saving his brother.

What that told her was if she gave up control with people who really cared about the outcome, it would all work out.

And she had to admit, she really liked the sense of teamwork, of being part of something.

But whether they could continue to work as a team inside the keep remained to be seen.

Still carrying cargo, they approached the tower. Raghnall pushed the heavy door open and entered. There were about fifteen warriors there. Many of them sat and played cards. Others stood and talked, drinking wine and ale. The room wasn't big but was full of stuff—boxes, chests, casks, sacks, firewood.

As heads turned to him, Raghnall froze on the doorstep. Rogene's hand slid to the handle of her dagger under her cloak. For what felt like an eternity, no one said anything.

"What are ye waiting for, man?" said one of the warriors. "Come inside. 'Tis raining."

Rogene sighed out with relief. They went inside. Raghnall put the sack in the corner and looked around, water dripping down his cloak and hood into the reeds on the floor. It smelled like a London subway car during rain—wet wool and stones. Rogene elbowed her way through the gathering of warriors and put the roll she'd been carrying on a stack of boxes.

Catrìona went inside, too, but not all their warriors could fit in. As she laid the box on the floor, all eyes of the enemy men landed on her, and they frowned.

"Who are ye, lass?" one of them said.

Rogene felt blood wash down from her face. She quickly glanced at Raghnall but couldn't see his face from under his hood. Goddamn it! Was he just going to stand there like a statue?

Panic gripped her throat. She had to do something. She was wrong to trust Raghnall. He was no good.

"She's just a lass," Rogene said with a fake Scottish accent. Faking—so badly!—the voice of a man.

They all glanced at her, looking under her hood.

"And who are ye?" said another one.

"Who're all of ye?" said a third.

"Ah, lass, who asked ye to interfere?" cried Raghnall, drawing his dagger and throwing back his hood. "I said I was going to talk."

"*Tullach Ard!*" the Mackenzie men cried and drew their

weapons, and Raghnall started the battle by launching himself at the nearest warrior. One stab and the warrior fell dead.

Around Rogene, a fight started. It was mostly a fistfight, as there was little space. Small blades of knives and daggers flashed in the dim light of the torches. The room filled with pained grunts, thuds, and cracks. Someone launched at Rogene. Bared white teeth flashed before her. Panicked, she stepped back, but Raghnall grabbed the man by the collar of his *leine croich* and pressed the edge of a dagger into his throat.

"Where is Angus Mackenzie?" he growled.

"Go to hell," the man replied.

Raghnall grabbed him by the throat, his fingers digging into the man's neck, and raised him up. "Where. Is. He?"

The man grunted in pain as he struggled to breathe.

Raghnall let him stand on the ground and pressed the edge of the knife into his beard.

"Ye think I am jesting?"

A shiver ran through Rogene as she saw yet another version of Raghnall. The Raghnall who was death. "I will slit yer throat if ye dinna say where the Mackenzie prisoner is."

The man's mouth twitched.

Raghnall pressed the blade into his neck, and a thin trickle of blood crawled down the man's throat. "Now." Raghnall pressed harder.

The man's eyes widened in horror, in surprise, and he closed his eyes in panic.

"Third story, Lord. Second door to the right."

Raghnall glanced back at Rogene. "Hear that? Go!"

Rogene stood frozen a moment, not quite believing they really had gotten the information out of the man. On wobbly feet, she turned and took the only flight of stairs leading up.

As she looked over her shoulder, she saw Raghnall open the man's throat in a fountain of gore. Rogene suppressed a shocked scream. Who was Raghnall? A rogue or a noble knight?

She went up and up. The floors were empty. From each landing, two corridors ran, one to the left and one to the right, with doors on either side. Torches illuminated the way, and the higher she climbed, the dryer the air was.

Finally, on the third floor, she stopped, breathing heavily, her heart drumming.

To the right. Second door. She walked to the right wing of the landing, stepping softly against the wooden floors. The sounds of a battle came distantly from down below.

There it was, the second door. Nothing distinguished it from the rest. She laid her hand on the massive door, pressed the heavy wood, and entered.

CHAPTER 27

A ngus couldn't believe his eyes. Was he dreaming or was she really standing there, in the door to his prison?

Her eyes were as large as pound coins.

Yes, his wrists hurt and were bruised from being cuffed for days, and he was still naked—though Euphemia had graciously covered his lower body with the blanket after she fed him his dinner yesterday. He pushed himself up to sitting. Goddamn it, he hated being seen by her like this... Helpless... Naked...

His face was burning from embarrassment and humiliation, anger thundering hotly in his blood.

By God's bones, did she think he'd mated with Euphemia? He couldn't tell why she was so shocked and what she was thinking.

"I didna marry her," he said. "And I didna bed her."

She blinked and finally seemed to rouse from her stupor. She walked into the room, letting the door swing closed. But just before it did, a soft clanging and screams from below caught his attention. A battle?

But the door closed before he could be sure, and she approached the bed and leaned on the mattress with one knee.

She cupped his face, and her touch sent a tingle of energy across his skin.

"Are you all right?" she asked, her big, dark eyes so close he could move his head forward and kiss her eyelids. "Did she hurt you?"

"I'm fine." He swallowed hard, commanding himself to not fall into the depths of her dark eyes. "God Almighty, I'm glad to see ye."

It was like everything brightened around him, colors gained vibrancy, sounds grew louder, and he was warmer.

But there was no time to fall into any sentiments. Where was Euphemia? She hadn't come to him yet this morning. He glanced at the door and shook his arms, the handcuffs rattling. Futile, of course.

Rogene glanced at the chains. "Key?"

He shook his head. "I dinna ken."

She glanced around. "Could it be here?"

"Mayhap."

She left the bed and began searching through the chests lined against the wall.

"How did ye get here?" Angus asked.

She was dressed as a man and was soaked through, her woolen cape leaving pools of water on the floor.

"Raghnall and Catriona came, too," she said as she rummaged in a chest. "Laomann allowed twenty-four warriors to come to save you."

Angus closed his eyes. Two dozen warriors had come to save him, risking their lives for him—as well as his brother, his sister, and this woman he'd known for only a short time. She hadn't gone back to the future. She hadn't run. She'd come to rescue him.

His chest exploded in a burst of warmth.

"Are they all right?" he said.

"They were when I left them." She went to kneel by another chest. "They're fighting downstairs." She looked back at him and their eyes locked. Something ran between them—an understanding, a connection they'd had since the very moment they met.

The door opened and Angus's heart jolted. A blond figure in a pale-blue dress that highlighted the brilliant blue of her eyes.

Euphemia.

"Are ye looking for this?" she asked, dangling one key on a ring.

Rogene jumped to her feet, pale. She muttered something under her breath, retrieved a dagger, and pointed it at Euphemia.

"Yes," Rogene said. "Give the key to me."

Euphemia inhaled deeply and let out a long exhale. Her face took on an angelic expression. Without showing any signs that she was worried, she closed the door behind her and looked at Angus.

"Ah, Lord Angus, yer whore came to rescue ye. Mayhap 'tis true love?" She chuckled and shook her head. "Even better. I dinna need to send anyone to Eilean Donan for her. I can show ye here and now how I treat a harlot who dares to seduce my man."

ROGENE SHOOK AS THE PAIR OF ICY BLUE EYES STARED INTO hers. The woman wasn't big, or tall, or muscular. Or anything. How could she have such power over her? Immobilizing her like this, her feet rooted to the floor, her arms trembling as the handle of the dagger chilled her fingers.

"Leave her alone, Euphemia," Angus cried.

Her brave, strong, selfless Angus. Completely helpless now. And she was the one in control—a freaking PhD student who loved books and reading and speculating about theories.

Not killing.

But she had to be strong. As strong as she'd always been for David.

"Don't forget that I'm the one with the weapon," she said, but her voice shook.

She wasn't fooling anyone. She didn't believe she could really stab another human being. Based on the amusement in Euphemia's icy cold stare, neither did she.

"Aw, lass." Euphemia was slowly walking towards her holding Rogene in a steely gaze. "What are ye doing pointing that at me? Ye arenae capable of scaring a child, my dear. Ye keep making things easy for me."

With her heart drumming against her rib cage, Rogene watched Euphemia take one step after another until she came to stand so close that the tip of the dagger pressed directly under the woman's collarbone. Rogene stared at her with wide eyes, feeling her lips tremble. She could kill her now. There'd be no better opportunity.

Do it, part of her cried. *What are you waiting for?*

But her hands refused to move.

"Come on, Rogene," Angus growled. "Ye can do this. Just one stab and she'll be done."

"Aye, Rogene," Euphemia purred. "Kill me while I'm letting ye. 'Tis the only way ye can get the key and save this handsome man from my evil claws. Otherwise, he's mine. And ye're dead."

"Do it!" Angus cried, thrashing and beating against the chains.

To hell with this!

Rogene sucked in a breath and with a roar, shoved the dagger forward.

Only to find empty air. Losing her balance, she stumbled against Euphemia's leg and fell flat on her stomach. The dagger slid away, and Euphemia picked it up.

Rogene pushed against the floor to stand, but felt the sharp, cold edge against the back of her neck.

"This is how ye threaten someone, lass," Euphemia said. "Ye mean it."

She pressed on the dagger, and Rogene felt a sharp bite as the edge broke her skin.

"Get away from her," Angus growled.

"Stand up slowly," Euphemia said.

With her arms and legs shaking, Rogene stood up. What an idiot. She should have done it.

"Turn around," Euphemia purred.

Rogene turned around slowly. There they were again, her eyes—pure ice. Pure cold. Pure nothing.

"I should have killed you, bitch," Rogene spat.

The dagger was pressing directly against the artery in Rogene's throat. She felt it pulse against the metal. Rogene clenched and unclenched her fists in helpless fury.

"Ye should have," she said. She turned to Angus. "I want ye to see the woman ye think ye love die in front—"

Rogene grabbed Euphemia's shoulders, pulled the woman's body down, and kneed Euphemia right in the stomach. Euphemia doubled up with a gasp and fell onto her back.

With an angry groan, she struggled up, but Rogene sat on her stomach and grasped the handle of the dagger, working on wriggling it out of the woman's hands. She was so strong! She was pointing and jabbing the blade at Rogene, too close to her belly. The blade was swinging dangerously, an inch or two away from Rogene, but the woman wasn't letting it out of her grabby fingers!

Kicking her fear back into the bottom of her psyche, Rogene slammed her teeth around Euphemia's wrist. She tasted iron as warm liquid appeared on her tongue.

Euphemia screamed in pain and dropped the dagger.

This time, Rogene didn't hesitate. She caught the weapon and pressed the edge against the other woman's throat.

"It's over, you bitch." She spat her enemy's blood on the floor. "You taste like shit, by the way."

Euphemia was holding her wrist with her other hand and staring at Rogene like she was ready to kill her.

Yeah. She saw Rogene meant business this time. And inside, Rogene knew she wouldn't hesitate again.

"Key," she said. "Now."

Euphemia didn't move, only breathed angrily in and out.

"Now." Rogene pressed the dagger and, just as Euphemia had done to Rogene a few minutes ago, broke the skin on her neck. Euphemia raised her chin, trying to get away from the weapon. "Now!"

Euphemia went into the pocket of her dress and retrieved the key. Rogene took it and threw it to Angus. It landed on his chest. He had enough space between his hands to be able to open the handcuffs by himself. Then he undid the cuffs on his ankles and stood from the bed, rubbing his wrists.

"Let me," he said to Rogene, and took the dagger from her hands. Rogene was momentarily blinded by his nakedness—his gorgeous cock hung right before her, and despite the danger and the adrenaline rushing through her body, she remembered their lovemaking the night he was kidnapped.

He bent down and pressed the knife to Euphemia's throat. "Get on the bed, ye evil bitch," he spat. "Undress."

Rogene expected Euphemia to make more jokes about being naked with him, but Euphemia didn't say a word. A muscle ticked on her cheekbone as she began unfastening her dress. She let it slide down and the woman's white body flashed before Rogene.

"Get on the bed," Angus said.

Euphemia raised her chin, perhaps waiting for a look a naked man might give a naked woman. But Angus's eyes stayed on her face, and there was not a hint of appreciation. Only disgust. And anger. So much anger.

"Ye wilna get out of this castle alive," Euphemia said. "Ye ken that, right? There are hundreds of warriors, and ye have a band of what...ten men?"

Angus's jaw clenched tightly. "I'll take my chances. 'Tis better to die of a blade than to stay tied in iron at yer mercy. Climb. On. The. Bed."

Euphemia's face darkened. She did as he told her. He approached her and pressed the blade against the woman's throat.

"Rogene, cuff her."

Rogene took the handcuffs and put them on the woman's wrists. Euphemia looked full of venom, like a snake ready to sink in her fangs for the kill.

When both cuffs were on Euphemia, Angus returned the dagger to Rogene, found some clothes in the chests, and dressed.

He took the key from Rogene, went to the window, and threw it as far as he could.

"I'm sparing ye yer life, which is more than ye deserve. But if ye come for Kintail," he said to Euphemia, "I wilna be so forgiving."

He took Rogene's hand, his callused palm warm against hers, and pulled her after him. With Euphemia thrashing and screaming, they stepped into the dark corridor where the sounds of battle came somewhere from the floors below.

CHAPTER 28

T he ringing of metal against metal echoed off the rough, torchlit stone walls. Stepping down the stairs, Angus held the most precious hand in his, that of the woman who'd risked everything for him. Something no one else had done in his life.

Ever.

She'd gathered a band of warriors, she'd teamed up with his brother and sister, and she'd come to rescue him. Without knowing how to fight, with no money or any other advantage. Being an outlander in this time hadn't stopped her.

As they descended the stairs, he turned to her and looked into her big, warm eyes. "Thank ye, lass. Ye saved my life. Ye were my shield."

She blinked, and her eyes watered. "It's not just me, Angus. Your brother and sister came, too. Your warriors."

"Aye. I ken. But I dinna ken if that would have happened without ye."

"Of course they'd have come for you without me. I just couldn't—"

Footsteps pounded up the stairs towards them and Angus drew the dagger in front of him. Goddamn it, it was the only weapon that he had but better than nothing. The warrior was bloody and had wounds—and it wasn't anyone he recognized, so he must be of the Ross clan.

The man stopped for a brief moment, then launched. He had his longsword drawn, but they stood in the narrow flight of stairs, stone walls to their left and their right, and he had no room to swing at Angus. Having an advantage with the short dagger, Angus drove his blade under the man's ribs, and he grunted in pain and slid down on the stairs.

"Come, lass," Angus said as he bent to take the man's sword. "We must get through."

"No," she said behind him and turned to go back up the stairs. "We'll land right in a battle, and you're unprotected. No armor, no shield, nothing."

Her worry warmed his heart. Suddenly, all the yells and cries from downstairs faded away. There was just him and her. This woman wanted to be his shield, while his whole life was dedicated to being a shield for others.

She stood on the stairs above him, tugging him up and away from the battle. But he grasped her by her hand and pulled her into his embrace. Yes, he might die today. Yes, he might be wounded.

"My whole life I was a piece of meat, good for nothing but beating," he said, blissfully surrounded by the scent of her hair. "For my father. For my clan. For my king." He turned and met her eyes. "Today, I'll fight for you. I'll fight for me. I'll fight for a chance of us."

Her eyes watered. "Angus..."

He shook his head. "Nae. Not a word. Come. Stay behind me."

She opened her mouth, but he stepped back and descended the stairs, clinging to the wall and peering around the corner.

The next landing was empty, so he went lower, to the next floor. There, three men were fighting—two against one...

Against Ìona. He was clearly exhausted, his blond hair misted and clinging to his forehead, a gash on his upper arm.

With a roar that made both enemies look up, Angus launched himself at them. That gave Ìona a moment of advantage, and his claymore cut into one warrior's neck. He met the other enemy's sword with a loud *clang* and proceeded to thrust his claymore over and over. Each time he met resistance that reverberated in his body. His wrists were sore from days in cuffs, but he kept going.

The man was strong but not skillful, and finally Angus thrust his claymore into the man's gut, and he died, clutching at his wound.

"Ye all right, Ìona?" Angus said.

"Aye," his friend said. "'Tis a slaughter downstairs, Lord. More men are coming. We must leave."

"Aye."

"Is Catrìona all right?" Rogene asked.

"Aye, the last time I saw her, she finished three men."

Impressed, Angus shook his head once. Catrìona knew how to fight—Angus had taught her early on as he couldn't stand the thought that she wouldn't be able to protect herself against Father if Angus wasn't around. But as far as he knew, she'd never wanted to use the sword-fighting skills. She always preferred to choose a peaceful way. She couldn't stand the thought of taking someone else's life. "Don't kill" was one of God's commandments.

"Good," Angus said. "Protect Lady Rogene with yer life, aye? Let's go."

The three of them climbed down the stairs. Two men fought at the bottom of the stairwell. The rest of the room was dark in the dim light of the torches. A crowd of men had squeezed into the small space, and they banged against one another with swords too long to swing in the space available.

Mackenzie men always had knives or daggers with them, but

so, apparently, did the Ross men. Both sides used these shorter blades viciously, along with their fists.

In the middle of the skirmish, he saw Raghnall's tall, dark-haired figure. He had a black eye and a gash on his forehead, but otherwise looked whole, though tired. He was fighting William, the Earl of Ross.

Catrìona was in the corner with a face Angus had never seen on her before. Her teeth were bared, her eyes wide, her blond hair in wet strands. Clearly consumed by battle rage, she stabbed a man right in the eye with a roar.

She could be Morrigan, the goddess of war and death from Ireland, about whom Angus had heard from his MacDougall mother.

"How do we signal for everyone to retreat?" Iòna asked.

Angus looked around. There, to the left, was the entrance door—closed but not barred.

"This is how," he said and took a lungful of air. "Retreat!" he yelled so loud that he thought the walls shook.

All heads turned to him. Raghnall's eyes flashed with triumphant recognition.

"Retreat!" he echoed. "*Tullach Ard!*" he cried the Mackenzie war cry. And aye, it sounded strange to cry the war cry for retreat, but it meant they'd gotten what they wanted, they'd achieved their goal and could now leave. "*Tullach Ard!* Retreat!"

"Dinna let them pass!" yelled William.

Someone pushed the door open, and the skirmish spilled out into the storm-darkened courtyard. Thunder rolled and lightning flashed. Rain descended in a wet curtain, and the daylight was as gray as dusk. Seeing their loss, the Ross men were picking up the fight and attacking with renewed strength. Outside in the storm, Angus knew it would be a pig shite of a battle.

If the Ross men closed the portcullis, they would seal the Mackenzie group inside the courtyard. Ross archers would obliterate them, shooting from the walls.

If Angus and his men wanted to survive, their best chance was to run, not fight.

"Once ye're outside, lass," he said to Rogene, "run to the gates and dinna stop a moment whatever happens, aye?"

They could now descend the stairs as more and more people moved outside.

"I'm not leaving you!"

They pushed away and mixed with the crowd moving towards the door. As they moved, someone slashed at Angus with his knife, and he pierced the man with his dagger. It didna need to come to this, he thought. If only Euphemia didna have the need to spill blood and to own him, body and soul. They had to step over the bodies of the dead and the wounded that lay on the floor, and his stomach felt sick as he thought of how many lives had been lost here today.

Unnecessary.

And then, suddenly, there was more space as most people had made it outside.

"Ross men! Yer mistress lost!" Angus cried. "Stop fighting and let us pass."

"Dinna let him get away!" growled William, who was in the middle of the crowd but staring at Angus.

A man launched at Angus. Angus hit the warrior right in the nose, and he yelled, clinging to his face as blood rushed down over his mouth.

"She'll never have me," Angus growled.

He was shielding Rogene and pushing the Ross men aside. He had to stab, and slash, and hit them, as no one wanted to stop the fight. And then they were through the door and into the cold, wet air. An icy gust threw a handful of rain into his face, and he had to blink. It was like plunging into the loch—sprays of cold water flew right into his eyes. The Mackenzie men were running in the general direction of the gate as it was impossible to see even the walls through this storm, only the shapes.

"Shoot them!" yelled someone. "Shoot them!"

"Whom?" came a call back.

"The damned Mackenzies!"

An arrow flew past Angus and thunked into a black puddle. His feet slurped and mud clung to his shoes as he ran with Rogene's hand in his.

Then another arrow swooshed past and someone yelled, "Stop shooting! 'Tis me, Maol-Moire!"

"Ah damn, ye're shooting yer own men!" Angus jeered at the archers.

"Stop shooting!" Maol-Moire cried again. "Close the portcullis!"

Ah, goddamn it.

"Faster!" He tugged Rogene after himself.

They ran, losing their balance and landing in the sludge, but getting up again and continuing.

Finally, there it was, the gate. Another few steps or so... The portcullis was almost down!

"Quick, Rogene, go before me," he cried as he pulled her by the hand so that she was in front of him. "Roll!"

Just twenty inches or so remained between the sharp metal spikes and the ground. Rogene fell to the muddy earth and rolled under the portcullis. He threw himself to the ground, but as he rolled under the portcullis, it landed on his tunic and pinned him in place. He grabbed the tunic, pulling with all his might. The strong fabric finally tore, and he was free. Rogene grabbed his hand and they ran down the slope. He looked for his clan but couldn't see anyone.

"We have horses hidden!" Rogene cried to him through the raging storm. They were both soaking wet. "Can horses go through this storm?"

"They have nae choice. Do the rest of the men ken where the horses are?"

"Yes, of course. They all must be heading there."

"Aye. Lead the way."

CHAPTER 29

T *wo days later...*

ROGENE HUDDLED IN THE DRY, WARM HEAT OF ANGUS'S embrace and looked at the fire. His arm was around her shoulders, heavy and comforting and strong. Around them, the woods were quiet. Warm weather had replaced the storm, and the sun had shone the two whole days they'd been traveling. Thank goodness they'd found a horse, but the poor thing had been so terrified of the storm they'd had to make their way on foot at first, tugging the animal after them.

Once the storm had passed, they'd been able to continue on horseback.

Night birds were hooting, noises and rustles coming from somewhere behind the bushes and between trees, but Rogene wasn't afraid. She felt shielded and protected by Angus.

Her belly was full from the fish he'd caught in the nearby loch and roasted over the fire.

As she looked into the flames, she remembered she had most

likely killed a man back in Delny Castle. Even though freeing Angus from Euphemia's claws felt right, she wondered if she'd interfered too much with history. Angus was supposed to have married Euphemia, who was supposed to give birth to his child, no matter how much Rogene wished it wasn't true.

And as soon as she returned to Eilean Donan, she needed to go back to her own time.

No matter how much she wanted to stay.

"What are ye thinking of, lass?" he said.

"You don't want to know." She turned her face to him and looked into his eyes.

During their journey, they'd been mostly silent, listening for pursuers. Rogene didn't mind. She had so much to think about. She needed to tell him the truth about his son. She should have told him a long time ago.

"I do," he said softly. His eyes darkened and saddened. "Whatever it is, tell me."

She wanted to, she really did. The knowledge weighed at the pit of her stomach like a rock. But looking at him, so relaxed, so handsome, she didn't want to break his whole world apart.

Because he'd need to go back to Euphemia and marry her. Because he'd need to choose someone else.

Not his own happiness.

So she didn't tell him. Instead, she leaned closer and kissed him.

He responded, kissing her back with his impossibly tender and yet demanding lips. His tongue brushed against her lower lip. He dipped his tongue into her mouth, and wildfire seethed through her veins.

His strong arms wrapped around her, pressing her against him with a groan. She turned to him, wrapping her legs around his waist. He was already hard, and she was already shamelessly rubbing herself against him. He cupped her breasts through the tunic and massaged them, rolling her hardening nipples around his thumbs. Liquid pleasure shot through her, and she was already melting under his touch.

Suddenly, they weren't in a forest anymore, they were in a bubble of pleasure, of love, of desire.

He kissed her with such hunger, with such need, that she sagged against him. His arm was an iron bar around her waist. He was so big, and hot—as always, like a furnace—and his kisses impaired her thoughts. She wrapped her arms around his shoulders and brought him closer.

She was already making desperate noises. Her breasts tingling and swollen from his caresses, her sex hot and wet and needy. She felt drunk and disoriented, her blood like fire.

They were covered with her cloak, which was wide enough for both of them. But it fell from the intense movements of her body. They were both breathing heavily, and she was like human ivy wrapped around him in a desperate attempt to become his second skin.

He went under her tunic and cupped her breast with his bare hand, and she moaned. Bolts of pleasure went right through her sex, and her inner muscles clenched.

"Lass," he growled against her neck. "If ye keep making sounds like this, I wilna last long."

"I don't care," she echoed his growl. "I want you." She began fiddling with the thin leather belt at his waist.

"What are ye doing to me...?" he said as he pulled down his pants. "Ye need to be cherished." She pulled her own pants down. "And cared for." He took his erection into his fist and directed into her entrance. "And loved..."

They both froze at the word as he slid effortlessly into her slick core. She gasped slightly, still looking into his eyes as she took him into the very depths of her, stretching, filling, making her whole.

And when he was buried in her completely, she tightened around him automatically, and he groaned.

"I love ye," he said. "I love ye, lass. I desire ye like ye're my last breath of air. Ye're everything."

She blinked slowly as the meaning of his words seeped into her lust-filled brain. The man a Highland faerie had said was destined for her loved her... He loved her! And she...

"I love you, too," she whispered.

There wasn't anything else she could say, really. Despite the centuries separating their births, despite the fact that they could never be together, despite the fact that she couldn't possibly stay, she loved him.

Happiness flashed through his eyes and he took her mouth like he wanted her to be the last thing he remembered before he died. He started moving within her, slowly, rousing bliss within every cell of her being.

She hid her face in the crease of his neck as he intensified the rhythm and was pounding into her. His thrusts grew faster, harder. He breathed erratically, echoing the beats of her heart.

She whimpered, taking him all in, the pleasure so intense she was falling apart, unraveling, opening up her heart.

And then he was there with her, over the edge. He stiffened, cried out, bucked, and pounded into her with wild, mindless thrusts, losing himself in her body. She came violently with a gasp, and Angus cried out her name.

They sagged against each other, like one tired, satisfied being. Without pulling out of her, he covered them both with her cloak and took her into his big arms. They breathed one breath in unison, wrapped in each other, and Rogene refused to think of anything that lay beyond the here and now.

It was as though they were lost in time and space, in a capsule of happiness, and she wanted this to last for eternity.

Because it was more than just love and more than just sex. For the first time, she understood what the word "soul mate" meant. It was what she felt now. The absolute and full completeness. The satisfaction that went into every fiber of her being.

The feeling that she was home and everything was right with the world. Every. Single. Thing.

She breathed, inhaling his masculine scent. Yes. Everything was right with the world.

Except one thing that kept nagging at her somewhere deep within. She had to come clean. They had to talk about what would happen next for them. They'd just said they loved each other. In her time, it meant they were very serious.

But no matter how right they were for each other, they had an expiration date. She knew that.

Did he?

She leaned back and looked at him.

"I need to tell you something," she said.

He frowned. Oh damn. She hated herself. She was about to destroy everything. How she wished this wasn't true. She sat up, put on her breeches, and pulled her tunic back down over her breasts. He rose on one elbow.

"What is it, lass?" he asked.

She swallowed hard. "I'm a historian, right? So I know a lot of things that happened in the past...well, that happen now."

"Aye."

She fiddled with the edge of her tunic. "One of those things is about you and Euphemia."

He rose and sat up straight. "What about me and Euphemia?"

Wringing her hands, she sighed out sharply. "I wish this wasn't true. But there is a real, historical document that proves that you married her."

Angus went completely still, his jaw ticked under his beard.

"And more than that, you and she will have a son." Every word tore at her throat as she said them. "Paul Mackenzie. One day, in 1346, at the battle of Neville's Cross, your son will save the life of Robert Stuart, the grandson of Robert the Bruce. That will have dramatic consequences for the history of Scotland because when he becomes King of Scotland in 1371, he will start a whole dynasty of Stuart Kings and Queens of Scotland. Your and Euphemia's son will save a future king's life."

Angus closed his eyes as though she'd just slapped him. "Nae."

She felt as though a knife stabbed her in the heart. "I'm sorry, Angus."

He ran his fingers through his hair. "So if I dinna marry her and she doesna have my son"—he met her gaze, and there was so much pain in his eyes—"Scotland will lose its future king."

She nodded. "Without Paul, everything might change. If Robert III dies at that battle, there won't be a clear heir to the throne. There may be more bloodshed. England might interfere. Who knows what could happen. Such things might have consequences for the course of world history. Like the butterfly effect."

He frowned. "The butterfly effect?"

"Yes, it means that even the slightest change in history can have major consequences. It's like a butterfly flaps its wings and causes a huge storm. Of course, in reality, it doesn't work like that. But it's a metaphor to imagine the idea."

He growled out a sigh. "I understand the idea, lass. What I dinna understand is why did ye save me from Euphemia if ye still think I should marry her."

As though sharing Angus's outrage, a bird somewhere in the darkness screeched. Rogene winced and looked up into the bottomless night sky, stars like diamond dust against the inky space.

They were still under the same sky, even if she would be born hundreds of years in the future. They were still walking the same earth. Only time was different. Nothing else.

When she looked at him, the knife in her heart was turning. "Because I couldn't bear the thought of anyone hurting you." She put her hand on top of his. The touch sent a wave of tingles through her. "Because I wanted to be your shield."

He withdrew his hand and lay on his back, staring into the

stars. "But I dinna have a choice, do I, lass?" His Adam's apple bobbed, and his dark eyes met hers. "After all, nae matter how much I want to choose ye, I still have a duty much bigger than I've ever imagined." He closed his eyes and drew a deep breath. "My duty is nae to protect my siblings against my father nae more. 'Tis to protect Scotland's future, generations of people, thousands of lives. Including yers. Ye may never be born, is that true?"

She nodded. "It's a possibility, yes. I'm afraid so." Her voice cracked.

"And ye're sure 'tis what has to happen?" he said.

"Yes. I've seen the documents myself."

He shook his head. "By God's blood, lass. Why did ye have to come and stir up everything? I would have marrit Euphemia. I would have fathered Paul. I wouldna have kent love. I wouldna have hurt like I'm hurting now."

Her eyes watered, and he became a blurry, orange, glowing fleck. "I'm sorry, Angus."

They were silent. He stared at the sky and she stared at him. Emptiness and coldness filled the space between them. The bubble had burst, and she was the one holding the needle.

Wiping her tears, she said, "What happens now?"

He chuckled. "I had hoped to convince ye to stay with me. To marry me. But I see that 'tis nae possible, is it?"

She shook her head, her chest tearing at the seductiveness of that thought. "It was never an option, Angus. No matter how much I would have wanted to stay. I have David to think of. You have Euphemia, and you'll have a son you can teach how to be a good man..."

"As though I want a son from that woman." He met her eyes, and his were burning like coals. "I want a son from ye."

She felt a tear roll down her cheek. "That damn faerie. Why send me all the way here, give us love and hope, only to crush everything when nothing is possible, anyway."

His eyes softened. "At least I have ye with me for now."

He opened his arms and she fell into his hug as if into a soft cloud. As he wrapped his huge arms around her, she laid her head on his chest and heard the erratic thumping of his heart.

"I'll deliver ye to Eilean Donan," he said. "Once ye've gone through the rock, I'll return to Euphemia. Yer history will be safe, Lady Rogene, from the future. I'll choose duty yet again. It seems my father was right, after all, and I canna escape my fate."

CHAPTER 30

F *our days later...*

THE SIGHT OF EILEAN DONAN DIDN'T BRING ANGUS JOY.

It brought sadness. It meant losing the woman he loved forever.

As they rode down the streets of Dornie towards the small port, he was aware of her gentle frame pressed against his back, her arms wrapped around his waist as she hugged him tightly. God Almighty, what he wouldn't give to have her wrapped around him like that for an eternity...

The village wasn't as busy as usual, with most people gone to plant the fields of barley and oats around the village. People carried baskets and firewood, pushed barrels on wheels, swept their houses. A blacksmith was banging against his anvil somewhere, and a carpenter hammered against wood. The scent of baked bread and brewed ale hung in the air, mixed with the scent of sheep dung that was being spread on the fields. People greeted him as some recognized him.

Since only one horse had been left in the grove when they'd arrived upon fleeing Delny Castle, Angus had assumed Raghnall, Catriona, and the rest of the band had taken the horses and made their escape, as well. He hoped they had made it home safe already or would soon arrive.

As Angus and Rogene arrived at the small port, he descended and helped Rogene to get down from the horse. Their eyes locked, and hers were wide and sad. They both knew what this meant. As soon as they arrived at Eilean Donan, he'd accompany her into the underground and she'd be gone forever. Part of him still hoped the rock wouldn't work. Or that all she'd said about time travel wasn't true.

Then he wouldn't lose the woman he loved. He also wouldn't need to marry Euphemia. He wouldn't need to produce a son who'd save the future king.

Silent, they walked down the wooden jetty towards the boat. The loch was still today, with no wind. The sun shone brightly and a thin, misty fog hung over the surface of the loch. It made the castle look like it was in the realm of faeries, not of this world.

Nature was waking up before the summer. Young leaves on trees and bushes were green, shiny, and tender. Fresh, shy grass was growing. He could smell the delicate scent of flowers—must be the apple trees down by the shore, he thought. They were shedding small, white petals onto the ground and the surface of the loch.

All that peace and beauty around him made the turmoil inside of him spin faster. As he helped Rogene get into the boat, it careened from side to side, just as his heart was lurching.

His heart was full of the dread of voluntarily going into a prison. Of losing something so precious, so valuable that one found it only once in a lifetime.

He got into the boat and told the man to row to the castle. As the boat began moving, he met Rogene's eyes. She stared at him like she wanted to remember his every detail, and his heart gave another violent lurch.

They'd made love every night for the past four days after she'd told him about his son. Their lovemaking had been sad and desperate, and they'd known it would hurt them both later when they'd lose each other forever and would have only memories.

But he couldn't stay away from her. He'd take her in any way he could have her. And if he'd have only memories of her, well... so be it. He'd cherish and treasure them his whole life. He'd take them out in his mind and relive them when he was lying with Euphemia, when he needed to bed her, when he was old, and gray, and most of his days had gone.

After a short while, the boat arrived at the jetty of Eilean Donan, and the man tied it to a pole. As they went down the wooden surface towards the castle, Rogene took his hand and intertwined her fingers with his, locking their hands together. Her palm was cool and small and tender. Every step he took felt heavy, as if he were dragging boulders after his feet.

The closer they came to their love's inevitable doom, the faster his mind raced, searching for ways to avoid it. Searching for ways to keep Rogene here. Wondering, again, was the destiny of Scotland more important than his personal happiness? Could he find another way to resolve this, have the child that would protect the future king and still have the woman he loved by his side?

They walked through the sea gate and into the greater bailey where houses and workshops stood, then through a palisade and into the second bailey. There, he turned to Rogene to suggest that they think again about her returning to her time, when he noticed a woman running towards them at full speed.

Trying to see who it was, he squinted, and a huge smile spread on his lips.

"Catrìona!" Rogene exclaimed and waved her hand.

They walked closer to the keep, and Catrìona didn't stop but slammed into Angus, knocking the air out of him, and wrapped her arms around his shoulders.

"Ye're alive," she whispered. "Ye're here!"

He let go of Rogene and hugged his sister back. Catrìona's tears wet his cheek. Lord, it was like when they were kids. She'd seemed so fragile and so sweet, and when she'd had a scare, she'd come to him and he'd tell her it was all right and as long as he was by her side, he wouldn't let anything get to her.

Catrìona let go of him and hugged Rogene. "I'm so glad to see ye."

When they broke the hug, Angus said, "What happened to ye? Is Raghnall all right?"

"We lost ye. We all got lost, but thankfully, Raghnall found me and two others, and we made our way here as soon as we could. Raghnall said he saw ye by the gate, but they began shooting arrows again, and we had to run. We only arrived yesterday. Raghnall has small wounds on his ribs and shoulders, a scratch on his thigh, but he's all right otherwise. He's with Father Nicholas, who's now well and tending to him. The rest of the men are here in the castle, and I'm healing their wounds."

"How many came back?" Angus said.

Catrìona's eyes saddened. "Twelve."

"Only a dozen?" Angus said. His life was not worth the lives of twelve honorable warriors, especially given that he'd need to marry Euphemia, anyway.

"I'm afraid so. But they'll be so happy to see ye're alive, both of ye."

She grasped Rogene's hands and squeezed them. "Thank ye for freeing him."

Rogene smiled. "Don't thank me. I couldn't live with myself if I hadn't."

Catrìona's gaze saddened. "Neither could I, but—"

She glanced at Angus and he frowned. Did she seem different to him? Sadder? Turned inward in a way? It was as if she wore something heavy on her shoulders. Her skin seemed a little gray and her eyes tired. Even her golden hair seemed to shine less.

"But what, sweet?" Angus said.

She bit her lip. "I'm supposed to leave for the convent at the end of this summer. But how can I serve God when I killed so many men that I lost count?"

Angus paled. Yes, he'd seen her fighting like a she-wolf, and he knew she'd likely have some trouble coming to terms with that, and it looked like he'd been right.

"Are ye thinking of nae going?" he asked.

She wrapped her arms over her chest, her eyes filling with tears. "I want to go, Angus. 'Tis my calling. 'Tis what God wants. I just... I dinna ken if I can be a good servant to the Lord if I already broke his commandment."

Rogene rubbed her shoulder. "Maybe you should talk to Father Nicholas about that?"

Catrìona nodded. "Ye're right. I will. I need to finish tending to the wounded. I just saw ye two from the window and had to come see ye and make sure ye're both unharmed."

"Aye, dinna fash, sister. We're both well."

"Good, I'm so glad."

With that, they walked towards the keep. Catrìona climbed up the stairs to where the wounded were. Rogene went up to get her purse with the magical object she called a phone.

While she was gone, he went into his bedchamber and found the leather roll with the letter from the Bruce and put it behind the belt of his breeches, under his tunic.

When they both returned to the ground floor, they stared at the stairs leading down.

Angus looked at her. "Do ye still want to go?"

She sighed. "I have to, Angus."

His heart was tearing apart as she turned and walked down the stairs. The lower they descended, the faster his mind was spinning. Every step brought her closer to the rock.

Brought the end of their brief but wonderous relationship closer.

He'd never see her again. He'd never talk to her, never touch her, never say how much he loved her.

Never touch that possibility of happiness again.

They were now at the long hall of the basement. Angus took a torch from the sconce on the wall and they walked down the hall towards the door at the end. Time crawled, but he wanted it to stop altogether. That damned Highland faerie. Where was she? If she commanded time, mayhap he could persuade her, bribe her, convince her nae to do it...

But Rogene had already opened the heavy door and stepped inside the cave-like room. It smelled like mold and water and wet stone.

The light of the torch fell on the floor and the wall to his right. There it was, the rock, surrounded by the chests and casks and sacks. Where he'd lost the ring he'd meant to give to Euphemia and met the woman who'd changed his life forever.

He set the torch in a sconce above the rock. The flame threw dancing shadows around them, and darkness surrounded the spot of warm orange light in the middle of which Rogene stood.

Once she left, all light would be gone from his life, too. He stared at the rock with its curvy patterns and the handprint, and he hated it with all his might. He wished he could smash it into dust with his own hands and trap Rogene with him here forever.

"So, I guess this is it," she said.

She looked pale, and her eyes were big on him.

Only moments were left till they'd be separated forever. Nae, he couldna have it.

"I canna let ye go," he said and took her by the hand.

"But Angus—"

That familiar, sweet tingling went through him like every time they touched. "Nae. Listen to me. Ye can still stay. I ken 'tis nae what ye deserve, but listen. What if I marry Euphemia—and

God kens how much I dinna want to do it—but what if I do, and ye will be my mistress?"

She frowned, angry. "Your mistress?"

"Aye. I hate myself for suggesting this, but 'tis how we can be together. I can give ye a house—a small estate, men to protect ye, and I would come and visit ye every moon. Euphemia would never ken of ye, and my men would die protecting ye. Ye'll have everything ye want—"

"Except you," she said coldly. "And except my brother."

"Ye have me already, Rogene. Ye have me always. Always. I dinna want to marry her, and 'tis ye who tells me I must. For that child who'd save the Stuart kings."

"No. That would not be having you. You'd still be away. You'd still have her to think of. Your wife." She spat the word as though it tasted bitter. "You'll have your son..."

"Ye'll give me sons. Or daughters. I dinna care which. We'll have children."

She scoffed. "No, Angus. I won't abandon my brother for this. I couldn't stay even if you could marry me. I'm the only one he's got. No one else cares for him, and he's still seventeen years old."

Her brother... Oh Lord, he understood that more than anyone. He, whose life was dedicated to protecting his own siblings. And still...

She took a step towards the rock and something broke in him. This was it. She'd be gone forever.

He dropped to his knees as if a scythe had sliced through his ankles. He didn't beg her. He wanted to. He had to shut his mouth tight to stop the words.

She took another step, their hands still connected, their eyes locked.

Tears streamed down her cheeks.

Another step. So far away, he almost had to let go of her hand.

He had to let go of her.

He had to.

"I will always love ye, lass," he said.

With the last blessing of his words, he let go of her fingers. He pulled up his tunic. His hands refused to move, and he willed them with a strength he didn't know he had. He retrieved the leather roll and held it out for her.

Their eyes locked, and there was surprise in hers, and pain and sadness. She didn't need to ask what it was. She knew.

"Thank you. But I know it's important to you. I'll do the work to find it in my own time. Hide it somewhere safe. Somewhere new," she said through tears. Then she spun around and slammed her hand into the handprint. "I will never forget you."

With wide eyes, Angus stared at the carving, which began to glow. Something happened with the air, as though a tremor went through it, like a distant earthquake.

He blinked, and saw her turning to him, and their eyes met for the last time. And then she was gone.

Just gone.

And although the torch was still burning, his whole world went dark.

CHAPTER 31

O xford University, June 2021

"CONGRATULATIONS!" SAID DAVID.

Rogene looked up from the diploma in her hand. Her brother gave a soft chuckle and came to stand before her.

The University Parks were bright and alive with birdsong. Summer, contrary to common belief, was lovely in England, and Rogene inhaled sweet air full of the scent of greenery, blooming trees and flowers, and warm rocks.

She'd just defended her thesis. When she'd come back to her own time and told Professor Lenticton she wanted to work with a team to find that letter, they'd found it, thanks to Anusua and Karin. Anusua had checked through fifty letters from around that time, and had found evidence suggesting there might be a secret storage area in the underground rooms of Eilean Donan. They went to the castle as a team, and by carefully examining the wall, Karin had seen one stone that looked different from the rest and found the letter hidden behind a rock in the wall.

Rogene knew this used to be Angus's uisge brewery and the place where Bruce had hidden.

Once they'd pulled it out, there it was, the leather roll. The singed edges of the parchment reminded her of the day she'd thrown the letter into the fire only to have Euphemia take it out.

Thanks to that find, not only had Rogene honored her mother's legacy, but she'd also started a whole new direction of research. Suddenly her name seemed to be on everyone's lips—at least in the history department.

Rogene realized how great it was, to work on a team and trust her colleagues. She'd never have been able accomplish as much by herself in such a short period of time.

Professor Lenticton had already offered her a position as her assistant professor. Rogene would lead the research team on this topic. Professor Lenticton said she was proud of her, to see how she'd changed and was now open to teamwork.

David had flown back to his aunt and uncle after Rogene's disappearance. While Rogene was gone, he'd had his eighteenth birthday.

Once she was back, Rogene had called David's school principal and asked for him to allow her to homeschool David until his final exams, which were coming in two weeks. She felt incredibly guilty and just couldn't bear the thought of letting him remain with her aunt and uncle where he'd continue to be ignored and not supported with his dyslexia.

He was still waiting to hear about the football scholarship to Northwestern University, and was grateful to stay with her and have her help preparing for his exams.

She realized David had congratulated her and she'd never responded to him.

"Thank you," Rogene said.

They'd agreed to meet up here after her defense. Although her colleagues had suggested going for a beer, she'd said she'd join them later, after she celebrated with her brother. With an ice cream—just like they had when their mom and dad were alive.

"Why don't you look happy?" David said. "Before the wedding, you were all about this thing. You got the job with your supervisor. Isn't it what you wanted so much? The degree, job security, and proving Mom's hypothesis?"

She sucked in a breath. "Goddamn you and your observational skills. Let's go, we'll talk there."

They walked to a gelato shop where she bought him his favorite pistachio ice cream and a strawberry chocolate for herself.

"Actually, you haven't been yourself ever since you got back from that strange trip when you went like completely AWOL."

Karin had called the police the next morning when Rogene hadn't come down for breakfast in the hotel in Dornie. They had all been terrified while the police had searched for her, interviewed the wedding guests and the museum staff. David had stayed in contact with Karin every day until Rogene got back, hoping to hear some news about her, frustrated that he wasn't allowed to go and search for her himself.

Rogene sighed. "You have no idea." She licked her gelato and closed her eyes. Whenever she enjoyed something, she always thought Angus would have loved it. But there was no ice cream in the Middle Ages.

They crossed the street and slowly walked along the path. Oaks, which were planted along it at equal intervals, rustled gently in the wind. The big meadow of mowed grass was full of students sitting on blankets and sunbathing. Dogs barked, people laughed. It smelled like fresh grass, sunscreen, and barbecue. The sun was pleasant on Rogene's skin, warming her, and she waited for the aching tension in her shoulders to loosen. Now she'd achieved everything she'd ever wanted. The degree. The job. Mom's recognition. David was by her side.

She'd worked twelve hours a day after she'd returned, to submit the thesis on time. Then hours and hours of meetings and reading and learning and preparation for the defense. Now she could relax.

But the tension wasn't going away. And that nausea she'd had for a few days before the defense... She'd attributed it to nerves, but even now that she'd given her defense and gotten her diploma, it still wasn't going away.

Actually, it had gotten worse with the ice cream, and she couldn't even look at it anymore.

She rolled her shoulders back. She knew what the problem was. Angus wasn't here. He didn't exist in her time.

She hadn't been able to bring herself to check Angus and Euphemia's marriage certificate since she'd returned. But she'd briefly checked the history of the Scottish kings, and it had all worked out perfectly, just the way she remembered.

So he must have married Euphemia like he'd said he would. And she must have had Paul Mackenzie. Rogene didn't know. It was too painful to think of that, let alone look through the documents. And what would be the point? She'd only terrorize her heart, which already throbbed as though put through a meat grinder.

"I didn't want to talk with you about it until you'd defended your thesis," David said, "but I know you didn't run away with a secret boyfriend like you said. You have no boyfriends. Secret or otherwise."

Rogene sighed. "Yeah. You're too smart for your own good. What do you think I did, then?"

She felt her brother's piercing eyes on her. "I think...I think you disappeared."

"Yeah, Sherlock. I disappeared with Cameron. Like I told you. I'd had enough of the stress with the wedding, with the thesis, with Lenticton. He was walking his dog on the island and he talked to me. I went for a drink with him. The rest is history."

"Yeah," David said after he bit into a chunk of the ice cream. "But you would have called, or texted, or emailed. I know you.

You would have never left me. You text me daily when I'm in the States and get worried if I don't reply by the end of the night."

His brown eyes were serious and, as always, so intelligent, taking in her carefully. Could she really tell him the truth? He'd think she was lying, of course, but then she could turn it into a joke. And she really wanted to tell someone about her crazy adventure...about Angus.

What was the worst thing that could happen if she did confess? She would tell him she was kidding if he didn't believe her. Which would, probably, be a bit cowardly and mean, but she really didn't have the mental capacity to fight with anyone about anything. All she needed was a friend. Was support. And her brother was the best support she could get.

"Okay," she said, "let's go sit and talk."

He put an arm around her and hugged her to his side, reminding her of how huge he was, and how loving. "Okay."

They sat on a bench under the shadow of a large oak tree. David bit into the cone. He was half done with his ice cream. Looking at her now dripping cone, Rogene felt nauseated, and threw it into the trash with regret.

David turned to her, bending his leg on the bench so that he was facing her. "So? Where did you really disappear to?"

She let out a long sigh. "Back in time, David. To 1310."

He raised his brows with an amused chuckle. "What?"

She gave a nervous laugh. "Ha! Gotcha. Funny, right?"

But he didn't laugh. He narrowed his eyes as he chewed on the last of his cone. "Not really. You don't look too amused."

Rogene wiped her sweaty hands against her skirt. "Well. Then I suppose I was with Cameron, taking a break from everything and going AWOL for once in my life."

David rested his hand on her arm, looking concerned. "You're acting weird, and I want to know why. So, suppose you're telling the truth. How did you travel in time?"

"Forget it," she said. "Does time travel sound more believable than me running away with a guy?"

David chuckled. "No offense, but yeah."

"Well, offense!" she said. "Excuse me, I'm not so bad looking."

"That's not the issue. The issue is you're so organized and controlled. You'd never just take off for several weeks." He paused, eyeing her. "So maybe you were kidnapped. Are you covering for someone? Do you have Stockholm syndrome?"

"I don't have Stockholm syndrome. And I wasn't kidnapped. And I'm not protecting anyone. I don't want you to think I'm insane."

"Okay, don't worry about that. Just tell me what happened."

Rogene groaned. "Ugh. Okay. I'll tell you, but remember you asked for it."

"Sure."

And then she told him. About Sìneag. The rock. Angus Mackenzie being allegedly her soul mate. About the slap. The church and Father Nicholas. Then going back to Eilean Donan. Euphemia. Writing the contract. Bruce's letter. Angus falling in love with her and canceling the wedding. The kidnapping. Her journey to retrieve him. Their trip back. Her telling him about Paul Mackenzie and them breaking up. Her traveling back.

By the end, she was telling the story through hysterical, childish sobs. David hugged her and she pressed her forehead into his shoulder, smudging her running makeup against his T-shirt.

She cried for some time, letting the ache pour out of her like bad blood, letting her brother soothe her.

When she could finally speak, she looked up at him, wiping her eyes. "So, what do you think?" she said. "Do you believe me?"

He stilled, looking at her as though trying to decide how to tell her she was actually naked in a public place. "Uhm. I believe you seem to believe your words. You're not a great liar or a great actress. Never have been. So I can't imagine you'd be so upset if you didn't believe this to be true. Which makes me wonder what kind of pills you were given. And where you were held while you were hallucinating like that. And what the fuck they did to you while you were unconscious. You need to tell all this to the police."

Rogene sighed. Of course he didn't believe her. "Sure. I need to talk to the police again."

"I'm serious. Someone dangerous is out there, kidnapping women and drugging them."

"Probably," she said. She felt rejected and misunderstood, and although she knew that chances of him believing her were slim, she still felt hurt.

"Anyway, enough of that," she said. "Shall we go to the pub? You can't drink, of course, but you can hang out with my colleagues and me."

David looked at her with concern. "Uhm. Are you sure you want to go in this state? You look...like a panda."

"Ah, damn it." She sighed and brushed her hair with her hands. She retrieved her phone and unlocked it. The photo of Angus appeared on the screen. She'd looked at it for luck before her presentation, and her photos were still open. She tapped the camera app and pressed on the camera-reverse icon to take a look at herself and correct her makeup, so the photo disappeared.

But David frowned. "Who was that?"

She swallowed. "No one."

"No. Show me. Come on."

She sighed and returned the photo to the screen. There he was, overexposed by the flash against the dark background of the underground room. His beard, the small scars on his face, the black eye and the wound from Euphemia's whip, the clothes, the sword...all authentic. All real. A sconce with a torch was visible on the wall, too.

"He looks like he has a cool costume," David said.

"That's not a costume," she mumbled.

"So, a guy kidnapped you and drugged you and pretended he

was Angus Mackenzie. That's fucked up. You should show this face to the police."

"I will," she lied. "Now let's go."

"Rory—"

She quickly wiped away the rest of her smudged black mascara and stood up.

"Enough about that. Are you coming or not?"

David pulled her into a big hug, then stood back and looked at her dubiously. "Are you okay? Is it something I said? I'm really worried you were abused, and I just want to make sure you're okay."

"I wasn't abused. I'm fine. I made my choice, and now I have to live with it. Now, come on. I need a big glass of wine. After all, I did get everything I wanted."

And as they walked towards the bike parking area, she tried to ignore the fact that she was already regretting the choice she'd made. Because now that she had gotten what she wanted, the emptiness within her only felt wider.

And deeper.

And all she wanted now was to return to Eilean Donan and go back in time to Angus.

CHAPTER 32

D elny Castle, June 10, 1310

"ANGUS MACKENZIE?" CRIED THE GUARD FROM THE gatehouse.

There was a sudden clatter of several armed men running along the curtain wall.

Angus stared at the gate as if it were made of poisonous snakes. Was he seriously doing this? Going to talk to Euphemia felt like putting his bare hand into hot coals and expecting it to feel cool.

"Aye, I'm Angus Mackenzie," he said. "I came to talk to Lady Euphemia. I'm alone. Go get her this minute."

One of the guards left the wall and disappeared. After a while, the portcullis was lifted and he rode in, feeling the heavy glances of his men and Raghnall on his back.

He rode in under the scowling glances of the Ross men. The damned castle felt like a cage—one he'd never imagined walking into willingly again.

A man took his horse's reins, and when Angus descended, another one came to him and pointed a spear at him.

"Is this necessary?" Angus said.

"Aye," William said as he appeared from the door to the keep. "My orders. What do ye want?"

Angus sighed. "Nothing bad. If I wanted to hurt her, I wouldn't have come alone."

William had just opened his mouth to say something when another man-at-arms appeared from the keep. "Mistress says to let him in."

William glared at Angus for a few moments, then shrugged and nodded curtly. "Whatever the mistress wants. If he kills her, well, that'll be her fault."

The man-at-arms touched Angus on the shoulder with the tip of the spear.

"Move," the man said, and Angus walked.

He thought he'd be led to the great hall, but the guard told him to climb the stairs. On the first floor, he was ordered to go down the hall and enter one of the rooms.

When he did, he froze and closed his eyes, nausea rising in his stomach. On a large canopy bed was Euphemia, with her legs spread, and a man positioned with his head between her thighs.

Her eyes were half closed, her back was arched, and her mouth opened as she moaned sounds of pleasure that made bile rise in Angus's stomach.

For Scotland, he thought. For hundreds of thousands of people. For Rogene.

"Forgive me, Lady Euphemia," he said, shielding his face with his palm and looking down at the floor. "I have ye at a disadvantage. I'll come back later."

"Nae," she moaned. "Nae. Stay."

Surprised, he glanced at her. Her face was in complete ecstasy, and she was looking right at him. He realized she must be imagining him instead of that man.

By God's blood, he wasn't going to be part of that. Without

another word, he pushed the astonished guard back into the corridor and shut the door after him.

The guard frowned and exchanged a puzzled look with Angus. Angus crossed his arms over his chest and leaned against the wall. She was sending him a message. She didn't need him, and she could have any man she wanted. He had refused her, but she wouldn't wait for him.

But he didn't care if she wanted to sleep with the whole army. If he was to have a son with her, he had to make sure the boy was his. If anything, what she did gave him an advantage in negotiations because she was impure, and before the wedding, he needed to make sure she was not with child.

After a while, the man left the room, and Angus entered. Euphemia was dressed and tying up a long, golden braid before a large mirror. Mirrors were a luxury he hadn't seen often.

"Lord Angus," she said, looking at his reflection. "Too bad ye didna stay. I did have a large appetite, enough for two men."

"I never share my woman."

As he said "my woman," she threw a sad, longing glance at him, and her expression changed from a sly, smug mask into the face of someone who'd lost something important.

"I'm nae yer woman nae more," she said. "Is that what ye're implying?"

He slowly walked farther into the room. It was richly decorated, and he'd never seen one quite like it. Large, with a big canopy bed with beautifully carved poles and a rich blanket with gold-and-silver threads. A bearskin lay by the fireplace. Beautiful tapestries hung from the wall, showing women gathering herbs and flowers, a hunt, and the image of the crucified Christ. Several carved chests lined the wall. Two chairs flanked the mirror, again with masterfully carved arms.

The room smelled of the expensive rose water she preferred. The scent made him sick as it brought back memories of him handcuffed in her possession.

"Ye're nae my woman," he said. "But I came here to renegotiate our marriage."

As he said the words, something hung heavily in his chest, sucking all the life out of him.

Euphemia turned to him, her eyes wide, frowning.

"Dinna jest with me, Lord Angus," she hissed.

"I dinna jest."

She stared at him, her cheeks flushing. "Why did ye change yer mind?"

He couldn't tell her exactly what Rogene had told him, but he could give a version of that. One that would likely make her accept his terms, because there was something she equally wanted.

A son.

"Someone who kens the future told me that we're destined to be marrit. That we'll have a son who will one day save the life of a Scottish king."

Her lips parted in surprise, her eyes shining in delight. "A son..."

"Aye."

"But...what about what I did to ye? Are you ready to forgive me?"

Angus frowned at the change in her. Where was the arrogant, self-righteous woman who was so sure in her power and her beauty? She stood looking at him almost sheepishly. Was it an act? Or was she revealing a side of herself he hadn't known she had?

"I will have to, wilna I?" he said.

She came to him in three large steps and took his hand. Her hands were small and pale and cold, and unlike Rogene's touch, they caused an urge to pull away.

But he didn't. If Euphemia could be humble, if she could open up to him and be more human, he could imagine their marriage to be functional in some way.

A deep, aching, sucking wound opened in his gut. The

longing for Rogene that he knew would never go away as long as he lived.

"Lord Angus, I was desperate. I...I wanted ye, and I hated that ye took a lover, and that ye didna want to bed me. I always get what I want. I'm of a strong mind, and even my brother is afraid of me. But ye're the first man who showed me ye can be my master."

To his surprise, she dropped to her knees, still holding his hand and looking up at him.

"Only ye. And I didna ken how to behave. What to do. And still ye didna want to bed me, even though I forced ye."

Uncomfortable, he pulled her up so that she stood. "Please, Lady Euphemia. There's truly nae need for that. I will bed ye of my own will. Ye're right that ye canna force me. Especially if ye want my respect and my..."

He trailed off. He couldn't say love, because as long as he lived, he'd never love a woman who wasn't Rogene.

"Love?" Euphemia finished.

With reluctance, he squeezed her hand back. "I will promise that as long as I'm yer husband, ye will be the only woman for me. I wilna have a mistress and I wilna bed servants. 'Tis nae in my nature to do that. And I must insist that ye do the same."

Her blue eyes sparkled, and she beamed. "Of course."

She looked pretty.

Almost.

"Before we marry, I must make sure ye're nae pregnant from another man. The lad will be my son. Mine."

"Aye. I'm nae pregnant. I was angry at ye, and I did bed one man, but I took precautions."

"We shall see. With yer agreement, I'd like a healer to examine ye. Or we must wait for half a year to make sure."

"I dinna mind if a healer examines me. I'm nae pregnant as I just had my course. Anything else?"

"Ye accept all the conditions we had tried to negotiate in the contract. Kintail stays with Mackenzie clan. The dowry. We live on my estate."

She blinked and something dark flickered through her face but disappeared. "Aye."

He nodded and still held her hand.

"Do ye forgive me now?" she said.

He inhaled deeply. "Aye."

She smiled, then her face gained a more menacing expression, and his blood chilled.

"Good, because I do have one condition of my own."

"What is it?"

"That Lady Rogene dies."

He inhaled sharply, feeling as though a knife sliced his stomach. "Ye dinna need to worry about her. She's gone. As good as dead."

She frowned. "How?"

"She's gone overseas. So far away, ye can never reach her. Forever. Ye may consider her dead."

She narrowed her eyes. "How can I trust ye? Can ye swear?"

"I swear on God's name, Lady Euphemia. She's gone."

She studied his face for a while, then relaxed and gave a satisfied nod. "I believe ye." And then she beamed and laid her hand on his chest. "I didna think that ye'd come back to me. I thought I'd lost ye."

She caught his eyes, and for the first time since he'd known her, he saw a human soul behind them. Her eyes watered. She was vulnerable, and open, and fragile before him. And he thought that if she could be like this, this marriage could go better than he'd ever thought it could. He could respect this woman and get to know her and mayhap even become friends with her.

"I'd like to see more of this side of ye," he said.

She blinked. "No one ever does. I dinna let anyone so close to me because people have betrayed me in the past. My husbands cheated on me. My brother told my secrets to my da and he punished me. Even ye..." She shook her head. "But ye've come back to me and made the first step. I will do the same, Lord Angus. I already let ye in way too deep. I've fallen in love with ye..." She whispered the last words.

Angus swallowed. He'd never asked for her love, but he would accept it as a gift because love was not to be wasted. Unfortunately, he knew he'd never be able to reciprocate. But he'd give her the respect and appreciation that her love and openness deserved.

He wrapped an arm around her shoulders, and she pressed her head to his chest. If he was right, she was trembling ever so slightly.

"But if ye ever betray me again," she whispered, "I'll give ye nae mercy. I will destroy everyone and everything that's dear to ye."

CHAPTER 33

O xford, July 7, 2021

"FUNNY," ANUSUA SAID WITHOUT TURNING HER HEAD FROM the computer screen. "I've seen this document but never noticed this inscription before."

"Which one?" Rogene asked as she continued looking at her own screen, scrolling through the archive's scans of letters from the Wars of Scottish Independence.

She stopped scrolling at the Declaration of Arbroath, dated April 6, 1320, which was the letter of the Scottish parliament to the pope from fifty Scottish barons and leaders. They pleaded with the Pope to reconsider his support in the English-Scottish conflict. There were nineteen red and green wax seals attached to the document; the rest had been lost through the years.

"This record of the marriage of Angus Mackenzie and Euphemia of Ross…"

Rogene's heart lurched. She spun on her chair so fast a vertebra in her neck clicked. The small office shrank around her, the paneled walls pressing in on her. Sounds intensified, and her back misted with sweat.

"What about it?" Rogene asked.

"Well...I've always thought it was in May 1310, but here it says July 14, 1310. I must have mixed up the dates."

Rogene breathed out. That made sense because she had caused quite a hubbub and Angus had probably needed some time to renegotiate the contract and to convince the Earl of Ross and his sister to continue with the wedding.

"Oh. Yes. Well, we read so many documents it's impossible to remember everything."

"Yes, but that's not the strange thing about it," Anusua continued, zooming in. "I don't remember this bit. And for the life of me, I have no idea what this means. Look."

On shaking legs, Rogene stood and walked to stand behind Anusua's chair. There, on a yellowy-beige page, was the church record of the marriage: Angus Mackenzie married Euphemia Ross on July 14, 1310. Both parties gave consensus, both parties were of age, and no blood kinship was found between them. All that was written in a typical, calligraphic script.

But then underneath was a different inscription, clearly from a different writer. One who wasn't that experienced in calligraphy. The letters were different from each other, the tails of the letters too fat, or too thin, or too crooked.

Just like the letters of the contract she had been writing for Angus and Euphemia.

"Crikey," Anusua said. "Does it seem like it resembles modern English to you? That's so strange."

With a horrific wave of cold tingling, Rogene read the inscription.

"He is not marrying her. He is marrying you."

Feeling the ground slipping from under her feet, Rogene searched behind her with her hand until she found a chair, rolled it towards her, and plumped her behind into it.

Anusua chuckled. "It's as though someone from our time

traveled to 1310 and wrote it as a joke." She looked at Rogene with a chuckle. "Sort of like 'Peter was here.'" Her smile fell, and she narrowed her eyes. "Are you okay, hun?"

Rogene's throat contracted as she swallowed. *He is not marrying her. He is marrying you.*

This sounded terribly like it was a message—for her. From her. From 1310. It sounded like Angus was marrying Rogene.

Rogene.

Not Euphemia.

Which meant...

Her hand clasped around the blouse on her belly. She was still nauseated from time to time, and she had missed one period since she got back. They'd had unprotected sex, but she'd been on a pill —which, of course, she hadn't taken with her to the Middle Ages...

So, of course, she could be pregnant. Why hadn't she considered this before? She had thought of it, briefly, but always ignored it. Oh yes. She was in denial.

Another wave of cold tingles ran over her.

"Wh-when was Paul Mackenzie born?"

Anusua squinted at her. "Who?"

"Th-their son, Angus and Euphemia's... When was he born?"

"Oh...the Paul Mackenzie who saved Robert III's life. Why?"

She didn't reply. She pushed off the desk and rolled to her computer. Her hands were so cold and shook so much that she was hitting the wrong keys as she typed "Paul Mackenzie wars of independence." Wikipedia was not a reliable source, but it was a hell of a lot faster than searching through the archives. She could always confirm later.

Paul Mackenzie, born February 15, 1311 in Eilean Donan to Angus Mackenzie and a woman presumed to be Euphemia of Ross, though the identity of the mother is disputed by historians since there are other sources claiming Euphemia's presence in Ross at the same time. Other sources claimed she had died, possibly of childbirth.

Rogene's head spun, and the world darkened around her. Suddenly she lost the ability to move her limbs. She knew distantly she might be about to faint, but she held on to the handle of her chair and willed herself to stay alert.

"Can you please find the source...the church registry for Paul Mackenzie's birth?"

"Why?" Anusua asked, but already she was typing the search into the archives database. "I think it's correct. He was born in February; I have the same date in mind."

"Just to check that Wikipedia has it right."

Deep breath in and out. Needles prickled in her lower belly —it had been happening on and off for a couple of weeks, and she thought it must be from the shock of returning to her own time and adjusting to modern food. But could it be another symptom of pregnancy?

"Yes, Wikipedia is correct." Anusua chuckled. "For once."

"And the mother?"

Anusua peered at the screen. "Euphemia of Ross. Why?"

How could that be? Oh dear God. If Rogene had traveled in time and married Angus, and if she was pregnant now and Paul Mackenzie was indeed her son, why had she had the wrong mother written in the registry?

But if it wasn't Rogene who'd traveled back in time, who would have written that message, and why? *He is not marrying her. He is marrying you.*

"Okay. Seriously. What's going on?" Anusua said.

Rogene shook her head. "Can you please send the links to both documents to my email? I'm not feeling well. I need to go lie down but I'd like to take another look at them at home."

"Sure. Yeah, you don't look well, hun. Go lie down. Eat something."

Rogene took her purse and walked out of the office. Outside, the warm summer air calmed her down a little. All this was strange, but she shouldn't jump to conclusions before she knew and was sure. She hadn't felt well since she'd come back, and her nipples were hurting like crazy.

What if this was another indication she was pregnant?

First things first, she needed to buy a home pregnancy test. Maybe a dozen, just to be sure. As she sat on her bike and rode to a drug store, she wondered if it wouldn't harm the baby that she rode a bike? And what about last week when she'd had a couple of glasses of wine to celebrate her graduation?

And the junk food she'd eaten. She didn't take any vitamins; she should start...

On weak legs, she went into the drug store and bought a heap of pregnancy tests from different brands. When she got home, David was in the second bedroom, having an interview for college via Skype. She heard him talk and the other voice, computerized.

Thank God she didn't have to explain anything to him. She went right into the bathroom and quickly read the instructions. Pee on the stick, not rocket science. She did the deed and put the test on the vanity to wait for a couple of minutes. She set the timer on her clock and fired up her email program to click on the links that Anusua had sent.

She opened the images of the scanned documents and zoomed in, studying every letter, every detail, and every hook of the calligraphy. There was even a scratched part, just like when she'd made a blot and had to scratch away the upper layer of the parchment.

And then the inscription was in English. Modern English! Did she write this message to herself to go back in time? What other explanation was there?

Be with Angus. Marry her soul mate, the man of her destiny. The man she loved.

The timer went off, the beeping echoing off the tile walls of the bathroom. She looked at the test, and she could already see.

Two lines.

With a shaking hand, she picked it up and studied it. The

second line was weaker than the first one, but it was there. She looked again at the package. One line—not pregnant. Two lines —pregnant.

Joy spilled within her in a sweet burst of sunshine. She put her hand over her lower belly. Was he there, her son? Paul Mackenzie?

Was her life about to change again?

She had to be sure. With a tremor in her fingers, she unwrapped another test and peed a few drops on it. Her bladder was empty. She had to drink more water to do more tests. But as a couple of minutes passed and a smiley face appeared on the screen, she knew the surest way to know was to make an appointment with a doctor. She needed to read all the books about pregnancy. She needed to start taking vitamins. She had to double-check the date of the wedding...

July 14.

A week from today, in 1310.

A week!

If she was going to go back in time, it had to be before the wedding.

But what should she do about David?

She left the bathroom and went into the kitchen, making herself a cup of tea. She needed to breathe, calm down, and assess the situation as she always had—with a cool mind.

She knew she had to discuss it with David. She had no answers as what to do with him, but he was the most important part of her life, and she wouldn't go back in time without knowing he was okay and taken care of.

But what that would look like, she had no idea.

CHAPTER 34

J uly 9, 2021

CLUTCHING THE PLASTIC BAG FULL OF NINE MONTHS' WORTH of prenatal vitamins, Rogene opened the door of her apartment. In her bag was an early ultrasound showing a small, gray pear surrounded by a big black bubble.

Her and Angus's baby.

It was still too early to tell if it was a boy or a girl, and she kept asking herself if it was him—Paul.

Hard rock music blasted from David's closed room, and Rogene knew right away that something was wrong. He listened to it only when he was struggling with his studies or he'd made a mistake because of his dyslexia.

With a sinking heart, she knocked on the door. She had an idea of how to take care of him, but she was terrified of letting go of him, of letting him out from under her wing.

Besides, she still wasn't sure going back to the past was the best plan. She had no idea why she would call herself Euphemia of Ross to marry Angus. That didn't make any sense.

And that note—yes, it was written in modern English, but perhaps someone else had added that later? And it did seem to her that Anusua's suggestion was right—it sounded more like a joke, more like a "Peter was here" sort of message than anything that was meant to be read as a command.

But there were only five days left before the wedding in 1310. So if she did, by some miracle, decide she could go, if she could find the strength and trust and confidence in herself and in David, and forgive herself for leaving him, she needed to return to 1310 like right now.

She opened the door a slit and peered in. He lay on his bed with his hands behind his head and stared at the ceiling. The music blasted from a speaker on his desk.

"Hey!" Rogene cried over the music.

David looked up, touched a button on his phone, and music grew quieter. "Hey, what are you doing home so early?"

"I had an appointment," she said, walking into the room.

She was still nauseated and a little dizzy, so she sat down on his bed.

"Is everything okay?" she asked.

"Yeah. Why?"

"The music."

David's face was impossible to read. She never knew whether he was in a bad or a good mood. Without saying anything, David picked up an envelope and handed it to her.

Northwestern.

With shaking hands, she took it.

"It's not opened," she said.

"Your ability to notice things is uncanny."

She chuckled. "Is that why you were playing the music? Are you worried?"

He shrugged, but his eyes were on the envelope, burning holes in it.

"You know that even if you don't get the scholarship, you can still get into Northwestern. I can pay your tuition."

He kept staring at the envelope.

"Shall I open it?" Rogene said.

She took a deep breath. Not only would this decide his future, but hers, too.

"If you please, my lady," he said.

Ever since she'd told him about time travel, he'd been good-naturedly teasing her with such titles. But even so, she had found him watching YouTube videos about the Wars of Scottish Independence and documentaries about medieval Scotland. He'd even asked her a couple of questions, like what did people really eat, and how the toilets were, as though he was testing to see if she'd told the truth or not.

She ignored his gentle teasing, tore the short edge of the envelope, and took out the letter.

"'Dear David,'" she read. "'We are pleased to inform you—'"

She cried and jumped to her feet, hugging him. Her brother roared and hugged her back with such force that she feared her ribs would crack. He lifted her off her feet and spun her around.

When he put her down, he pumped his fist in the air. "I got it! Yeah!"

Rogene felt the tears stream down her face. They both knew what this meant. Despite his struggles with dyslexia, he'd gotten a scholarship into one of the best universities in the world.

Which meant, he'd be taken care of financially. And he was now eighteen.

Which meant...

If she trusted herself, and him, and really talked to him about this...maybe she could go.

She hugged him again. "Well, let's celebrate with ice cream!"

Though the thought of ice cream made her sick again.

"Not ice cream," he said. "I'm not a kid anymore."

"Okay, how do you want to celebrate?"

"How about that good scotch you have in one of the cabinets?"

"No way, mister," she said. "Not on my watch. Not for three more years."

"Drinking age is eighteen here."

"I don't care."

He sighed, but his eyes sparkled. He gave her a carefree grin —a rare sight, and one that made him look even more like Dad... She wiped a sudden tear. "How about a good old steak dinner? I'll take you out tonight."

"Can I have a beer then?"

"No."

"Ugh." He sat on the chair, dwarfing it with his large frame. "As if I haven't tried alcohol before."

"I won't enable you. And don't roll your eyes. Look, David, I need to talk to you about something."

She sat on his bed and leaned on her elbows. She wanted to take his hand in hers, but she knew he'd be uncomfortable.

"I'm pregnant."

He frowned, looked her up and down, then his eyes widened in horror. "What? By who?"

"By Angus Mackenzie."

He shook his head, wincing, as though he couldn't believe what he was hearing. "The guy you said you traveled in time to?"

"Yeah."

"Ha-ha. Funny. Nice prank."

"I'm not kidding, David. Just listen to me."

Under his skeptical gaze, she told him about the new inscription in the church registry, the changed wedding date, the fact that there were other documents that said that Euphemia was in Ross while Euphemia was also in Eilean Donan, giving birth to Paul Mackenzie. She showed him Paul's birth registry and the letter from the doctor stating her estimated delivery date.

He stared at the screen of her phone with the "He is not

241

marrying her. He is marrying you" message written in modern English in bad calligraphy.

He lifted his gaze from the phone and looked at her with concern. "Do you hear how you sound? It's clear you were raped and drugged and abused and now you're pregnant by the freaking monster! You need to call the police."

She pinched the bridge of her nose. "I know it sounds insane. But I...I want to talk to you about this. I want to go back, David."

"Go back where? To the rapist?"

She sighed. "Back in time. I think it's me who's marrying Angus. Not Euphemia. And I think *I'm* carrying Paul Mackenzie. Not her."

He stared at her like she were clinically insane. "Fucking hell."

"Don't swear," she said through gathering tears. "You got the scholarship. You're eighteen. I...I also got the news that the university press wants to publish my thesis as a book, and they offered me an advance of ten thousand pounds, which I'll transfer to you, so you'll have some money and won't have to depend on anyone."

He shook his head. "You're not serious."

Tears were streaming down her face now. "I am." She stood up. "I didn't expect you to believe me right away, I do know it sounds completely nuts. But I did hope you'd give me the benefit of the doubt."

He jumped to his feet. "I don't care about money or anything else! I just want to protect you from whoever did this to you. I'll fucking kill the guy!"

"Stop swearing."

"Stop talking about leaving, about going back to the guy who hurt you!"

She looked at her hands, which were blurry from tears. "He never hurt me. He saved me. I-I'm sorry to be leaving you again.

I left you with our aunt and uncle when I went to England. And now this... But I need to go."

"Okay, if you don't call the police, I will."

"Call the police all you want," she said as she walked to the door. "I'm going."

CHAPTER 35

Oxford, July 13, 2021

IT TOOK ROGENE FOUR DAYS TO SIGN THE BOOK DEAL AND TO get the lawyer to transfer all royalties and the advance to David —record time. Being of age now, he didn't need to be left under the protection of a legal guardian or social services.

So Rogene knew he didn't technically need her, other than she was the only close family he had left.

And he hers.

But she knew she needed to live her own life. She couldn't control David, his opinions, and his decisions. She couldn't shield him from everything, and he no longer needed her protection. With a scholarship to Northwestern, he could now start a new, exciting life on his own.

Since she'd told him she was leaving, they'd barely talked other than that he continued trying to get her to go the police. He stared at her with concern as she packed the bag of necessities she'd take with her to the fourteenth century. Vitamins.

Antibiotics—different kinds for different bacteria. Clothes for the baby. Warm socks. Shoes! Good, sturdy, warm shoes. Books... Damn, she couldn't take many, and they were heavy, so she settled on a children's book, a book on biology and the basics of medicine, one on herbalism, and one on the basics of engineering.

All the paperwork had been done superfast. She'd even prepared a will and left everything to David. But she hadn't told him that. She'd also left a suicide note. Her death would probably be easier for the police to accept and David would get his inheritance faster.

She realized those thoughts were cold and calculating, but, she supposed, that was her historian's mind.

It was afternoon the day before the wedding when she felt like she was ready. She had her backpack on her shoulders, and the most authentic medieval costume she could find online was in the small messenger bag that she wore across her body.

She had about ten hours of driving ahead of her. She'd probably need to stop for a few hours and nap, but she had no more time to waste.

Four days was as fast as she could get all the legal stuff done. If she was going to stop the wedding, she had to do it as soon as possible.

She opened the apartment door to walk out into the hall and looked back at David's closed door. There was no music. And she thought she'd said everything there was to say. He didn't believe her. She didn't blame him. But she wished this all was different.

Knowing she'd never see him again, she at least had to say goodbye.

"David," she said, half turned to the door, "I'm going."

The door flew open. He stared at her, his broad shoulders tight, lips pursed in a fierce line and shook his head.

"I love you," she said. "Will you hug me?"

"No. I'm not saying goodbye because you're not going."

Another blow to her gut. "I love you. Remember that."

She turned and started down the stairs when she heard steps behind her.

"Come on, Rogene, don't leave," he said as he climbed down the stairs with her. "Let me help you. We'll find a shrink. You probably have PTSD."

"I don't have PTSD. And I need to hurry."

"If you think I'm going to let you go to some sort of a sick psycho, think twice."

They were now outside the building and walking towards the tiny car she'd rented. She opened the trunk and threw her backpack in.

When she closed it and walked to the driver's door, David was blocking it. "Rory!" he said helplessly.

"Move," she said. "I'm not kidding."

They stared at each other in that familiar siblings contest she'd always won. She did, again, and David sighed and stepped to the side, letting her open the door.

"Bye, David," she said with a sinking heart.

She closed the door and started the car, but before she could press on the pedal, David opened the passenger door and flopped onto the seat next to her.

"Let me at least make sure you're safe," he said.

Something warmed in her heart, and tears blurred her vision. She was so hormonal and emotional, damn her. "Okay. Thank you," she said.

He nodded and looked in front of him. She tapped the address into the GPS and drove.

After hours of driving, they stopped for dinner, then for a coffee at midnight, after which David told her he'd drive and she could rest.

He stopped to rest during the night, too, and they arrived at the castle in the early morning. They were the first in line for tickets to visit the castle. She bought two tickets and they went inside.

When there were no museum workers around, she sneaked past the rope blocking the stairway to the underground rooms, and David followed her. She had no idea if this would work. Would Sìneag even come? Would the rock work again?

"Where are you going?" he asked.

"To the rock."

"I must be out of my goddamn mind to go along with this," he mumbled.

When she opened the door to the cave-like room with the rock, her heart beat in her chest like a drum. Was she too late? Was the wedding already happening?

Oh God! What if the rock didn't work?

She stood before the pile of rocks, in the middle of which was the one with the carving and the hand. David frowned at it. "So it does exist..." he said thoughtfully.

"It does."

He looked around. "And where's the guy?"

"Back in time. Through the rock."

The scent of lavender and freshly cut grass reached her nostrils. Sìneag?

Rogene's palms broke out in cold sweat. David squinted in the dim light, looking around. Then Rogene blinked, and Sìneag appeared. David jumped back a little. Rogene beamed.

"Whoa!" David cried. "Who the hell are you?"

Sìneag studied him with wide eyes and the curiosity of a child.

"I'm Sìneag," she said. "And who are ye, young and handsome man?"

"My brother," Rogene said.

"Oh!" Sìneag beamed. "Right! Is he coming with ye?"

Rogene's smile fell. "What? No, of course not."

Sìneag cocked her head with a mysterious smile. "Well..."

"No!" Rogene exclaimed. She thought of all the dangers, and bloodshed, and sickness, and cold, and she didn't want him to go there.

Sìneag kept smiling and staring at David.

"What?" David said.

"Nothing," Sìneag said. "Yer sister does oppose ye going."

Then David's face fell. "Wait. I had thought it was that Angus guy who abused Rory and lured her back here, but are you involved in that plan, too?"

Sìneag blinked. "Forgive me, but what plan, lad?"

"To rape her and abuse her and keep her captive."

"Nae, lad, I dinna do anything like that. I send people through time so that they can meet their soul mate, the person they're supposed to be with. Like yer sister and Angus Mackenzie."

David shook his head. "Unbelievable. It's like you both are brainwashed."

"So, lass," Sìneag said. "Ye want to go back, aye?"

Rogene nodded. "Yeah. It's still possible, isn't it?"

Sìneag nodded. "Aye. For the last time. Only three times per couple."

Her back sweating, Rogene nodded and glanced at David, who was scowling down at them. "Good. I'm ready."

He stepped forward. "No, you're not."

"Mayhap ye are, lass," Sìneag said. "But there's still the question of payment."

"Payment?" Rogene frowned.

"Well, 'tisna payment in the sense of yer human money. But I do like to treat myself to yer delicious human foods. Do ye happen to have something?"

Rogene gave out a soft chuckle. "You're sweet. Of course I have something for you... Um. I think I had a chocolate bar. Does that work?"

"Oh aye, I like the sound of that."

"I ate it last night," David said.

Rogene's face fell. "That's okay. Do you have something else?"

"I have gum."

Rogene lifted her brows at Sìneag.

"What's that?" Sìneag asked.

"You don't know what gum is?" David said.

"It's not food," Rogene said. "It's just...to chew...for taste."

Sìneag pinched her lips in consideration. "That doesna sound very appetizing."

"I think I have soda..." Rogene said and peeked inside the messenger bag that hung over her shoulder. There it was, the smooth metal surface. She grabbed the can and showed it to Sìneag. Thank goodness she didn't pack any food in her backpack, which she wore on her back.

"It's a drink," Rogene said.

Sìneag's eyes sparkled. "Aye, I'd like to try."

She took the can and turned it around, puzzled. Rogene realized Sìneag didn't know how to open it.

"Let me." The can opened with a small *hiss*, and Rogene handed it to the faerie.

After one small sip Sìneag giggled and touched her lips. "Oh!" she exclaimed. "What is this? It tickles..."

David shook his head in disbelief. "Come on, lady, it's nice acting you've got going on, but don't you think you're taking it a bit too far?"

But Sìneag offered him a wise smile. "Ah, lad. So young. So clever. So mistrustful and so...lonely."

Stunned, David blinked, looking like a young boy again—open, and vulnerable, and sweet. The boy she'd known all her life. The boy who had grown into a young man but still was only her little brother. Rogene wanted to take him into her arms and shield him and keep protecting him. Was she right to leave him here by himself? Was she right to leave him period? He was such a big guy, but he was still so young.

She had to, she told herself. She had to.

And he'd be all right. He must be. He had his whole life to live.

"So," Rogene said. "Is this enough, Sìneag? I have a wedding to crash."

"Aye," Sìneag said. "But are ye sure? Ye wilna get another chance to return to yer time."

The carving on the rock began glowing, and David stared at it, narrowing his eyes with a WTF expression.

This was it. She fingered the straps of her backpack on her shoulders. Was she really ready? Had she really thought everything through? If it wasn't for David, she'd already be on the other side of that rock.

"Rory..." he said in a warning.

She reached out to him for the last time and squeezed his hand. "I'm sorry, David. I have to." He grasped her palm and didn't let go.

"Rory, this looks fishy as hell."

"Bye, David." She kissed him on the cheek and with an effort, freed her hand.

Moving her heavy feet, she walked to the pile of rubble and sank to her knees before the stone, her backpack heavy. She threw a last glance at Sìneag and David, and her brother's eyes were huge and fixed on her face. He breathed heavily, clenching and unclenching his fists.

She smiled at him and put her hand into the cool surface of the handprint. There it was, the familiar vibration, the sense of falling and of water, and darkness started consuming her—

"Rory!" came a distant cry, as if from another world.

Someone grabbed her by the elbow of her other arm, the sensation foreign and strange.

And she was falling and falling through the darkness until she blacked out.

CHAPTER 36

She jerked upright. Inky darkness surrounded her. And that smell—the mold, the water, the wet dust... It smelled differently from where she'd been a moment ago —or, rather, hundreds of years ago.

In 2021, electrical lamps had illuminated the cave-like room. The time-travel rock must have worked and she was back in 1310. Of course, she couldn't be sure until she asked someone who knew what date it was.

But this time she was prepared. She had a flashlight in her messenger bag. Her backpack was still on her shoulders and she let it slide to the ground. Searching around herself for the bag, she touched something warm covered with some sort of fabric...

A body?

Gasping, she drew her hand back and covered her mouth with her hand. Who was that? She needed her light.

With her heart racing, and her pulse loud in her ears, she kept searching around herself and finally got a hold of her messenger bag. Her mind raced as she went through the contents.

Clothes, medicine, a book, silver coins... Her hand wrapped around a plastic cylinder. The light!

With a shaking hand, she found the button and pressed it. Momentarily blinded, she blinked. The round, white circle of light danced against the rough walls of the space, the vaulted ceiling, the rock with the Pictish carving...

There.

She stopped the light on a figure lying on the floor.

Her heart stopped. His eyes were closed, he was pale and looked like he was sleeping or unconscious.

David.

She rushed to him with her stomach sinking. Two fingers on his neck—he had pulse, thank God! She shook his shoulder gently.

"David. David!" she called.

He moaned and winced. Reaching to his head with his hand, he opened his eyes and blinked blindly into the light.

"Thank God, you're alive!" Rogene said.

Then she slapped him on the chest. "What the hell were you thinking? Why did you come after me?"

"What?" he croaked. "Rory, is that you?"

"Of course it's me, you idiot." She shone the light at her face. "I said, what were you thinking coming after me?"

"Coming where? What happened?"

She sighed. "What happened is that you traveled back into 1310 with me when you were not supposed to." She stood and held out her hand to him. "Stand up. You have to go back to the 2021. Quick."

He slowly rose. "My head is killing me. How are you so full of energy?"

"I don't know. Go on. There's the rock. Put your hand into the print."

"This is ridiculous."

"Okay, smart-ass. What do you think happened?"

"I don't know." He looked around. "That crazy woman drugged us and kidnapped us?"

"Is that your explanation for everything?" She sighed and

grabbed his hand. "Come on. Time to go back. I need to find Angus and stop the wedding."

He followed her slowly, still looking around and peering into the darkness. When Rogene focused the flashlight beam on the rock, it didn't glow. With her pulse pounding, she pulled David to the rock and put his hand in the print.

Nothing happened.

"Oh no," she muttered and pressed his hand harder into the print. "No, no, no! Sìneag! Sìneag!"

She looked around.

"He needs to go back to 2021!" she called.

Her voice echoed against the walls, then silence.

"Rory—"

"Damn it!" she cried, tears springing from her eyes. "She said this would be the last time. Didn't she? She said that, right?"

"Yeah, she did, but that doesn't mean anything."

"Oh, no, no, no!" She hid her face in her palms.

What should she do? How could she call Sìneag to take him home? And what about the wedding? She had no idea how to make Sìneag appear or how to make the rock work without her.

Looking up at David, she sighed. "It looks like you're stuck here, buddy," she said. "At least for now."

"Yeah. No shit."

"Which means you have to come with me. We don't have time to look for period clothes for you, but at least you're not showing cleavage or a lot of skin like I did." She looked skeptically at his simple gray hoodie and black jeans with ripped knees. "Your military boots will come in handy." She nodded. "Hold on to them. Medieval footwear is pretty horrible."

He looked at her as if she were crazy. But what else was new?

"Hold on to this, I need to change." She gave him the flashlight and retrieved the medieval costume she'd bought online. David turned around, and she quickly changed, shivering of cold. She'd tried to find something as historically accurate as she could, but the costume was made of cotton and had a zipper, about which she may have some explaining to do.

When she was ready, she gave him the backpack and put the bag over her shoulder. "Let's go. And please, don't freak out too much, okay? Remember, we traveled back in time. This is all real."

He blinked and shook his head, not saying anything.

Following the light, they walked out of the room and down the corridor. Opening the heavy door, they entered a long space with a curved rock ceiling. A few torches were lit in the sconces on the walls. Just like she remembered this long storeroom, there were still sacks, barrels, crates, swords, shields, and firewood.

David stared at the space with a deep, puzzled frown, no doubt wondering where electrical light had gone, along with the cabinets and boxes, and tables and chairs with protective covers.

"Where are we?" he asked as they walked down the hall.

"It's still Eilean Donan," she said. "But fourteenth century."

When they reached the curved stairs, she stopped him and turned to him. "Now listen. You will see men with swords and weapons, and women in medieval clothes similar to mine. The castle will look different. All I'm saying is, be ready and don't freak out. We don't need any additional attention, because in the Middle Ages, attention may mean death. They may think us witches, they may think us spies, they may think other crazy things. Just...keep your cool."

"You're already freaking me out."

They climbed the stairs and entered the square room. There were torches on the walls, and casks, barrels, and sacks filled it.

"Uhm. Where's the hall with the paintings and so on?" he asked. "You must be mistaken. We can't be in the same castle. What kind of trick—"

She opened the entrance door and he stopped talking. Through the arched door, they could see the inner bailey of the castle with its small household buildings, and the dirt-packed ground, and the well, and the post where Rogene had almost been whipped. The bailey was uncharacteristically empty.

With her heart thumping, Rogene walked out of the tower and tugged her brother after her. The air was full of the smells of grilled meat, ale, and cooked vegetables. A feast? Well, of course, if the wedding was today, there had to be a feast.

A servant walked out of the kitchen building carrying a giant tray on which laid a grilled boar. Rogene hurried towards him.

"Good day," she said. "Is the wedding today?"

He frowned at her, pearls of sweat glistening on his forehead. "Aye."

"Where? Where are they?"

"At the church, I suppose."

"Thanks!"

She hurried back to David, who looked around with an open mouth. "What the hell is all this, Rory?"

"We have to run. They're getting married now!"

CHAPTER 37

A ngus barely heard Father Nicholas's prayer for the wedded. Euphemia stood in front of him, her eyes silky and wet, her face glowing with joy. She wore a beautiful pale-blue dress with doves and flowers embroidered in silver thread. With her shiny golden hair done in a thick braid that lay on her shoulder and white heather woven into a crown on her head, she could be a queen. Her posture was straight and her head high, her beauty shining.

But she wasn't the bride he wished to see before him.

The door to the church was decorated with white heather, too, and he had a sprig attached to his tunic—it was the symbol of luck and happiness. Around Angus and Euphemia was clan Mackenzie, including Raghnall and Catrìona, as well as Laomann and Mairead, who was holding Ualan. A few people of clan Ross were there, too, including William himself. Several allies of clan Mackenzie were there: Craig and Amy Cambel with their daughter, Craig's cousin Ian and his wife, Kate, and Craig's father, Dougal. There were also other clans as well as villagers of Dornie.

Father Nicholas, solemn and wearing his best robe, made the sign of the cross over the couple. He was squinting from the sun that shone right into his eyes. The air was full of the scent of incense and flowers.

"Do ye, Euphemia of Ross," Father Nicholas said, "take Angus Mackenzie as yer husband, willingly and of yer own agreement?"

Her smile broadened and suddenly she looked so young, and so fragile, and hopeful. God, he wished he could love her. He wished he could scrape his heart empty and allow it to be filled with a new beginning, with his new wife.

But that was impossible. His heart didn't even belong to him anymore. He didn't desire this woman. He desired one that could never be his.

"Aye," Euphemia said.

"And no one is forcing ye to enter this marriage?" Father Nicholas said.

"Nae. I am taking Angus willingly." She leaned a little closer to Angus and whispered, "Very willingly."

He returned a smile that felt polite and strained on his face.

"And are ye of age?" Father Nicholas asked.

"I am," she said.

He turned to Angus. "Do ye, Angus Mackenzie, take Euphemia of Ross willingly and by yer own accord?"

Angus's throat tightened before he could answer. Was he? Was it all his own accord? Yes, he'd come to her. Yes, he'd proposed. But he was—again—following his duty. Not his heart.

Not his desire.

"Wait!" someone cried from the distance.

Father Nicholas narrowed his eyes at the marketplace. With the smile washed off her face completely, Euphemia turned her head, her eyebrows snapped together, her eyes wide. Everyone else was looking, too.

And that voice... He went as stiff as a statue. By God's blood, the voice sounded like it belonged to Rogene... He turned and looked.

"Wait! Please!" A woman was running towards them, navigating through the small crowd of people. Behind her, a tall, broad-shouldered young man hurried, with a huge sack on his back that swayed as he ran.

As she came closer, the raven hair flapped on the wind, the red skirt of her dress was bright and rich, and she had a bag over her shoulder that he'd never seen before...

"Wait!" Her hand was up in the air as though she were carrying something towards them.

Towards him, as her eyes were on him. And then she was close enough that he could see.

His heart must have stopped. He blinked to make sure this was real, that she was real.

Euphemia turned to him, an expression of sheer panic on her white face. "Lord Angus, ye were about to say aye, I believe?"

"Uhm..." Angus couldn't look away from Rogene, taking in every movement, every detail that he could see from this distance.

"Lord Angus!" Euphemia cried.

And then, an eternity later, Rogene stood before him, panting.

"Wait..." she said as she doubled up and breathed, holding her knees. A murmur went through the crowd of wedding guests.

"Lady Rogene?" he said quietly.

"Ye said she was gone!" Euphemia gritted through her teeth.

He didn't reply to her. The woman of his heart stood before him, and his whole being was focused on her. Nothing else existed. No one else mattered but her.

"Lady Rogene?" Father Nicholas said. "I am glad to see ye're well, but why should we wait with the wedding? Is anything the matter?"

She straightened up and looked at Angus. "You're not supposed to marry her, Angus," she said. "You're supposed to marry me."

Euphemia grabbed Angus by the upper arm and turned him to her. The expression on her face was terrifying. Nostrils flared, glaring at him from under her eyebrows, her teeth bared, she looked like a wolf ready to tear his throat out.

"Angus," she growled. "Did ye lie to me?"

"I didna," he said, returning her stare. Without saying another word, he freed his arm of her and slowly walked to Rogene. It felt like a storm was cooking somewhere nearby, so charged was the air between them, so slowly went the time.

When he stood before her, and she straightened and breathed easier, their eyes locked. And he was lost. All the reasons to stay away from her—Scotland, Euphemia's threat, his son—all that didn't matter anymore. Because only now that she was by his side did he feel like everything was right in the world.

Like life was better. Fuller. Like his heart could beat again inside his chest, instead of aching like an open wound.

"Why are ye here, lass?" he said.

"To marry you," she said, and something clicked together within his soul and became whole.

She stepped closer to him and whispered so that only he could hear, "Because it's not Euphemia who's the mother of Paul Mackenzie." She laid her hand on her belly, and the ground shifted under his feet. "It's me."

His eyes widened like an owl's as he stared at her hand. "Are ye carrying my child, lass?" he said.

"I am." She gave the sweetest smile in the world, and he was ready to scoop her up and kiss her until she couldn't breathe. She'd come to marry him.

"My God..." he whispered.

But he couldn't touch her yet. He had to deal with Euphemia first, or her wounded ego would unleash all the hounds of hell.

"Wait here, lass," he said and turned to Euphemia, who stood by Father Nicholas with a stony expression.

"Lady Euphemia—" he started.

"Angus, what in God's bones are ye doing?" Laomann growled, stepping closer. "Dinna ye dare break this off. Ye have a duty to this family—"

But Angus had had enough. Ignoring the astonished faces of his guests, he turned to Laomann.

"Dinna ye dare say anything about my duty, brother. I've protected ye and this clan my whole life. I will continue to do that until my last breath, but I also deserve to find my own happiness with the woman I truly love. The woman who crossed distances ye canna even imagine for me. The woman who is destined for me."

His eyes locked with Rogene's and hers glistened with tears of happiness as the broadest smile brightened her face.

Laomann's face twitched as he scowled at Rogene.

Angus turned to Euphemia, but before he could say how sorry he was, she interrupted him.

"Please, spare me the humiliation, Lord Angus," she said, her back as straight as a pole.

Her fists were clenched as though she were holding invisible knives. "Ye tricked me, again. Yer whore came back, and ye love her so much that ye will betray yer word to me. Twice. Am I right?"

He inhaled the air sharply. "I am sorry. I never meant to hurt ye, Lady Euphemia... Ye have my highest resp—"

She didn't even stop to listen to him. She walked off, hitting his shoulder with hers. She stopped before Rogene and said something to her with a face full of venom. Rogene paled and watched her as she made her way through the crowd.

"Ye will regret this," William said to Angus and followed his sister, together with the other Ross clansmen.

Her words rang in his head... *If ye ever betray me again, I will destroy everyone and everything that's dear to ye...*

He felt cold sweat trickle down his spine as he walked towards Rogene. He took her away from the curious glances of the guests and brought her to Father Nicholas.

"Father Nicholas," he said. "Ye asked me if I was marrying Euphemia willingly. I was, but I also wasna. I was marrying her out of duty." He looked at Rogene. "But I do want to marry this woman because I desire that more than anything in the world. Would ye marry us?"

Father Nicholas looked at her. "I can. But the registry of the wedding would need to be changed."

Rogene's eyes widened. "You've written the registry already?"

"Aye. Nae me, that is. One of the friar boys. I like when things are done and ready."

A slow smile spread on her lips. "So that's how the marriage registry stayed there," she muttered. "I could keep the name Euphemia in the book," she whispered to him, "and for the child's birth registry so that official history wouldn't be altered." She turned to the priest. "Um... I'd like to help you with that."

He cocked one eyebrow. "Ye, child?"

"Yes. I'm sure you have enough on your plate."

He nodded. "Aye, child. Well, I do need to strain my eyes and see much less these days. I thank ye."

He looked at the guests and sighed. "I suppose, Lord Angus, ye want to set up a different wedding?"

"NAE," ANGUS SAID. "THE GUESTS ARE HERE. THE BRIDE IS here. We have the feast ready." He took Rogene's hands in his, and that jolt of electricity darted through her again. "If the bride would have me..."

Her smile spreading on her face, she swallowed a knot, her throat tight from emotion. "Of course I would."

Angus lit up like a Christmas tree.

Father Nicholas shook his head and chuckled. "'Tis most unprecedented—"

"Hold on a minute!" David cried. He'd already put the backpack down on the ground and strode towards Rogene, looking more like a protective warrior than the boy he'd been just a few months earlier. "Can I talk to you in private?" he said as he came to stand next to her.

Angus cocked his head in careful apprehension. "Who's that, Rogene?"

"It's okay," she said. "It's my brother, David."

"Ah..." Angus's eyes burned with curiosity. He clapped David's shoulder in a universal sign of manly approval. "Welcome, lad..."

But David blocked Angus's arm and shoved him back. "Don't you touch me or her."

"David!" Rogene gasped.

"You kidnapped my sister, hurt her. Held her here in this weird role-playing game thing. Keep your hands off her, or you'll answer to me."

Rogene blinked. David was tall but lean, not yet a mountain of a man like Angus, though he might be once he'd filled out more. And yet, he glared at Angus, his neck cords standing out, his lips tight in a snarl, ready to protect her with his life. She loved her brother so much at that moment.

"Calm down, lad. I love yer sister and want to marry her."

"Yeah, we'll see about that. Rogene, come with me."

David took her by the elbow and dragged her behind the corner of the church.

"Rory, what the actual fuck?" he growled.

"Language!"

He waved his hand dismissively. "Time travel...marrying a guy who hurt you...this medieval reality... I don't know what is really going on or where we are, but I won't let that guy hurt you again."

She hugged him tight, then pulled away and looked up into his worried face. "Look, say time travel was possible...by some miracle, by an advanced alien technology or whatever...by things we can't explain," she said. "Can you imagine for a moment that this is real and we are back in the fourteenth century?"

He rubbed his forehead but kept silent.

"If this was real, what would you do?" she asked.

"Go back to the twenty-first century, of course! I got the scholarship to Northwestern."

She nodded. "That's what I want for you, too. These times are too dangerous, and I'd want you safe."

"But I don't believe this…"

"You do, a little bit. Don't you?"

He sighed. "I do think that there are things we can't always explain. After all, at one point people thought the earth was flat, didn't they?"

"Yes. I think, around this time, actually."

He looked around. "But…are you seriously going to marry that dude? Wasn't he about to marry someone else?"

"Only because he thought she was going to have his son. But she's not. I am."

"I don't like it. I don't like him. This is crazy."

She hugged him again. "I know. I'm weirdly glad you're here with me. Now, whether you like Angus or not, you'll have to get along with him because I am going to marry him." She locked eyes with him. "All right?"

He shook his head. "I still don't accept your explanation. And if he does anything to hurt you, I swear I'll take him down."

"Sure. Now, let's go and get me married."

They came back to the entrance of the church and David stood protectively by Rogene's side.

"Do I have yer blessing, lad?" Angus said with a soft chuckle.

"No," David said.

"He's fine," Rogene said and took Angus's big, callused hands in hers. "Father Nicholas, please… I'm ready."

"Come here, lad," Raghnall said. "It looks like we're going to be brothers."

He gestured for David to come closer. Puzzled, David went to stand next to him. Catrìona leaned over to him and said something quietly, and David nodded with a smile.

Father Nicholas raised his thin eyebrows and smiled kindly, the skin around his eyes wrinkling.

"Dearly beloved, we're gathered here to marry Lord Angus Mackenzie and Lady Rogene Douglas. Are the parties present here on their own accord and nae forced into this marriage?" he asked.

"Yes," Rogene said.

"Aye," Angus echoed.

Her head spun. She felt light-headed and so deliriously happy she thought her heart would burst. Her brother was with her, and she was marrying the man of her dreams.

"Do ye, Angus Mackenzie, take Rogene Douglas as yer wedded wife?"

"Aye," Angus said solemnly, like a vow.

Rogene's heart gave a lurch.

"And do ye, Rogene, take Angus to be yer wedded husband?"

She paused, her hands shaking. She realized that this was the moment when she'd forever be bound to the man she loved. The moment that would make them one. The moment when they would become a team, and when neither of them would be bound by duty but rather blessed by desire...by love.

She looked at David, as though asking for his blessing one last time. He caught her eyes and gave her a nod and a smile. She knew that even though he was worried about her, he wanted her to be happy. And he saw that she was.

She turned to Angus, feeling like she were floating.

"I do," she said.

"Then I pronounce ye husband and wife. Ye may kiss the bride, Lord Angus."

And as cheers and hoots sounded around them, Angus took her into his arms and kissed her. She was back in the safe confinement of his lips, inhaling his masculine scent. He picked her up, cradling her like a real groom carried his bride.

He stopped the kiss and leaned back a little, staring at her with eyes wet and sparkling like the night sky.

"What is it?" she asked.

"I love ye, lass," he whispered against her lips.

"I love you, too, Angus. Even though I never knew it, you and this baby are everything I ever wanted."

"Ye came back to me. I never thought ye would. But now, ye're giving me a bairn, and ye became my wife... Ye and the bairn are everything I've ever desired."

EPILOGUE

E ilean Donan
Two weeks later...

ANGUS'S LARGE, WARM PALM RUBBED ROGENE'S BACK, soothing her. She was leaning over an empty bucket, her breakfast of porridge threatening to spill out.

"Get pregnant, they said," she muttered. "It will be great, they said."

"They said what, love?" Angus asked.

"Nothing. Just wondering why any woman would choose to get pregnant." Her stomach was aching with a need to vomit, but she couldn't. It wouldn't come. That was how she'd lived for the past two weeks. She supposed it was a good sign that the baby was fine and growing and just taking what it needed from her.

What *he* needed from her.

Rogene sat back down in the large chair by the fireplace in the lord's hall and wiped her misty forehead. Angus, who took a seat in another big chair by her side took her hand and pressed it against his lips, his short beard sending tingles all over her body. His dark-gray eyes sparkled as they met hers, his mouth curving in a chuckle.

They'd been so blindly happy for the past two weeks. Earth disappeared under her feet when Angus was near her. There was a slight tug at her heart every time he entered the room even when she didn't hear or see him.

Her husband... The love of her life... The father of her child...

She could trust him with her life. The thought was so simple and so natural, she couldn't believe there was ever a time she couldn't get herself to trust people.

They'd stayed in Eilean Donan for a while after the wedding, to prepare and pack for the journey to Ault a'chruinn. Then this terrible nausea had hit Rogene, and she'd begged Angus to stay until it would pass. Spending several hours in a boat, adding seasickness to morning sickness, sounded to her like a death wish.

Besides, there was still the question of David...

The lord's hall was lit in golden sunlight from two slit windows, dust floating in the sunrays. Catriona glanced at Rogene with sympathy, the stone weights on her loom clanking as she moved the handle up to form a row in the fabric.

"Doesna ginger help, Rogene?" she asked.

"Nothing helps," Rogene replied. "Only your brother's presence."

"In that case, I wilna take a single step away from ye. Dinna fash, wife."

Rogene beamed, already feeling like her nausea was subsiding. Maybe there was truth to the whole endorphins making pain go away thing. Or maybe her love for Angus could heal anything.

"You better not," she said, intertwining her hand with his.

David groaned softly at their almost constant display of affection, glancing up from carving the handle of a dagger. He sat in a chair by the table, his elbows on his knees. In the two weeks since he'd arrived, he hadn't shaved because the medieval razor—which looked like a mix between a miniature scythe and a tiny ax—"gave him the creeps." The short beard added ten years. Physical labor, which included working at the smithy, helping with the horses, and even starting sword training, had grown his muscles. That, too, aged him.

"What?" Rogene said.

"Could you guys be less happy, please? Just consider those of us mere mortals who have not found love across the ages and are not even necessarily eager to be here in the first place."

Rogene sighed. David missed home and was understandably worried about his future. They'd tried to send him forward in time almost every day.

Nothing worked.

And the more time that passed, the grouchier he became. The only times he seemed to be truly enjoying himself were during physical activities and when he was being useful—that was why he was always trying to find something to do, she suspected.

What he loved most was horse riding. It was like driving a car, he'd told Rogene, only better. Like partnering up with a living being. His eyes sparkled whenever he was near a horse, and horses seemed to like him, too. Angus had told her that he was planning to give him a horse of his own soon, to lift his spirits.

They haven't told anyone about time travel, keeping the pretense of being distant cousins of James Douglas; although, deep down, Rogene knew her new family thought she and David were odd at times. No doubt, they suspected there was something else going on with them, but no one questioned them.

Yet.

"Catrìona wants to be here," Rogene said, "don't you, hon?"

Catrìona raised her eyebrows and gave a polite smile. "Lord

David is right, sister," she said. "I am ready to head to the monastery. I am only waiting for the end of summer to honor my word to Laomann."

Rogene sighed. In the past month, Catrìona had become even stricter with her prayers. She'd given all her good clothes to the poor in the village and wore her mother's old dresses with fading colors and patches all over them. She was fasting, and her cheeks had become hollow and circles darkened under her eyes. Her translucent skin looked paler every day. The dresses hung on her as if she were a scarecrow. It pained Rogene to look at her, but she knew the young woman was punishing herself for killing and was even more determined now to dedicate her life to serving God.

Rogene sighed. "We didn't mean to make anyone uncomfortable."

"I know," David said, his eyes softening. "Sorry, Rory. I'm really happy for the two of you. It's just...it also reminds me, not everyone is so lucky. And of how much I'll miss you if I ever do get home."

Angus nodded and opened his mouth to say something when an excited "Ma-ma-ma!" announced his nephew's arrival. Angus's face spread in a wide grin. Laomann came into the hall with Ualan in his arms, Mairead walking after them. The boy was tugging at Laomann's beard, and Laomann was trying his best to show excitement and not yelp with pain.

Angus leaned closer to Rogene. "I must say, now that I have ye and our son on the way, I sympathize with some of the hard choices that Laomann had to make to protect them as husband, father, and laird." He met Rogene's eyes and she sank into the dark depths of him, her heart singing. "I would do anything to protect ye and our future babe. Plead, humiliate myself, or beg if my sword and my words didna help. We still have Euphemia to think of. And I ken we must be ready for whatever she throws at us."

Rogene squeezed his large palm and smiled at him, calling for courage to rise within her as the fist of anxiety squeezed her stomach.

"I know you'll protect us."

The family sat together around the fireplace, talking, laughing, playing with the baby. Rogene met David's eyes as their clan chatted around them. He smiled at her in encouragement. Even though there was sadness in his eyes, there was something else she felt, too.

The warmth of belonging to a family that she hadn't felt since their parents died. In all the years with their aunt and uncle, she'd never had that. And now, she knew she and David were accepted without a question, without a doubt, perceived as equal members of clan Mackenzie—perhaps not by everyone, but by the core family.

Was this it? The family she and David had always longed for? It certainly was for Rogene. She wasn't so sure it was for her brother.

The only one who was missing was Raghnall, who, after talking to Laomann after the wedding, had disappeared. Rogene wasn't sure what they'd talked about, and Angus said it wasn't his secret to tell.

After a while, the servants brought lunch, which consisted of a vegetable stew with barley and bannocks. Rogene ate a little, but stopped as soon as her nausea returned.

Later that night, Rogene lay—sated, warm, and heavy—in Angus's secure arms in their bed. Lazily, she traced a soft line down his hard chest, smoothing her fingertip over his soft, dark hair. She gently kissed his skin and laid her head on his rib cage, listening to the beat of his heart. It sounded like music to her.

She'd never again take this sound for granted. Not when she knew what a dark, lonely place her world was without him.

Angus brushed his fingers down her spine. "Ye have such soft skin, lass," he said. "Softer than silk."

She smiled. "Thanks. We aim to please."

She put her chin on his chest and looked at him.

"I love when you're so relaxed," she said. "You're so handsome when you have no worries in the world."

"'Tis because ye and the babe are in my arms. And when 'tis just ye and I on our estate, I wilna let ye out of the bedchamber. I will love ye every day until ye're sore and my cock canna stand nae more. Though I dinna think 'tis possible with ye."

Rogene giggled and slowly moved her hand down his hard stomach to the apex of his thighs and covered his gorgeous cock with her palm. Already semihard, hot, and velvety, he jerked under her palm and grew harder.

"Lass..." he whispered. "Didna ye have enough just now?"

She put her leg over his hips and pushed herself up, straddling him. His cock was pressed against her clit, still sleek from their recent lovemaking, and sent a small jolt of pleasure through her. She began to gently thrust her pelvis to and fro, rubbing herself against his hard length. His dark eyes became black bottomless pools as he devoured her, slowly looking her up and down.

Breasts, then waist and slightly rounded belly.

He laid one palm on the small swell. "By God's blood, lass, ye become more and more bonnie every day. So feminine... So..." He reached out with his other hand and thrust his already stiff cock deep inside her. It went in smoothly, effortlessly because of how wet she was, and filled her still swollen and sensitive core.

She gasped as her walls stretched, accommodating him within her, adjusting to the sweet pressure and all the bliss that radiated through her.

"So delicious..." he said with a thrust that spiraled her higher. "My wife..." Another thrust. "My love." He sat up and wrapped her legs around his waist. He looked deeply into her eyes, his own gaze dark. The gaze of a conqueror. The gaze of a warrior. The gaze of a man who loved her more than anything in the world.

"My desire..." He groaned and began thrusting into her.

She knew then that he'd let go—let go of the sense of duty, of limitations, of expectations—and given in to desire, to love, to happiness.

And as she was falling apart around him, feeling like she was no longer a separate person but had become one with him, her heart was full.

Right after sunrise, an urgent knock on the door woke Rogene up. Angus grunted, his heavy, warm arm bringing her tighter to him.

"Go away," he croaked.

But the knock repeated.

"My lord Angus," someone said from behind the door. "'Tis me, Iòna. Come quick. Lord Raghnall is back. He's hurt, and he brought another wounded man with him. He asked me to fetch ye..."

Angus rose immediately, blinking sleep away, worry on his face. He reached for a tunic that lay on the chest by the bed.

"I'm coming," he said, and footsteps sounded from behind the door, growing quieter.

Rogene reached for her dress, fighting a new wave of nausea.

"Stay," Angus said, fastening the belt on his trousers. "'Tis early."

"No, I want to help."

When they were dressed, they hurried down the curved stairs.

They walked into the fresh air of an early morning, rich with the scent of lake water, wet grass, and flowers. Birds sang, roosters crowed, and sheep bleated from the pastures on the mainland. The inner bailey was empty, except for Iòna and another guard. A still sleepy Laomann and a pale Catrìona arrived right after Rogene and Angus.

Raghnall pressed his hand against his side, the tunic under his palm brown with blood. A tall stranger who stood on one leg had his arm around the guard's shoulder. His head was bandaged, covering one eye.

"Raghnall, what happened?" Angus said.

"And who is this?" Laomann asked.

The wounded man looked up at them, and Rogene distinguished a handsome face. His ear-long hair and beard were the color of dirty gold. The tan of someone who'd been outside most of his life colored his high cheekbones. His intelligent green eyes were clouded with pain and exhaustion.

One moment, Rogene was studying him, the next, Catrìona gasped and fell. On instinct, Rogene turned and caught her sister-in-law, supporting her by the elbows.

Catrìona clenched her dress over her heart and whispered, "Good Lord..." She crossed herself hastily and pressed her wooden cross to her lips.

"Catrìona, I wish you ate more," Rogene whispered to her. "Stop starving yourself—"

"'Tis nae that," Catrìona replied in a hot whisper.

Raghnall frowned, his dark eyes on Catrìona. "Are ye all right, sister? 'Tis only Tadhg. Ye remember him, right?"

Tadhg's eyes were on Catrìona, and he was clearly as astounded to see her as she was to see him.

"Tadhg," she said. "I didna ken ye were alive...or would ever be back."

"Who is he?" Rogene whispered.

"The only man I've ever loved," Catrìona said. "My betrothed..."

"Yer who?" growled Angus quietly.

But she didn't reply. She let go of Rogene, rushed to Tadhg, and supported him from the other side.

Raghnall looked at Laomann. "Is it all right with ye, brother, if Tadhg stays here until he gets better? Ross men attacked on my way back from clan Ruaidhrí and he saved my life. Euphemia isna going to leave us alone."

Rogene's skin chilled. Laomann nodded and gestured to the keep. "Of course. Stay, Tadhg. Ye need help, too, Raghnall."

"I'll help ye get better," Catrìona said.

"Thank ye," Tadhg said, his voice rasping.

"I'll make sure Tadhg is all right," Raghnall said, "but then I'll go stay with Father Nicholas. He can heal me."

"Ye're nae going anywhere until I care for yer wound," Catrìona said. "Dinna argue with me."

They slowly walked towards the keep and disappeared through the door.

"Did you know she had a betrothed?" Rogene asked Angus as she watched the door closing behind Laomann.

"Nae. Father wanted to marry her to a wealthy man but didna find one that was rich enough or had a high enough title. She was his prized possession, a bonnie, shiny thing to sell off for a fortune."

"So Tadhg must have been her secret love..." Rogene whispered. "Do ye think he might change her mind?"

Angus sighed. "I dinna think so."

"We'll see. I hope whatever she decides she chooses her happiness. You did. And thank God!"

The first rays of sun appeared from behind the curtain wall, promising a hot day. But as Rogene squinted and nestled into Angus's hug, her world didn't get brighter and warmer. Instead, dread weighed heavily in her chest, sending her heart into an erratic rhythm and misting her skin with sweat.

Somewhere out there, Euphemia was preparing her revenge, gathering warriors and sharpening yet another dagger.

At the wedding, the scariest and happiest day of Rogene's life, Euphemia whispered something to her. Something Rogene had desperately tried to forget and ignore.

Something that, she now knew, wasn't an empty threat said in the heat of the moment.

How would it feel to ken that everyone ye love and hold dear would perish, and it all would be yer own fault? If only ye'd stayed away...

But as Angus's strong arms brought her closer, she knew that even though they had a powerful enemy, they were one clan, one family. Destiny was on their side. Because they had found the greatest gift of all. Something that Euphemia didn't have.

Love and trust.

THE END

Loved Angus and Rogene's story? Get excited for Catriona's story next in **Highlander's Vow.**

NOTE ON HISTORICAL ACCURACY

Taking a creative license is always fun, and I particularly enjoyed mixing things up in this book. Historical facts intertwined with my imagination and created a couple of people who didn't exist and events that didn't happen.

First, Eilean Donan got a new dungeon, underground rooms that don't exist, and a room with a Pictish rock that sends people through time. If you ever visit the castle, please don't go looking for those rooms. But I'd like to hope that if you do, you might find them.

Second, Euphemia, Countess of Ross, is a real historical figure who had survived two husbands and kidnapped a Mackenzie laird to marry him. Although that didn't happen until 1427. When I read about her, I was so fascinated by this woman that my imagination went wild. Most of the kidnappings we read about in the Highlands are done by men, and I was intrigued that Scottish women were so fierce that they were also capable of kidnapping a man they fancied.

Often we get a feeling that history was written by men, but this simply can't be true. It was fun to come up with a female character who is capable of shaking things up at such a magnitude her actions span across several books.

Third, and most important, there is absolutely no evidence that Robert the Bruce wanted to give up when he visited the Mackenzie clan or wrote a letter about it. On the contrary, historians believe that he came to Mackenzie lands to recruit men. Although I do wonder if through all his hardships in 1307 and the beginning of 1308 if he really ever thought about abandoning his cause. He is a fascinating man on all accounts, though not always as heroic and honorable as we may think, once you start digging, but undoubtedly an unforgettable man who shaped history, and I love writing stories around the Wars of Scottish Independence.

I hope you enjoyed this cocktail of history and fiction!

Mariah

ACKNOWLEDGMENTS

Writing this page is my favorite part of the book creation process, partly because the work is done, and partly because a book always has several people without whom it wouldn't have existed.

I'm very fortunate to work with a great team of editors. As always, the biggest thank you is to my sounding board and my creative partner who helps me pick the best ideas and make the story exciting and emotional, the talented editor, **Laura Barth**. A new and great addition to my team, **Beth Attwood**, helped to check facts, kill repetitions, and smooth out the writing. And, as always, a careful and meticulous proofreader, **Laura LaTulipe**, caught the last "slippery bastards," a.k.a. the typos and tough errors that made it through despite the efforts of several editors.

This novel was written in the toughest year I have ever lived through, which is something millions of people and I have in common. 2020. The COVID-19 pandemic crippled traveling and made it impossible for me to go to Scotland and visit Eilean Donan personally. However, when I turned to my readers and asked for help figuring out the geography of the castle and the details of interior that are impossible to catch from photos and videos, I was humbled to receive dozens of emails and messages.

As a result, several readers spent a lot of time answering my questions, sending me detailed descriptions, photos, and links. Essentially, they were my eyes and ears. They were the ones who helped me bring the setting of Eilean Donan to life and make it authentic. My immense gratitude to my wonderful readers: **Sandra, Cindy R., Mindy D., Cornelia W., Georgine F., Lorna M., Diane C., Anca F., and Marybelle M.-C.** This book wouldn't have been the same without you!

And last, but not least, I'm so thankful to have such **amazing readers**. You, those who buy, read, and review my books, keep me inspired, keep ideas flowing, and through your support, allow me to write my books full-time, seeing my children grow up and hug and kiss my husband every day.

With love and gratitude,

Mariah

ALSO BY MARIAH STONE

CALLED BY A HIGHLANDER SERIES (TIME TRAVEL):

Sìneag (FREE short story)
Highlander's Captive
Highlander's Hope
Highlander's Heart
Highlander's Love
Highlander's Christmas (novella)
Highlander's Desire
Highlander's Vow (release 2021)
Highlander's Bride (release 2021)
More instalments coming in 2021 and 2022

CALLED BY A VIKING SERIES (TIME TRAVEL):

One Night with a Viking (prequel)—grab for free!
The Fortress of Time
The Jewel of Time
The Marriage of Time
The Surf of Time
The Tree of Time

CALLED BY A PIRATE SERIES (TIME TRAVEL):

Pirate's Treasure

Pirate's Pleasure

A CHRISTMAS REGENCY ROMANCE:

The Russian Prince's Bride

JOIN THE ROMANCE TIME-TRAVELERS' CLUB!

Join the mailing list on mariahstone.com to receive exclusive bonuses, author insights, release announcements, giveaways and the insider scoop of books on sale - and more!

Join Mariah Stone's exclusive Facebook author group to get early snippets of books, exclusive giveaways and to interact with the author directly.

ENJOY THE BOOK? YOU CAN MAKE A DIFFERENCE!

Please, leave your honest review for the book.
As much as I'd love to, I don't have financial capacity like New York publishers to run ads in the newspaper or put posters in subway.

But I have something much, much more powerful!

Committed and loyal readers

If you enjoyed the book, I'd be so grateful if you could spend five minutes leaving a review on the book's Amazon page.

Thank you very much!

SCOTTISH SLANG

aye – yes
>**bairn** - baby
>**bastart** - bastard
>**bonnie** - pretty, beautiful.
>**canna**- can not
>**couldna** – couldn't
>**didna**- didn't ("Ah didna do that!")
>**dinna**- don't ("Dinna do that!")
>**doesna** – doesn't
>**fash** - fuss, worry ("Dinna fash yerself.")
>**feck** - fuck
>**hasna** – has not
>**havna** - have not
>**hadna** – had not
>**innit?** - Isn't it?
>**isna**- Is not
>**ken** - to know
>**kent** - knew
>**lad** - boy
>**lass** - girl
>**marrit** – married

nae – no or not

shite - faeces

the morn - tomorrow

the morn's morn - tomorrow morning

uisge-beatha (uisge for short) – Scottish Gaelic for water or life / aquavitae, the distilled drink, predecessor of whiskey

verra – very

wasna - was not

wee - small

wilna - will not

wouldna - would not

ye - you

yer – your (also yerself)

ABOUT THE AUTHOR

When time travel romance writer Mariah Stone isn't busy writing strong modern women falling back through time into the arms of hot Vikings, Highlanders, and pirates, she chases after her toddler and spends romantic nights on North Sea with her husband.

Mariah speaks six languages, loves Outlander, sushi and Thai food, and runs a local writer's group. Subscribe to Mariah's newsletter for a free time travel book today!

facebook.com/mariahstoneauthor

instagram.com/mariahstoneauthor

bookbub.com/authors/mariah-stone

pinterest.com/mariahstoneauthor

Made in United States
Orlando, FL
11 November 2021